EXILE

THE SHORTEN CHRONICLES BOOK 3

ROSALIND TATE

Anacopia
Lift Cave
Atsq'uri
Mongol HQ
Kajet Queen
Rusa's Palace

We know what we are, but know not what we may be.
William Shakespeare

CHAPTER 1

20th November 1925. England.

The olive-green car roared along the winding lane, the engine reverberating and harsh in the hushed countryside. A cold wind tore over the open car's half-height windows, and the narrow tarmac road glittered with frost. Despite the speed, Freddy Lacey, heir to Shorten Manor, urged his chauffeur to go faster.

The car skidded around a bend and the chauffeur gave Freddy a nervous glance in his rear-view mirror. One of Reynolds' eyes was half-closed by an ugly purple bruise and his face was streaked with blood.

They rounded another bend. 'Stop,' said Freddy. The lift was still there. Thank God.

The size of a small room, the lift looked jarringly out of place, nestled in front of a tall hedge. The frame of the open doorway was gold, and above it was a shiny round dial showing a choice of three floors. But the slid-back doors weren't visible outside the structure and there was no shaft or haulage mechanism. Not a real lift.

The rectangular outer walls matched the drab winter shades and textures of the hedge and vegetation surrounding it, softening and masking its angular lines, but light from the interior fanned out over the road, dazzlingly bright.

Freddy caught his breath. There was someone inside, illuminated like a saint by a chandelier above her: a girl in an emerald-green dress.

Such a sight in a rural lane should have been alarming or sinister, but for Freddy it was a beacon of hope. He'd heard the stories all his life. His own mother had come to Shorten Manor through this device.

Only yesterday, he would have been eager to examine it for posterity and science, but today his mind was filled with the fate of his darling girl. Miss Sophie Arundel.

Freddy opened the door before the car stopped, and he stumbled as he jumped out. Sprawled on the frozen verge was a dead man, his forehead a disgusting red mulch. Freddy put his hand to his mouth.

Reynolds turned the car around, parked, but didn't get out.

'This is the man who attacked you?' said Freddy.

'Yes.' The chauffeur picked up a rifle from the passenger seat. 'Mr Parkes may still be here.' Reynolds checked both ways in the lane. 'He's gone entirely mad.'

Freddy had known Mr Parkes for years. Sane as the next fellow—

'Mr Harrington was lying by Miss Arundel's dog, over there.' Reynolds gestured towards the verge in front of the lift. 'Mr Parkes must have moved the bodies.'

Driving here, the chauffeur had been gibbering. Only now was he making sense. 'What about Miss Arundel?'

'Mr Parkes punched her, knocked her to the ground.'

Freddy's heart lurched.

'She told me to get away, so I put my foot down.'

Freddy took a shuddering breath, the cold air searing his lungs. 'How could you *leave* her?'

'She ordered me to. He meant to kill us, and nobody would have known what happened.' Reynolds scanned the lane again. 'I've never believed those stories, but perhaps they're true, and the invisible lift sent him insane?'

'The lift's right there. There's a girl inside.' Freddy pointed. 'You can't see it?'

'No.' Reynolds kept his expression respectfully blank.

Hugo had thought only those with a particular gene could see the lift and travel in it. Freddy exhaled, his breath creating pale circles in the air. He'd inherited the gene from his mother. 'The gamekeepers will arrive soon. Mad or not, Mr Parkes won't take them on.' He swallowed back tears. Sophie might be dead, her body hidden somewhere with Hugo's.

But that girl must have come from somewhere. Had the lift taken *someone* away and returned with the girl? He prayed that someone was Sophie.

Another thought came to him, and his stomach clenched. Deranged Parkes could have forced Sophie into the lift, gone with her to where the lift had come from. And if its doors shut now, the lift would vanish — and not return for decades.

Freddy sprinted across the verge towards the lift. The girl was the same age as his beloved Sophie. Her dress was draped in elegant folds, resembled gowns worn by native ladies in India, and on her feet were flat white shoes with rainbow-coloured laces. Her shiny black hair hung dishevelled to her shoulders and her dark eyes watched him warily.

Freddy stepped over a red patch on the grass and into the lift, and the girl dropped something that clattered to the floor. She clutched at a grey satchel slung over her shoulder. 'Where am I? Who are you?' She had a local Derbyshire accent.

'I won't hurt you. I'm trying to travel to the university.'

'I'm at the university. I mean … I was.' Her lower lip trembled. 'I'm dreaming.'

'You're awake. I'm not certain how this works, but I believe to return there, you need to wish with all your heart. I'll wish too.'

'Just wish.'

'Wish a lot. More akin to praying. Think about the university, and your home. Happy times.' Freddy knelt on the shiny floor, facing the threshold, his knees cushioned by his suit trousers and the thick material of his town coat.

'I *am* dreaming.' She picked up a smooth metal object by her feet. It looked like the tiny telephone Hugo had brought with him when he and Sophie had arrived at the Manor. The girl put it in her satchel. 'This is a weird dream.'

'I told you, it isn't a dream, and we need to pray.' Under Freddy's knees, the lift floor was transparent and beneath it, a large purple cobweb rhythmically flashed. He ignored it, put his hands together, and closed his eyes. He tried to picture the university. Perhaps it had some quirky feature he should concentrate on. 'Is the university similar to a Cambridge college?'

The girl giggled. 'More like a multi-storey car park.'

He could ask her to describe a multi … what she'd said, but that wouldn't help. He knew Sophie and Hugo's world was similar to his, but many things were different. They'd talked about an invisible network in the sky, space rockets and computers, but he couldn't visualise that. His thoughts turned to darling Sophie, his fiancée. 'Remember a person you love dearly.'

The girl sat with her back to him, cross-legged. She clasped her hands above her head and shut her eyes.

Odd way of praying. But each to their own.

Sophie's lips, soft and searching under his … no, too

distracting. Remember her face, her smile. The first time they'd met, she'd been riding a bicycle, wearing tight navy trousers that showed off her shapely legs. Her teeth were remarkably white and whenever she'd smiled at him, his insides had danced like butterflies over a flowerbed.

Freddy shifted his numb knees.

'Nothing's happening,' said the girl. 'Maybe we should try something else?'

He'd pictured Sophie so intensely he'd half imagined she was beside him. 'There *is* nothing else, as far as I know. We have to pray harder.'

The girl nodded.

Was Reynolds still by the car? No, checking on the chauffeur would disrupt his concentration. Freddy closed his eyes again. Kissing Sophie—

Loud rattling, and the lift doors shut.

'Keep praying,' said Freddy.

The lift lurched forward and down, and Freddy fell onto the doors that were now the floor. The girl pitched into him with a thump, landing on top of him.

She stood up hastily, as if he could give her some disease. 'What's happening?'

A ripple of fear. 'I don't know.' He leaped to his feet. They could be trapped in here. Dread joined fear. He pushed it away. Hugo had been clear how to make the lift work. *Focus on where you want to go. No doubts.*

Sophie…

The lift barrelled slowly, as if setting course, guided by an unseen wind. The girl did an elegant forward roll and so did he, in a bizarre dance.

He banged his head against a rail and grabbed it. There was another rail on the opposite wall. 'Hold on to that.' He sat on the floor.

The girl held the rail and sat down too. 'What the hell is this thing?'

'No one knows. Every so often, it appears in the lane. Apart from you, six people have arrived in the last thirty years. They all came from your world.'

The girl gaped. 'What do you mean?'

Freddy thought back to Hugo's parallel universes theory. 'Our worlds are similar, but our time runs slower than yours, so we're a hundred years behind. And not everything is the same. You had a big war with Germany, and we didn't. My friend Hugo called it the Great War or the First World War.'

The girl clenched her fist. 'You're a nutter.'

'I beg your pardon?'

'Keep away from me.'

This girl reminded him of Sophie, probably kicked and punched a bag on a stand for fun like she did. That part of Sophie he'd never understand. But he understood Hugo. A most splendid chap. Freddy's eyes watered. Hugo dead… No, too horrible to contemplate. He blinked. Don't break down. That would upset this girl.

The lift was upright and motionless, and to distract himself, Freddy studied the chandelier. It emitted a perfect light. When the lift had turned over, why hadn't it shattered? Or swayed, even a little?

No, think about Sophie, couldn't risk being entombed in here, or landing in an unknown place. What had Hugo said… *How do we get to the right universe? We might end up in a really strange one, or a world that seems like home but is crucially different.*

'I'm too hot.' Freddy took off his scarf, stuffed his gloves into his coat pockets, and reached up to remove his bowler. Not there. Must have fallen off on the verge.

He removed his coat, gripped the rail, and his mind wandered. Kissing Sophie on the cheek on the steps of the

Manor, her wonderful blue eyes fixed on him. He fancied he could taste her skin, cold against his lips. Her resolution to help Hugo return home was typical of her sweet nature. Always thinking of others.

The girl was still praying.

He should too. Almighty God, long-suffering and unknowingly good, I confess to you, I confess with my whole heart, my neglect and forgetfulness of your commandments, my wrongdoing, the hurts I've done to others, the good I've left undone. Please take me to Sophie. Forgive all my sins—

Rattling and a rasping noise, metal scraping along metal. The lift doors jerkily opened, and a clang rang out louder than a dinner gong.

They both stood up.

Beyond the threshold was only darkness, but the girl ran into it.

Freddy slipped on his coat and scarf, steeled himself, and stepped out.

Solid ground.

Blind, he waited for his eyes to adjust. According to Hugo and Sophie, this should be the students' union. He walked cautiously forward. After the sterile air of the lift, traces of sweat and dust tickled his nose, and he sneezed.

A bright light shone into his face, turning him blind again.

CHAPTER 2

*W*hen two students disappeared from a university in the north of England, the police found no trace of them, and three months later, when they reappeared in the same location, safe and well, the police were baffled.

The students claimed they'd joined an obscure cult, cut off from the modern world and, with no evidence of a crime, the police closed the case. But the cult story was a lie, concocted because the truth would have branded the students insane.

Sophie Arundel and Hugo Harrington had walked into a lift in the students' union, expecting to step out into a corridor in a tower block. Instead, they'd crossed universes, into an alternate 1920s and a grand country house: Shorten Manor.

By the time they'd figured out how to return to their own universe, Sophie had decided to stay with Freddy. But she hadn't counted on a murderer with his own reasons for keeping the way home secret. Forced into the lift with Hugo, she was carried back with him to the students' union.

After travelling to Hugo's house in London and telling his family their made-up cult story, Sophie finally lay down in his parents' guest bedroom, ready to sleep for a week.

But she was wide awake.

04:01. The illuminated digital time on the bedside radio mocked her in the night-gloom, and she sighed. Her dog, Charlotte, a large brown labradoodle, snored peacefully beside her. Charlotte had sleeping *totally* sussed. Maybe it was easier for dogs.

Sophie snuggled further down under the cosy duvet. Was it the prospect of getting in the lift again that was troubling her? Returning safely to Freddy would require focus and mental strength, even with double-gene power. Charlotte possessed the lift gene too, and dearly wanted to return to Shorten and to Jack, her retriever companion.

Sophie pictured Reynolds speeding away from her in the lane, imagined the car careering onto the Manor drive. How must Freddy have felt when she wasn't in the car? Didn't bear thinking about.

But she should rest today, travel tomorrow. Better to arrive late in Shorten, than land somewhere ... wrong.

Hugo had worried about that. He was downstairs, comforting his mother. A few more hours in his house was do-able. He'd no clue she was in love with him, only saw her as a friend.

She'd acted her socks off, trying not to react, when he'd laboriously unfastened the buttons on the back of her century-old gown so she could shower and sleep...

Music might soothe her? Sophie turned on the radio but couldn't change it from a rolling news channel. She switched it off and stared at the ceiling.

Marrying Freddy in a few weeks didn't seem real, as if it were happening to someone else. But his ring on her finger was big and sparkly. One hundred-per-cent real.

Hugo's family had assumed she was engaged to Hugo. Awkward, but they'd gone with it. And the whirlwind romance fiction fitted neatly with dropping out of Uni and joining an imaginary cult.

Her mind drifted to Shorten, to Freddy's kisses … tender, steamy moments snatched in private, in the library or in the small drawing room.

But the memory of Hugo's fingers on her dress buttons was stronger.

CHAPTER 3

'You shouldn't be here. Told the girl the same.' Looming out of the dark was an overweight chap with a battery-powered torch. His jacket was an unfeasibly bright yellow.

'I hope you can help me, sir,' said Freddy. 'I'm looking for my fiancée, Miss Sophie Arundel.'

'Her and Hugo Harrington have gone to London with the police.'

Freddy exhaled. Not dead. But why were they with the police? And why had they travelled to London, hundreds of miles away?

The man frowned at Freddy's coat. 'You're here for the interviews.'

Freddy only hesitated for a moment. 'I lost track of time.'

The man narrowed his eyes, perhaps considering something. 'It can take a while to find your bearings. Best you get on your way. It's late.'

Freddy looked at his watch. The second hand had stopped. Broken. 'Do you have the time, sir?'

The man checked his watch. 'Just gone four.'

An ungodly hour. 'I've ... lost my keys and telephone. Stolen.'

The man sighed. 'Don't tell me, you don't have insurance.' He didn't seem to expect a reply. 'Come on.' He turned and marched away, and Freddy followed.

Now the air smelled stale and institutional, like a school or a deserted office.

The man slid a playing card into a slot in a door. A tiny green light appeared and there was a click. The bottom half of the door was metal, the top glass. The man pushed it open but hesitated. 'Are you sure you're here for the interviews?'

'Yes, sir.' Freddy remembered how he'd felt waiting to start his Cambridge entrance exam. 'I'm a bit nervous. I *really* want to read maths here.'

The man nodded and gestured for Freddy to walk through the doorway. As he did, an electric bulb dangling from a low ceiling blinked on.

Strewn by Freddy's feet were newspapers and post, and on the right was a wooden door with a metal number: 0001. The first 0 had slipped, half adrift.

Hugo had mentioned there were undergraduate rooms off from the students' union. Freddy nodded at the numbered door and the man inserted the card into it. The door swung open.

Freddy thanked the man, stepped inside, and hastily closed the door. He cast about and found a light switch.

He was in a tiny parlour, neat and warm. A row of cupboards lined one wall and in the centre of the room was a sofa and an armchair. On a coffee table was a steel book with a silhouette of a discarded apple.

Two inner doors. A suite of rooms? And a slight scent of dog reminded him of home.

He should announce himself. Wouldn't do to be arrested for burglary. 'Hello?'

A scuffling noise erupted on the other side of the nearest interior door. A light showed at the bottom and the door was wrenched open by a young man wearing nothing but short drawers. 'Who the hell are you?' He dashed to the cupboards and from a drawer took out a large knife.

Freddy stepped back in alarm. 'I apologise for disturbing you at this hour, but it's an emergency.'

'An emergency?' The boy paused but kept hold of the knife.

'Mr Frederick Lacey. How do you do?'

'What?'

'I'm trying to find Miss Sophie Arundel.'

The boy rubbed his eyes with his free hand. His dark hair was a tumble of curls that reached past his ears, like a young Lord Byron in his prime. 'Lorna, stay in the bedroom.'

A girl appeared in the doorway and at the same moment a black labrador shot towards Freddy.

'Hello.' Freddy reached out to pat the dog.

'Don't hurt him,' said the boy. 'Or I swear—'

'Fudge, come here.' The dog returned to Lorna's side, and she stepped into the room, pausing to adjust a tie on her wrap-around garment. Though it had been cut off to finish at her knees, it resembled his mother's gown, worn when he'd had chicken pox and she'd slept in the nursery.

Lorna's eyes were unfocused, and he suspected she couldn't see him, but Freddy still averted his gaze, embarrassed she was in her night attire.

He went to remove his hat, then remembered he wasn't wearing it, and acknowledged Lorna with a courteous nod. 'Mr Frederick Lacey, at your service. How do you do? Again, apologies for calling at this hour.' He glanced at the boy and the knife. 'I mean you and your wife no harm. I desperately need your help.'

The boy stared. 'Are you from the government?'

'No.'

'With that coat, you look as if you're from the government.'

'Should I take it off?' asked Freddy.

The boy's stare didn't falter. 'Slowly.'

Freddy removed his coat and scarf and looked for a coat rack. In the absence of one, he laid the clothes on the sofa arm.

'He's asking after Sophie Arundel,' said the boy.

'What about her?' Lorna hugged herself. Her legs were bare and on her feet were sandals with a single strap between her toes.

'Miss Arundel and Mr Harrington have been living with my family,' said Freddy, 'and I need to find them. They could be in danger.'

'Living with your family?' The boy frowned.

'Yes. Would you mind if I sat down? I've had a rather stressful day.' Freddy sat on the sofa. Hopefully, they'd forgive his rudeness. 'I'm extremely worried.' He clasped his hands together. 'I realise that attempting to locate her in the dead of night is impractical.'

'Impractical?' Despite her brown hair being oddly short like a boy's, Lorna was pretty, with a pointed chin and a smooth complexion. 'Elliot, what's happening?'

'I don't know.'

'Impractical,' added Freddy, 'because she's in London with the police.'

Lorna looked bewildered.

They weren't going to help him. 'Could I ask you to call the police? Perhaps they'll take me to the same station.'

'Sophie hasn't been arrested,' said Elliot.

'They've been missing for months,' said Lorna.

'I'm intrigued by this guy,' said Elliot, 'and he's got no bag that could blow up.'

Blow up bags?

'He's our age,' said Elliot. 'Wearing a boxy suit and a bow tie.'

'How strange.' Lorna patted Fudge.

'Can I search you?' said Elliot. 'Put your arms up.'

Freddy got to his feet and held his hands in the air. 'What are you searching for?'

'A weapon.' Elliot was still holding the knife.

This university was nothing like Cambridge in his world. 'Shall I turn out my pockets?'

'Yes,' said Elliot.

The only thing in Freddy's trouser pocket was a worn penny he spun while pondering maths problems. Freddy laid it on the table making a clink sound, pulled a notebook from his inside breast pocket, set that on the table, and took off his suit jacket.

'Are we awake?' said Lorna. 'This is very odd.'

'I think so.' Elliot peered at the penny. 'You collect old coins?'

'It helps me think,' said Freddy. He spun the penny, and when it fell, it made a louder clink on the smooth table.

Elliot returned the knife to a drawer.

'Would you like a cup of tea?' said Lorna.

'That would be very kind,' said Freddy. Perhaps this world wasn't that different from home.

Lorna strolled over to the cupboards. 'How do you have your tea?'

Nobody had ever asked him that before. The servants knew how he took his tea.

'Milk, one lump of sugar … thank you.' This was awkward, imposing on them. But needs must.

Elliot offered Freddy an oversized cup of tea with no saucer. The cup had coloured squares on the rim and 'GAME

OVER' printed near the top. Peculiar. What had happened to saucers and why had cups become so big?

Lorna sat in the armchair, and Elliot set two more large cups on the table and sat beside Freddy on the sofa.

'Did anyone else go with Mr Harrington and Miss Arundel with the police?' said Freddy, concerned about Mr Parkes.

'You've not seen the video?' said Elliot.

Sophie had told him about 'videos,' but those had been stories. Freddy shook his head.

Elliot opened the steel book. It resembled Hugo's telephone, though it was bigger. Hugo's device hadn't worked, as it had 'run out of juice.' Presumably, this device had enough juice.

Elliot tapped it. 'Only Sophie's dog was with them when the police arrived.'

Freddy gaped. Moving pictures inside this machine! The people holding their hands up had their backs to the camera, but the taller one looked like Hugo, and the girl was wearing Sophie's dress. And that was surely Charlotte, Sophie's dog? The cars weren't the same as home, nor were the police uniforms. Freddy drew a relieved breath. No sign of Mr Parkes. 'I believe that's them.'

Elliot frowned. 'Everybody thinks they were kidnapped by terrorists.'

Hugo had talked about terrorists, but Freddy couldn't recall who they were or why they were hurting people.

'It was front-page news for weeks,' said Lorna. 'We were interviewed. Everybody was.'

Freddy drank his tea. 'It's good the police are diligent.'

'A no-brainer given his father,' said Elliot.

'Whose father?' asked Freddy.

'How can you *not* know about Hugo's father?' said Lorna. 'He's the Foreign Secretary.'

Neither Lorna nor Elliot used formal forms of address. Stick to Christian names. 'Hugo never mentioned his father's profession.' He shouldn't pretend he'd known. Too late for that. 'It didn't come up.'

'I don't believe you.' Elliot sat back, his face set and his arms folded. 'You don't seem surprised.'

Freddy shrugged. 'Everyone's father has to do something.' Hugo and Sophie were in London, so he should travel there. 'Do you still have trains?'

'Why wouldn't we have trains?' said Lorna.

Freddy finished his tea. 'Hugo said most people drive everywhere.'

'We have trains,' said Lorna. 'Where do your family live?'

'Not far from here.'

'Right,' said Elliot. 'And yet the road-blocks and the media frenzy somehow passed you by.' He pressed his lips into a sceptical line.

CHAPTER 4

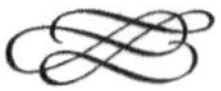

Shortly before five in the morning, in his parents' house in London, Hugo trudged upstairs.

His unlooked-for adventure had taken a heavy toll on his family and lying to his traumatised mother had wrung him out. But he couldn't regret his time with Sophie in Shorten.

There'd been moments when he wondered if she felt as he did, though those moments had been rare and fleeting. Yet an hour ago, when he'd unbuttoned her dress, she'd trembled under his fingers. Given him hope.

He sat on the bed in his room, exhausted but wired, his brain buzzing. A week after they'd arrived in Shorten, he'd sworn on the bible to keep Freddy's confidences secret, to help Freddy court Sophie and marry her. And he'd kept his promise, even when acting as go-between became so horrible, he'd dreaded every day.

The only aspiration for middle-class girls in Shorten was a good marriage and Sophie would have been happy with Freddy.

But that was there.

Hugo got to his feet, went to the bathroom and brushed

his teeth, his mind still racing. One chance to seize happiness… There must be a way to tell her how he felt *and* honour some of his vow to Freddy.

He rinsed the toothbrush in the sink and glared at his messy hair reflected in the mirror. 'Don't screw this up.'

~

Hugo woke with a start, registered it was light, and peered at his bedside radio. 08:14. Three hours sleep… He groaned.

Pulling on his towelling dressing gown, he shambled downstairs to make coffee but stopped on the first floor. Scratching was coming from behind a door.

From the guest bedroom — likely Charlotte wanting to go out.

Hugo opened Sophie's door and the labradoodle bounced up, nearly knocking him over. Sophie was sound asleep, her face hidden in a pillow. Oh, to lie beside her, draw her close… No, she'd freak out.

He continued down the stairs to the kitchen with Charlotte.

The expanse of floor-to-ceiling glass facing the garden gave the space a bright, modern feel, despite traditional Shaker cupboards and an old-fashioned Aga cooker.

He unlocked the French windows. Charlotte leapt outside, and Hugo yawned and switched on the coffee machine.

Unbidden, the memory of Freddy kissing Sophie in Shorten, happily bringing forward their wedding, loomed up, taunting him…

Focus. Freddy was a universe away.

The machine hissed and he pressed the symbol for a latte.

All he could do was choose his moment and hope beyond hope she felt the same.

CHAPTER 5

Three hours earlier, in the student flat in Derbyshire, Elliot frowned and tapped on his telephone. 'I'm calling the police.'

Freddy acknowledged the decision with a nod. 'They'll take me to Sophie.'

'I don't think they will.' Elliot smiled unpleasantly. 'It was you posting sick crap on how she's been murdered, wasn't it? And what you'd do to her if she's still alive?'

A horrible panicky feeling. Had someone been sending poison pen letters? Elliot seemed sure the police wouldn't help him. Freddy hadn't committed a crime, but perhaps habeas corpus didn't exist here? The authorities might imprison him, throw away the key—

'Hold on,' said Lorna, standing up and placing her hand on her husband's shoulder. 'He doesn't sound like one of those trolls. We're missing something. What did you say your name was?'

'Frederick Lacey.' Did she say *trolls*? Monsters in fairy tales. Those earnest discussions with Hugo about multi-verse theory... This could be the *wrong* world, with ogres and witches and vampires, where a different Hugo and Sophie had disappeared and returned. Hugo had said that in parallel universes there were other versions of the same person, so the Sophie here might not be *his* Sophie.

Keep calm. If this wasn't the right universe, he wouldn't travel to this version of London … go back to the lift, try again.

'How are you spelling that?' said Elliot.

Freddy frowned. 'What do you mean?'

'Your name,' Elliot said slowly. 'How Do You Spell It.'

Elliot thought him an idiot. Freddy spelled his name and Elliot tapped in the metal book.

'How would you describe Sophie?' Lorna looked more curious than suspicious.

'Beautiful, kind, brave, clever, and quite wonderful. We're engaged.'

'Engaged?' Lorna made it sound ridiculous. 'How long have you known her?'

'About four months.'

'O … kay.' Lorna sat down.

Freddy glanced at Lorna's left hand and fingers. No ring or wedding band. Did people not marry in this world?

Fudge sat beside Lorna's chair, watching Freddy, his head on one side, and like his mistress, the labrador seemed more curious than suspicious. Strange that the dog hadn't jumped up or barked when presented with an unfamiliar person. 'Fudge is very well behaved.'

Lorna didn't acknowledge the compliment. 'The police have been doing fingertip searches, on campus and off, searching for Sophie. Why didn't you tell them at the beginning that she was safe?'

'I couldn't. I wasn't here.'

'Where were you?' Elliot stopped tapping in his book.

Living right beside the lift and they didn't know about it?

At home, it was a mystery even the cleverest scientists couldn't solve. When Sophie and Hugo had arrived at the Manor, they'd been distrustful, frightened. If this couple thought him mad, he would be locked up. 'The lifts here … what do you think of them?'

'They're not pretty,' said Elliot, 'but they work. Have you a special interest in lifts?'

'Yes, I want to be an architect, like Sir Christopher Wren.' Freddy stared into his empty cup. They knew nothing about the lift.

'Have you any proof that Hugo and Sophie were staying with you?' said Lorna.

Freddy sensed her patience wouldn't endure much longer. 'Actually, I have.' He opened his notebook on the table. Pressed between the pages was a photograph of him, Sophie, and Hugo at the summer ball. He handed it to Elliot.

'What is it?' Lorna asked Elliot.

'A sepia photo of Hugo and Sophie. He's in black tie, she's wearing a fancy, old-fashioned dress.' Elliot looked at Freddy. 'And that's you.'

'Yes.'

'When was this taken?'

Freddy hesitated. In one sense, the photograph had been taken a few months ago, but if you took strict account of *where* — in another universe where time passed more slowly — the year had been 1925. 'At our ball.'

'Does she know you carry her photo around?' Elliot's tone was doubting.

'Of course,' said Freddy.

'Has she any photos of you?' said Elliot.

'I don't believe so, but she admired my guns picture.'

Lorna gripped Fudge's collar as if preparing to launch the animal at his throat.

'It was of Hugo and me at the shooting party,' said Freddy.

Elliot gave him back the photograph. 'Do you have a licence?'

The only licences Freddy knew of involved establishments selling liquor. 'I'm not in trade.'

'A licence for your guns,' said Elliot.

'I've no idea.'

Elliot stood up. 'We have to phone the police.'

'I realise this is impolite,' said Freddy, 'but do you have an indoor facility?' Couldn't risk incarceration, should leave via a window.

Elliot stared at him. Perhaps they didn't have a lavatory.

After a moment, Lorna said, 'Absolutely.' She pointed at the far interior door.

Despite her lack of sight, Lorna exuded confidence. She must have memorised the layout of this small home.

'Thank you.' Freddy hurried into the bathroom. It was the size of a cupboard, barely room to turn round. With difficulty, he closed the door.

The window was also tiny, and a bolt stopped it opening more than a few inches. A useful feature for a jail.

The lavatory and sink had been shrunk to fit and there was a tall glass box. One of the glass sides opened, and within the box was a flexible metal pipe attached to a wall. A drop of water dripped from a saucer fixed to the ceiling. Bathing equipment?

Elliot and Lorna were talking in hushed voices, but Freddy could hear every word. The walls were remarkably thin.

'The police got fed up being pestered for news while they were on campus,' said Lorna. 'If we use the non-emergency number, they won't come by for weeks, and they won't be happy if we call 999 for nothing.'

'This might not be nothing.'

'He could have been let out of somewhere, into the community.'

'He talks like a member of the royal family, wears a formal coat like my father at Remembrance and is ludicrously polite,' said Elliot. 'Go figure.'

'Describe him more.'

'About my height, sandy hair. How do you feel about him? You're pretty good at sussing people out.'

'He's not telling the whole truth,' said Lorna, 'but he was honest about feeling stressed, and I don't sense malevolence.'

'If I'd known how good your instincts were when we met, I might not have been so full of myself.'

A squishy sound. They were kissing. Freddy winced.

'Love, we should tell the police,' said Elliot. 'If he is a nutter or a stalker, he needs locking up.'

Freddy swallowed. A stalker? And the girl in the lift had called him a 'nutter.' Did that mean insane?

'He's not smooth enough to be a con man,' said Lorna, 'and he doesn't strike me as a closet terrorist.'

'No, too well dressed.'

'But why would Sophie get engaged? According to the 'Find Sophie' campaign, she was saving up to visit India this summer. She wanted adventures, not a teenage wedding.'

Freddy finally worked out how to flush the lavatory by pressing a button on the wall and returned to the parlour. He cleared his throat. 'Thank you for the tea, but I've taken up too much of your time.' He put on his jacket and picked up his coat.

Elliot stepped forward, his face resolute.

He meant to detain him here by force. And Lorna probably practised kicks and punches like Sophie—

'Don't go yet,' said Lorna. 'Why didn't Sophie phone her family and friends?'

Freddy reluctantly sat on the sofa, one eye on the front

door. How could he explain, without being arrested as 'a nutter'? Scientists in this world might believe in parallel universes, but Elliot and Lorna might not accept he was *from* one.

He could invite Elliot to accompany him to call the lift, but if Elliot didn't have the gene, he wouldn't see it.

He needed them to help him find Sophie, to check she was *his* Sophie.

Think. A believable reason why Sophie couldn't contact anybody… 'Her telephone had run out of juice.'

'Why couldn't she charge it?' said Lorna. 'Doesn't your house have electricity?'

On the wall behind Lorna was a line of sockets and wires, similar to the wiring for the telephone in the Manor. His father disliked new-fangled gadgets, had initially been reluctant to install it. 'My family disapproves of modern devices. And we're self-contained. We take no part in society.'

Elliot raised his eyebrows. 'You're from a *cult*?'

'I'm not sure what it's called,' said Freddy, 'but that's why, after Hugo and Sophie arrived, they couldn't tell anybody they were there. Sophie found it difficult at first and so did Hugo, but they adapted. Nobody expected them to leave.'

'Oh my God,' said Lorna. 'How did they escape?'

'The same way I did,' said Freddy. Keep it vague. 'In the middle of the night.'

'What would have happened if they'd been caught?' asked Lorna.

'Um, they'd have been punished.'

'You were being held too?' said Elliot.

Stick to the truth as far as possible. 'No. I'm part of the family. But I fell in love with Sophie.'

Lorna sat back in her chair. 'What religion does your family follow?'

'Church of England,' said Freddy, without thinking. 'Sophie's an atheist, but I don't mind.'

Lorna looked surprised. So did Elliot.

Sophie had told him that not believing in God was common in her England. Perhaps he'd misunderstood and Lorna thought he was insulting Sophie. 'She respected our customs. One day, she even went to church.' He smothered a yawn.

'You sound tired,' Lorna said to Freddy.

'I'm exhausted.'

'You could have a nap on the sofa.' Lorna stood up.

Freddy exhaled in relief. 'That would be very kind.'

She opened a cupboard. 'We've a spare pillow and a blanket.'

It was easy to forget Lorna was blind, save for her dog. Fudge was lying on the floor, his button eyes trained on Freddy.

'I promise to be a good house guest, and once I've recovered myself, I'll take myself down to London.'

'If you've only known life with your family,' said Elliot, 'this must seem … strange.'

Freddy nodded, glad he could be honest.

CHAPTER 6

Freddy woke up, and for a disorientating moment, couldn't remember where he was.

A weak sun filtered through flimsy curtains, making the parlour look even smaller, and his neck and back ached. A couch was a rotten substitute for a bed.

Elliot's voice was clear from the bedroom, though he was whispering. 'Two local matches for Freddy Lacey. One's sixty-something, the other's a baby. Both live in Shorten Manor.'

'Cult HQ?' said Lorna.

'Unlikely.' Elliot's tone was dry. 'It's a stately home, open to the public.'

Of course. Those Freddy Laceys must be his descendants. No, descendants of another version of him in this universe. Perhaps he should visit the Manor? Did the elderly man look like an older him? There might be a portrait of the other him a century ago in the Manor's dining room. But how would he explain who he was? He wiped sleep-sand from his eyes. The most complex maths equations were simpler than the parallel universe theory. Perhaps if he read that book Hugo had mentioned, he'd understand it better. *A History of …* something.

'Latest from the *Find Hugo* page,' said Elliot's voice. 'He's at his parents' house, with Sophie.'

Freddy's stomach rumbled and he sat up.

Lorna came into the parlour, wearing a navy skirt that reached her ankles and a loose, long-sleeved shirt. She walked to the cupboards.

'I do appreciate you letting me sleep here.' Freddy stood up from the sofa and looked out the window. Densely packed buildings.

'So, you'll go to London?' said Lorna.

'Yes.' Though how he'd pay for a train ticket, he had no idea.

Lorna handed Freddy a large saucer-less cup of tea just as Elliot emerged out of the bedroom wearing drawers and a short white shirt with cut-off sleeves.

'I'm going to hit the shower.' Elliot went into the closet.

Lorna sat opposite Freddy, and they drank tea in uncomfortable silence.

This was excruciating. 'I should leave.'

'Bathroom's free.' Elliot's words echoed through the flat.

Lorna smiled at Freddy. 'Would you like a shower?'

If the shower involved the glass box, he didn't, but out of politeness he said, 'Thank you.'

'I'll sort you a fresh towel.' Lorna strolled into the bedroom and returned with a towel.

Freddy shuffled into the bathroom, closed the door, and washed his face in the sink. The towel was fluffy and incredibly soft.

He opened the glass door. So much glass in this world. He twisted a knob on the wall. A rush of cold water drenched his head and shoulders, and he hastily adjusted the knob. He patted his hair with the towel, dabbed at his clothes, and sheepishly stepped into the parlour.

Elliot strode in, dressed in a black shirt and baggy, indigo trousers.

'Have you Hugo's parents' address?' Freddy asked him.

Elliot's eyes turned suspicious. 'Given Hugo's father's in the Cabinet, the address won't come up in a casual search. Security and all that.'

'Even if you could find the address, I don't think you'll be able to see him, or Sophie,' said Lorna. 'Have you any ID?'

'What's that?'

'Driving licence, passport,' said Lorna.

'No,' said Freddy, 'but Hugo will let me in.'

Elliot pulled on a hip-length jacket with a hood and took a dog lead from a drawer. 'Fudge!'

'Join me for a walk, Freddy.' Elliot put a coat on the labrador while the dog stood to attention. Fudge was unusual. Most dogs anticipating a walk would have leaped in delight.

The dog garment was the same glowing yellow as the jacket worn by the man with the torch. Printed across Fudge's jacket in bold black letters was *Don't Pet Me When I'm Working*.

Freddy slipped on his coat and scarf and Elliot led the way into the narrow hallway, through the students' union and outside.

Buttoning up his coat against a brisk morning breeze, Freddy looked up at the building they'd left. Elliot's rooms were at the base of a tower that was as tall as a cathedral. The turret had large bold squares painted on it, each a loud, primary colour. Garish—

'Let's go to the old chapel.' Elliot hadn't attached the lead to Fudge's collar, but he evidently didn't need to. Fudge was walking perfectly to heel.

They strode up a steep path between angular grey buildings with flat roofs, turned a corner, and Freddy gasped. In the middle of this soulless place was a medieval church.

He walked closer. This was the building that Hugo and Sophie thought existed in two places at once: here, and in his local village at home.

Two parallel universes. One church.

Above the familiar stained-glass window was the Janus carving, standing proud from the stone wall: two youthful faces looking in opposite directions. A stone's throw from the lift in the students' union, this was a symbol of a Roman god, of a doorway between worlds — and a warning not to travel.

Freddy touched the Janus frieze and felt dizzy. He drew a deep, calming breath.

'Are you okay?' asked Elliot.

'Yes. It's just … getting here has been an adventure.'

'I bet.'

What had betting to do with anything?

Fudge had availed himself of a narrow strip of grass and returned to his master's side. 'Let's go meet Lorna.'

They retraced their steps and followed a different path to a café.

Lorna was inside, seated by a window. Despite the store door constantly opening and shutting for customers of its own accord, the establishment's heating greeted Freddy in a friendly wave.

'Need to wash my hands, won't be long,' said Elliot.

Lorna gestured for Freddy to sit opposite her, and Fudge lay beside her feet.

Freddy draped his coat and scarf over the back of a chair and sat down. The table was covered with a sort of glass. Grey and shiny.

Elliot was now by the counter. 'How do you take your

coffee, Freddy?'

Freddy smiled at him. 'Milk, one sugar lump please.'

'Better opt for a flat white,' said Lorna.

Gobbledegook. A flat what?

'I'll get some pastries,' said Elliot.

'Thank you for this,' Freddy said to Lorna.

'You're welcome.'

Fudge put his head on the floor, but his eyes were alert, watching the door.

A boy came into the café and Fudge wagged his tail as he approached. The boy's skin was dark, and his hair tumbled over his shoulders in thin plaits. A male Medusa.

Freddy stood up and offered his hand. 'Freddy Lacey. How do you do?'

After a moment's hesitation, the boy shook Freddy's hand. 'Ziggy.'

Ziggy sat at the table and addressed Freddy. 'You're an intriguing guy. *No* digital footprint.' He pressed Freddy's arm. 'Flesh and blood but, digitally, you don't exist. Yet the unhackable man needs a dodgy hack. Ironic.'

There was one word Freddy recognised. 'You can't beat galloping over fields.'

'Not that sort of hack,' said Ziggy. 'Is he simple?'

Could be the easiest way to fit in here—

'He's not simple,' said Lorna. 'Just been cut off from the world.'

Ziggy stared at Freddy, his eyebrows raised. 'You've done time?'

In despair, Freddy whispered to Lorna, 'What does he mean?'

'Prison.'

Freddy sat up straighter. 'Of course not.'

Ziggy's lips twitched. 'Pity. I read this article yesterday

about a reformed criminal, genius with computers, and now he's joined the good guys.'

Lorna grinned.

Ziggy had been joking.

The café was crowded with young men and women, every table taken. One young lady had bright pink hair. 'Is there a circus nearby?' Freddy asked Lorna.

'Not that I know of.'

Another girl had been in a factory accident, a metal ring in her nose, and a metal clip through an eyebrow. So brave, appearing in public. And like Lorna, these women were chattering, confident and fierce. Perhaps all women here were as formidable as his Sophie.

Elliot set out cups, plates, and pastries.

Freddy scanned the table. 'Are there any napkins?'

'Napkins, Elliot,' said Lorna.

'Oh, right.' Elliot went to the counter and returned with a pile of thin tissues.

Freddy didn't help himself to a pastry. He was a guest, after all.

Elliot handed him a steaming cup. 'Dig in, Freddy, you'll feel better after breakfast.'

Freddy picked up a plate and a tissue and selected the nearest pastry. The confection was too dry, but the dark chocolate slivers were delicious. He finished it, sipped his coffee, and made a face.

'Sugar,' said Elliot, handing him a tiny paper envelope.

Freddy looked at him blankly.

Elliot tore off a corner and emptied sugar into Freddy's mug.

Freddy stirred the coffee with a teaspoon and tasted it. Lovely. What had happened to sugar bowls?

'Have another pain au chocolat, Freddy,' said Elliot. 'The way you ate the first pastry, you could do with it.'

After eating the pastry and sipping coffee, Freddy felt almost normal.

'Wicked suit.' Ziggy lounged in his chair, appraising him.

Freddy gave him a nervous smile. Was he being nice or horrible?

'This morning, I established you have *zero* visibility.' Ziggy watched him, apparently in admiration. 'No birth certificate, not even a fake. No record of attending school, living anywhere, or buying *anything*. If you were an undercover cop, there'd at least be a false trail. But you, Freddy, have zilch.'

Freddy swallowed. *Zilch* sounded bad.

'You found all that out so fast,' said Lorna.

'Nothing Ziggy the Geek can't crack. Finding Hugo's place only took a few minutes.'

Elliot gave an appreciative whistle.

'Not very reassuring for the security of the realm,' said Lorna.

'How did you find it?' said Elliot.

'You don't want to know.' Ziggy grinned. 'And it's your lucky day, Freddy. I'm doing gigs this week in London, so you can come along.'

Freddy nodded. What were *gigs*?

'And on the road trip, I can learn more about the invisible man.' Ziggy swallowed a big gulp of coffee.

'Ziggy, what's a road trip?' Freddy couldn't help himself.

'Jessica will get us to London safe and sound.'

'I thought she'd died,' said Lorna.

'False alarm,' said Ziggy. 'Patched up, good as new.'

'I'd still take it easy,' said Lorna.

'You're hurting my feelings.' Ziggy's tone suggested this was well-rehearsed mutual teasing.

Lorna looked in Freddy's direction. 'Jessica is Ziggy's ancient car.'

Freddy perked up. This was something he could talk about. 'How fast can she go?'

Ziggy considered. 'Open road, well over a hundred.'

'Miles per hour?'

'Obviously.'

'The speed limit's seventy.' Lorna seemed to sense Freddy's alarm.

After breakfast, as they walked to her rooms, Lorna said, 'If you and Sophie are together, why didn't you escape *with* her?'

He'd had time to invent his answer. 'I was planning to, but I fell sick the day before. The day they'd planned was their best chance. Everybody was tired after a big dinner, so I told them to go ahead, and I'd catch up.'

'But wouldn't it have been harder after they got away? Presumably your family beefed up security, after they left.'

She could work for Sherlock Holmes. 'I was family, not like Sophie and Hugo, so they weren't expecting me to leave. They didn't suspect about Sophie. We kept our engagement secret.'

Lorna nodded. 'I wish we'd known. It's been dreadful. Their families thought they'd been murdered.'

Back in the parlour, Elliot sat down on the sofa.

Freddy sat beside him. 'I'm sorry Hugo and Sophie staying with my family has caused so much trouble.'

'A *lot* of trouble.' Elliot opened his metal book, tapped, and swivelled it towards him. 'Press coverage when they disappeared.'

In the machine was a colour photograph of Hugo and underneath, a smaller one of Sophie, followed by printed text.

Former public schoolboy Hugo Harrington hasn't been seen since Monday. If he's been the victim of a targeted kidnapping, this marks a new development in the war against terror. Security for high profile figures and their families is under review...'

'And this is today.'

The new paragraph was only a few sentences, with no photographs.

The son of Edward Harrington, missing since September last year, has been found safe and well in Derby. Another student, Sophie Arundel, has also been found unharmed.

At the top of the text, a date brought home the enormity of what he'd done. Freddy swallowed.

This really was the future: the twenty-first century.

CHAPTER 7

Shortly after noon in the guest room ensuite, Sophie splashed her face with cold water. 'People have created incredible poetry, and beautiful sad novels about this,' she confided to Charlotte, 'but basically, unrequited love *sucks*.'

Despondent, Sophie slipped on her long cardigan and picked up her bag. 'Right, let's go.' Once she was on the train to the university — and the lift — this stupid hesitation, her 'hope-over-reality' mindset, would fade and, when she was back with Freddy, it should entirely disappear. She patted Charlotte and pictured the black retriever in Shorten, waiting for Charlotte. 'You'll see Jack soon.'

Downstairs in the hall, she collected Charlotte's lead from the coat rack and went to the kitchen to say goodbye. She'd already said her other goodbyes, to her best friend, and to her aunt.

She left her phone on the worktop. It wasn't fair to leave Hugo to field calls, but the phone was useless where she was going.

As she clipped the lead to Charlotte's collar, Hugo stood up from the table and Sophie briefly hugged him.

She turned on her heel, slung the strap of her bag across her chest, and walked into the hall towards the front door with Charlotte.

Hugo stood awkwardly in the doorway to the kitchen.

She'd never see him again. Finish this. 'I fell for you, head over heels.'

He stared at her, stunned. A muscle tensed in his jaw. 'I made a promise to Freddy, but I'll break it.'

Oh? This was new.

Fifteen minutes later, back in the kitchen, she was struggling to catch up, re-evaluating how he'd acted in Shorten. Memories shifted, over-written with fresh insight. Her breathing hitched, became shallow and shaky. Under thankfulness and surprise was a wrenching twist of Freddy-guilt, but she pushed it away.

Here, in the twenty-first century, Hugo could act on his feelings. His feelings for *her*.

And yet she hesitated. Was this happening? Could she believe it?

Hugo's eyes gave her the answer. He wanted her. Really wanted her. 'So, you'll stay?'

His casual tone didn't fool her. 'Obviously.' She kissed him, and when he responded, she wanted to drown in him, his touch and scent irresistible, inevitable. 'We can do anything we want.'

He mumbled against her mouth. 'Upstairs, right now?'

'Definitely *now*.'

CHAPTER 8

Ziggy's car was hurtling along a road wider than the Thames. Close beside Freddy was a truck several storeys high, longer than many cars, and beyond a low fence to his right, an endless sea of traffic raced towards them.

A bridge overhead whipped past, more deadly than a tree branch, and Freddy's heart lurched.

'How you doing?' Ziggy was resting one hand on the steering wheel and drinking from a water bottle.

Freddy kept hold of his seat, despite being tied to it with a strap bolted to the floor. It made him feel trapped, but Ziggy had insisted. 'What happens if somebody makes a mistake? Everything's going so fast, too close together.'

'If there's a pile-up, there's nothing we can do.' Ziggy gave him an odd look. 'You need to chillax.'

Chillax? He stared at the dashboard. Less alarming than the road. 'If you don't mind me asking, what's your real name?'

'Ziggy Stardust.'

'That's beautiful.'

'I'm kidding.'

'Kidding?'

'Joking.' Ziggy frowned. 'Are you sure you're English? You don't seem to get a lot of words.'

'Of course I am.' Surely that was obvious.

'Ziggy's short for Siegfried. My surname's Cameron.'

'My mother's maiden name,' said Freddy. 'Gosh, what a coincidence.'

'Not really. That name was forced on my family centuries ago by a slave owner.'

Freddy shifted in his seat. 'I'm glad we outlawed slavery.'

'We?'

'Britain—'

Ziggy veered off the terrifying road and parked in an area bigger than a field. But there was no grass, only tarmac and more cars.

Freddy couldn't release the car strap, so Ziggy did it. Freddy lurched out and concentrated on not being sick.

'My driving's not *that* bad.' Ziggy leaned against his car.

'You're an excellent driver,' Freddy managed.

In a busy café, Ziggy bought Freddy a round sandwich and potatoes cut into tiny strips. The sandwich was awkward to hold, overpacked with hot meat and unfamiliar fruit, and a bright yellow sheet of … something. Freddy bit into it and chewed. *Wondrous.* 'This is the best food I've ever tasted.'

'Your first burger.' Ziggy chuckled. 'I like you, Freddy Lacey.'

Freddy took another delicious bite and tomato sauce spurted onto his jacket. He ignored it and continued eating. The potatoes were just as tasty. He felt rejuvenated, invincible.

Back in the car, Freddy fastened his seatbelt by himself and stretched out his legs.

It was mid-afternoon when Ziggy stopped the car on a quiet street lined with trees and detached houses.

'We're still in London?' Freddy asked him.

'Wimbledon.'

'Near the tennis courts?'

Ziggy nodded. 'Hugo's house is the next on the left.'

Freddy drew a calming breath, inexplicably nervous. 'Thank you for bringing me here.' He pushed the button to take off the car strap.

'If things don't work out, call me.' Ziggy handed him a card. Below a curved line of musical notes was printed *Ziggy Cameron* and a long number. 'I could teach you to play the guitar.'

Freddy smiled, acknowledging Ziggy was joking, and climbed out. He retrieved his coat and scarf from the rear seat and waved as Ziggy drove away, grey fumes swirling from the car.

No point in putting on the coat. He'd be indoors in a jiffy.

Hugo's home was square and Georgian, fronted by a circular gravel drive. Closed iron gates prevented entry at both ends of the drive and a metal railing topped with ornamental spikes ran between the gates. Behind one gate, a policeman sat in a booth and up at the house, two officers flanked a red front door.

He hadn't expected the house to be guarded. Chin up. Faint heart never won fair lady.

Imbedded in a brick pillar by the guarded gate was a grey panel with a button. Freddy pressed it.

'State your name and business,' said the officer in the booth.

'Mr Frederick Lacey. I'm a friend of Mr Harrington and

Miss Arundel.' Using their surnames and titles was appropriate when dealing with a police officer.

'Give me a minute, sir.'

After at least five minutes, the officer said, 'You're not on any of our lists, sir, so you can't come in. No exceptions.'

Freddy's heart sank. He'd come so far, only to be defeated by mysterious lists...

Think.

'I'm not on your lists because Mr Harrington's so recently returned. If you ask him, or Miss Arundel, you'll find everything's in order.' Speaking politely and with authority should assist, or perhaps he should be more respectful, as he was with the butler. 'I appreciate the importance of following procedure, officer, but I assure you they'll vouch for my character. In fact, they're expecting me.'

That wasn't quite true, but they wouldn't be surprised. The lift had carried them home. Entirely logical it had also brought him.

The officer talked into his telephone.

What would he do if he couldn't go in? He couldn't bear it. Where would he sleep? He had no money. He checked for the calling card in his trouser pocket. If it came to it, he could borrow a telephone, contact Ziggy.

More minutes crawled by.

Then the front door opened. *Sophie*. And one of the officers was petting Charlotte.

The voice spoke from the button panel. 'Miss Arundel says she knows you, sir. Just a moment.'

Relief washed over Freddy in a rush, but he said calmly, 'Thank you.'

The metal gates opened by themselves, and Freddy waited until there was a good gap before stepping through.

'I need to search you, sir. Your coat, please.'

Freddy handed it over. The policeman went through the

pockets and draped it on the chair in the booth. 'Arms out, sir.'

The officer patted his chest, then his legs, including between them. Freddy flinched. 'Nearly done.'

This was outrageous. He should ask to speak to this man's superior.

The officer examined Freddy's notebook, the ball photograph, the penny, and Ziggy's card, and returned them. 'On you go.'

Freddy hurried up the drive towards Sophie, his heart hammering. She was wearing a night robe like Lorna's, only the garment was white towelling and much too big.

He smiled, and she gave him a nervy smile in return. Her blonde tresses were tousled, flowing over her shoulders. Freddy hadn't seen her hair undressed for months, back when she'd first arrived at the Manor. 'Sophie, am I glad to see you!'

'Ha, me too.'

The policemen on either side of the door stepped aside to allow him passage and Charlotte leapt up. Freddy scratched her furry head.

Sophie's face was rosy, as if she'd recently taken a bath. No. Something was wrong. She was leaning against the door jamb, taking dogged breaths as if she were about to faint.

'My darling girl, are you ill?'

'Came down with a nasty bug.' Sophie drew another focused breath. 'You'd better come in.'

Not wearing her engagement ring or the watch he'd given her. Yes, must have had a bath. But where was Hugo's butler, or his housekeeper? How awkward that Sophie had been obliged to greet him personally. He shouldn't have called unannounced. Ziggy could have obtained the property's telephone number—

Sophie kissed him on the cheek. 'Go through into the

drawing room. I'll be right back.' She gestured to a door off the hall and walked up a pretty staircase, gripping the balustrade for support. Perhaps the lift had made her sick? Was Hugo ill too?

Charlotte ran around Freddy, still wagging her tail, and a different dog joined in. He hung his scarf and coat on a rack and frowned at his appearance in a mirror. Dishevelled, and in need of a shave.

Hugo's drawing room wasn't that different from the small reception room in the Manor, except there was more space between the furniture. Freddy caught a familiar scent of wood polish. Many routines endured, even after a century.

Beyond a sash window was a pleasant garden. Raining now. What excellent timing.

The dogs sprinted from the room, alerted to someone in the hall, and Freddy followed.

Hugo was walking down the stairs, smiling broadly. His sleeveless pullover was familiar, but not his other clothes: slim navy trousers, a pale blue shirt, and no tie. Sophie was behind him, in her fetching cream tea dress. The art deco watch was on her wrist and his engagement ring sparkled on her left hand. Around her neck was her late mother's necklace, the single opal an eye-catching swirl of layered blues. This was the correct version of Sophie. *His* Sophie.

'Good to see you,' said Hugo.

Freddy offered his hand and Hugo shook it firmly.

'I'll make tea,' said Sophie, going through a door at the end of the hall. Charlotte raced after her.

'Let's sit down,' said Hugo, gesturing towards the drawing room.

Freddy sat on a plump sofa before a coffee table that was constructed completely of glass, even its legs. Prudent investors here presumably bought shares in glass companies.

Hugo flopped onto a sofa opposite, covered his mouth, and yawned.

'Did the lift make you sick?'

For an instant, Hugo looked confused. 'I'm fine, but Sophie has some sort of bug.' He yawned again. 'How did you get here?'

'Through the lift.'

'I get that.' Hugo's dark hair was quite awry, as if he'd forgotten to comb it. 'How on earth did you travel down to London?'

'It was difficult.' Freddy leaned forward. 'Reynolds said Mr Parkes went insane in the lane, tried to kill you.'

Hugo rubbed his eyes. 'It's a long story.'

Freddy patted the arm of the sofa. Like the ones at home. Real. Solid. The adrenaline enabling him to cope with the strange and the new had dissipated, leaving him weary. After he'd rested, they should all return to the lift, then settle into the Manor for the wedding—

'I'll go help Sophie with the tea things.' Hugo stood up.

As Freddy began to stand, Hugo said, 'Don't worry, I've got this.' He put his fingers through his hair, a very Hugo-gesture.

Freddy smiled at his retreating back. The perfect best man.

CHAPTER 9

Sophie followed Hugo into the drawing room and Freddy jumped up from the sofa.

Yes, it really was Freddy.

Hugo set the tray on the table.

'Milk, one sugar.' Sophie handed Freddy a mug, and he shot her a huge grin, clearly pleased she remembered how he took his tea. She'd believed she'd never see him again and, bizarrely, despite sleeping with Hugo, part of her was *glad* Freddy was here.

But how was he here? It had taken a seriously wacky theory and sustained concentration for her to call the lift. A fluke they'd got home at all. And yet Freddy had followed, apparently as easily as hailing a cab.

Sophie almost sat down beside Hugo. No, that would be weird.

She sat beside Freddy instead. He had a messy red stain on his jacket and her heart missed a beat. She hadn't noticed that on the doorstep. 'Is this blood?' she pointed. 'Are you hurt?'

'No.' Freddy patted her hand. 'Tomato sauce.'

In Shorten, he'd always been immaculately turned out, but there was a shadow of stubble on his chin that made him look older. Sexier. Freddy beamed at her, and her stomach flipped. Surprising … and perverse. An interesting highlight from the last few hours popped into her head and lingered like an X-rated movie trailer.

Get a grip. This was an excruciating mess… 'Sorry there's only biscuits, Freddy. You probably haven't eaten.'

'I'm not at all hungry.' Freddy drank his tea. 'I had the most wonderful meat and cheese sandwich. Beat the Ritz into a cocked hat.'

'Is that when you spilled sauce on your jacket?' said Hugo.

Freddy nodded. 'Sophie, I'm so glad you're still wearing your tea dress. At the café off the busy road, some women wore skimpy … unbecoming attire.'

'We got back very late last night,' said Sophie. 'I've ordered regular clothes, but they won't arrive until tomorrow.' She smoothed out a crease on her silk skirt.

'Isobel keeps clothes here,' said Hugo. 'You should borrow some.'

Isobel was one of Hugo's sisters. 'Thanks.' Sophie sipped her tea without tasting it and put down the mug. 'Is Reynolds okay?' Without the chauffeur, she wouldn't have survived the attack in the lane.

'In a terrible state. He said Mr Parkes *punched* you.' Freddy's full lips compressed into a grim line. 'My darling girl.' He held Sophie's hand in his.

'Tell us everything Reynolds said, and we'll fill in the gaps.' Hugo glanced at Sophie, his blue eyes sending a clear message.

In Shorten, Hugo had been adamant that only he would get into the lift and return home. But just before Alan Parkes attacked them, Hugo had urged Sophie to go with him. If the chauffeur had told Freddy that, Hugo would somehow need to explain it away.

'Reynolds said a man assaulted him,' said Freddy, 'and that Mr Parkes had *murdered* you.'

Freddy squeezed her hand, and Hugo's shoulders relaxed, an almost imperceptible change in his body language. The chauffeur had been fighting for his life, so Hugo urging her to get into the lift was a trivial detail. Not worth remembering, or recounting to Freddy.

'Parkes punched me unconscious,' said Hugo, 'thought I was dead. He stabbed Charlotte and tried to strangle Sophie. We only escaped by getting in the lift.'

'He went after us with a knife,' said Sophie, 'but as he reached the lift, the doors shut and sliced off his hand.'

Freddy gaped.

'My nose was bashed in,' said Hugo, 'and Charlotte nearly died.'

'Your nose looks fine, and Charlotte's fine too.' Freddy stroked Charlotte who was leaning into his legs.

'We believe the lift put us into comas, to heal us,' said Hugo. 'And it somehow disposed of Parkes' hand.'

Freddy held his mug as if it might wriggle from his grasp. 'The lift broke my watch.' He made a face.

'Ours only needed winding.' Hugo wore a wind-up watch, his great-great-grandfather's. Despite being an antique, it still worked.

With every passing minute, Freddy's expensive gift on Sophie's wrist, a century-old timepiece, seemed more showy, heavier.

Freddy wound his watch. 'You're right. It's working.' He grinned. 'We're an exclusive group, aren't we? Having the gene.'

'I don't have it,' said Hugo. 'I only travelled because I was with Sophie — and Charlotte.'

'Interesting,' said Freddy. 'However it works, it's efficient. I wasn't in there for long.'

'We think our journey actually took days, maybe weeks.' Sophie picked up her mug. 'And while we were asleep or unconscious, time didn't pass. We weren't hungry or thirsty and Hugo didn't need a shave.'

'Perhaps the real time varies,' said Hugo. 'Like the outward leg to the States taking longer because of the jet stream. No, that's idiotic. Space and time don't have winds.'

Freddy smiled, had missed these musings. 'There may be a sort of wind in space. Streams of electrons ejected by the sun.' He sipped his tea.

'There's an episode of *Star Trek* where solar winds are harnessed by a sail to fly through space.' Sophie had spent hours in Shorten explaining how science fiction had expanded from classic books into television and films.

'Can I watch it?' asked Freddy.

'Absolutely, but later,' said Hugo. 'Tell us what happened from when you left the lift.'

As Freddy talked, Sophie's mind whirred. He'd landed at the university not long after them. And he was okay, just tired.

'I hope I won't catch your bug, Sophie.' Freddy finished his tea.

She flushed. The only thing she was coming down with was an addiction to sex. Well, sex with Hugo. She lifted the teapot and topped up Freddy's mug.

Freddy's gaze was on her mouth, and she made herself smile at him, keen not to catch Hugo's eye or she'd turn beet-root red. She was having flashbacks, but good ones. If Freddy hadn't turned up, she'd have been enjoying a real-life repeat—

Hugo put down his mug with a clank. 'What happened to the girl in the lift?'

'I've no idea,' said Freddy. 'She ran off.'

'Must have the gene,' said Sophie.

'She'll never go near the lift again,' said Freddy. 'She was terribly frightened.'

'There must be stairs in the tower block that would take her to her room,' said Sophie. 'And there's another regular lift beside our gold one.'

'She'll use the stairs,' said Hugo, looking sombre. 'I would.'

'Her gown was lovely,' said Freddy.

'After we got back, we saw her go into our lift,' said Sophie. 'She was wearing a sari, an Indian style of dress.'

'I wonder what she's doing in England?' mused Freddy, half to himself.

'Likely born here,' said Sophie. 'Indian heritage.'

'I didn't see her,' said Hugo.

'You were in a daze after the crossing,' said Sophie. 'Completely out of it.'

Hugo rolled his eyes and she gave him a pretend frown.

'You two are funny,' said Freddy. 'You've always done this.'

'What?' asked Hugo.

'Playfighting. Like Jack and Charlotte, before they, you know…'

Sophie swallowed. Charlotte and Jack had loved playfighting in the Manor gardens.

Hugo's square-jawed face was carefully blank.

'Sorry, I'm not comparing you to dogs.' Freddy shook his head, as if he had water in his ears.

Charlotte was dozing against Freddy's legs, seemed content, but as she drank her tea, Sophie's guilt and self-loathing resurfaced. When she'd learned that Hugo had feelings for her, Sophie had abandoned her plan to return to Shorten, trading Charlotte's happiness for hers. Charlotte would never be with Jack—

'You don't look well,' said Freddy, eyeing her with concern. 'You should go to bed.'

Sophie's tea went down the wrong way and she lurched into a coughing fit. Freddy hit her on the back.

Note to self. Don't drink tea in stressful situations.

'Freddy's right,' said Hugo, giving her a meaningful look.

Retreat, regroup. Sophie scurried to the bathroom off the hall and splashed cold water on her face. The thought of hurting Freddy made her feel sick, but as soon as he'd recovered from the crossing, she'd explain — and break off the engagement.

For now, though, Hugo had resurrected his acting skills. And she needed to perfect hers.

CHAPTER 10

Five minutes later, Sophie came back into the drawing room from the bathroom, feeling more composed, and sat beside Freddy again.

Freddy put his arm around her shoulders. 'You're not well. You really should go to bed.'

Ouch. Stop talking about *bed*.

'I think you have a temperature.' Freddy had always treated her like fragile china. 'You are *my* Sophie, aren't you?'

Her heart missed a beat. 'What do you mean?'

'Not a different Sophie, in the wrong world?'

She silently exhaled. Just parallel universes stuff. Different versions of her. 'I'm the right Sophie.' She stroked Charlotte, who was now stretched out by her legs.

'And this is the right version of home,' said Hugo.

'I'm not sure about that.' Freddy finished his second mug of tea. 'When Elliot wanted to call the police, he thought I was a magical creature.'

'Sorry?' said Hugo.

'From a fairy tale.' Freddy placed his mug on the coffee

table. 'Someone had sent them poison pen letters, saying horrible things about Sophie. They said it was a troll.'

'Makes sense,' said Hugo.

'No, it doesn't,' said Freddy.

'Trolls are people who write nasty stuff online,' said Sophie.

'Why are they called trolls?' asked Freddy. 'Trolls don't write letters in stories. Too busy guarding bridges, making travellers pay tolls. Perhaps the words became mixed up. Trolls and tolls—'

'Hello.' Pamela strolled in with George, the Harrington's golden labrador. Pamela was a friend who lived in Hugo's house. Why she did, Sophie didn't know.

George bounded towards Hugo, who scratched him behind his ears, and Charlotte leapt up and ran towards Pamela.

'This is Freddy,' said Hugo. 'His family took us in when we were … away.'

Freddy got to his feet and offered his hand in a formal handshake. 'Freddy Lacey. How do you do?'

'How do you do. Pamela Beeching.' She shook his hand.

'Could he stay in the Stables?' said Hugo. 'Sorry about the short notice.'

Pamela smiled at Freddy. 'No problem.'

'Come on,' said Hugo, standing up. 'Let's check it out.'

Concern registered in Freddy's soft brown eyes. 'I've never slept in a stable.'

'It's *converted* from stables,' said Hugo. 'There's a sitting room, as well as a bedroom.'

Beyond the kitchen, in the utility room, Hugo selected a key from a box on the wall and Sophie followed the boys along a short path.

The Stables' ground floor was stacked with boxes, but

upstairs, the double bedroom, sitting room, and bathroom had been finished to a good spec.

Hugo opened a linen cupboard. 'If you need more pillows or something, Mrs B will sort it.'

The sitting room hadn't long been decorated, smelled of paint.

Freddy bent down to examine the TV. 'Mrs Bee?'

'Pamela. I've called her that from when I was little.'

'Is she your housekeeper?' Freddy picked up the TV remote and peered at it. 'You said nobody had servants.'

'Mrs B isn't a *servant*, Freddy,' said Hugo. 'She's an old friend of my mother's. She's been staying on and off since I disappeared.'

Freddy turned over the remote in his hand, then randomly pressed buttons. 'You said machines did everything.'

'Not *everything*,' said Hugo. 'A girl called Ania comes in to clean. She works when she can, around her family responsibilities.'

'Your society seems to be at an unsatisfactory in-between stage,' said Freddy.

'Sorry?' Sophie flopped down on the small couch.

'Too few servants, and not enough machines.'

'You may be right.' Hugo looked through the window. 'My mother's back from work.'

'She *works*?' said Freddy.

'As a solicitor.'

'Goodness.' Freddy waggled the remote. 'What does this do?'

Hugo switched on the TV plug at the wall, took the remote and pressed a button.

The screen lit up and so did Freddy's face, like a child on Christmas morning.

Hugo caught her eye. 'You look done in. I've got this.'

Sophie shot him an appreciative glance and made her way down the Stables stairs. She hurried along the path to the main house, through the utility room, but paused in the doorway to the kitchen.

Charlotte lay by the French windows, George asleep beside her. Pamela was by the cooker, talking to Hugo's mother.

Fiona Harrington's pencil skirt and matching grey jacket were crease-free and business-like, but her immaculate make up couldn't conceal the shadows under her eyes. A cruel legacy of so many days not knowing if her son was alive or dead. She looked up. 'Pamela tells me we have another guest.'

'Yes,' said Sophie, feeling awkward. 'He's … the son of the family we stayed with.'

Fiona nodded. 'Part of the cult.'

'He's very polite and well-dressed,' said Pamela, stirring a spoon in a teapot.

'Freddy's had a sheltered life,' said Sophie. 'No exposure to television, mobile phones or the internet.' Inspiration struck. 'His family's similar to the Amish in America. They don't use modern gadgets.'

'I see,' said Fiona. 'Will he be staying long?'

Sophie had no freaking idea. 'Just a few days.' She sat down at the kitchen table.

Hugo's mother accepted a mug of tea from Pamela.

'I'll bring you up supper in a bit.' Pamela gave Fiona a reassuring smile and received a grateful nod in return before Hugo's mother walked away.

Pamela sat down opposite Sophie. 'You weren't expecting him.' It wasn't a question.

'No.'

Pamela drank her tea, her kind face thoughtful. 'I was young once, you know.'

Deep breath. 'Freddy's family doesn't approve of sex

outside of marriage, and Freddy would be appalled if he knew Hugo and I were together.' Sophie met her eyes. 'Could you ask Hugo's parents to keep schtum?'

'Of course.' Pamela hesitated. 'When you turned up last night, I assumed you'd led Hugo astray. Hugo giving up on university was *so* out of character.'

An illogical pang of guilt. Neither of them had chosen to cross universes.

'But it was clear to me this morning what's happened. He's fallen in love.'

Sophie bit her lip. Like Hugo, she had a huge sign on her head: *Clear the road, madly in love person approaching.* Freddy would twig within hours—

'It's magical when you meet the right person.' Pamela smiled, but it was wistful.

'Hugo is … special.'

Pamela's eyes twinkled. 'You must be too. Listening to Bizet for three straight hours.'

Sophie looked down. Pamela's rooms were next to Hugo's bedroom. The outpouring of romantic opera had been plenty loud enough to cover any untoward noise. Or so they'd thought. 'It was a random digital choice.'

'You're the first girl he's brought home.' Pamela stared at her mug. 'And he's never been into opera … so I knew it was serious.'

Hugo strode into the kitchen, Freddy in his wake. 'Freddy wants to use the family bathroom.'

'Is the Stables shower not behaving?' asked Pamela.

'Behaving perfectly, but Freddy would prefer a bath.' The boys tramped off upstairs.

'I take it Freddy's family doesn't approve of showers?' said Pamela.

'They're eccentric,' lied Sophie.

Where Freddy's family lived, showers had yet to be invented.

~

By ten that night, Hugo's house was silent. The sort of silence that said everyone was asleep or should be. Wearing Hugo's sister's sweatshirt and tracksuit bottoms, and with Charlotte at her heels, Sophie climbed the stairs to Hugo's room. Isobel's clothes weren't flattering. The tracksuit wrinkled in folds around Sophie's ankles.

Hugo's bedside light was on, and he was sitting on the edge of his bed in his dressing gown, frowning at his phone.

'What's up?'

'I've told my friends the cover story. I *hate* lying.' He put the phone aside.

'I feel guilty about Freddy all the time.' Sophie sat down next to him. 'The new normal.'

'Tomorrow, we tell him about us.'

Sophie clasped her hands together and Freddy's ring sparkled, the solitaire diamond caught by the light from the lamp. 'We should wait. He's reeling from the crossing and twenty-first century overload.'

Charlotte curled into a sleeping position on the floor.

'Perhaps you're right.' Hugo sighed. 'He took an age to accept he could have a bath without a valet.'

'A *future* alien place is a scary learning curve,' said Sophie. 'We had it easy in Shorten, had some idea how things worked from TV shows.'

'I want Freddy to enjoy himself before … we explain about us. I've given him my old pay-as-you go.'

'How old is it?' Her phone was positively ancient.

'Last year's model. I've topped it up and showed him the features.'

'He'll have fun with that.'

'Play Bizet's *Pearl Fishers Duet*,' said Hugo, and the aria started up through the smart speaker.

The beautiful sound was now indelibly associated with making love with Hugo. Sung in French, the lyrics were lost in the melody and not distracting. Just as well. An aria sung by two men in love with the same woman… 'Pamela mentioned hearing this music.'

'I played it too loud,' said Hugo. 'But I was rather preoccupied.'

'I think she's guessed that Freddy's more than a friend.'

'Nothing gets past her,' said Hugo. 'My mother came second on their law course, but Mrs B ranked first.'

'How come Pamela didn't practise?'

'Her husband died. Living with us, she was able to care for her new-born baby, helped look after my sisters, then me. When she moved to Suffolk, we kept in touch.'

'What happened to the baby?' asked Sophie.

'All grown up. Works in a hospital near here.'

Sophie peeled off Isobel's sweatshirt and tracksuit bottoms and dived self-consciously under the duvet.

'I can't believe you're embarrassed about undressing.' Hugo did his killer half-smile. 'After this afternoon.'

Sophie blushed. 'I'm still adapting to … *us*.'

'And now Freddy.' Hugo drove his hand through his hair. 'I'm so wired and tired, I want to bite somebody.'

'I'm up for pretend biting. Maybe we need to think up safe words. You know, *Fifty Shades*, so the person stops if the other person's hurting too much.'

Hugo threw off his dressing gown, slipped into bed beside her and drew her close. 'This Freddy mess is painful enough.'

CHAPTER 11

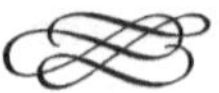

The next day, shortly after nine, Freddy lay in the bath, humming to himself. He'd bathed last night and was surely clean, but bathing first thing was an ingrained habit. And with no requirement to make conversation with his valet, the experience was more tranquil.

The tiny telephone lay on a bath stool, sleek and black. After texting Sophie, *I love you,* and texting Ziggy, *Good luck with your concert,* Freddy had been seized by a mysterious desire not to let the device out of his sight.

He washed his hair and ruminated on an article he'd read on the small screen, how algorithms had transformed the stock exchange. Fascinating.

After his bath, he dressed in Hugo's borrowed trousers and shirt.

Down the hall, a young woman in a floral apron walked towards him, pulling a sleek machine with a long handle. The scullery maid Hugo had mentioned—

'Hello. You must be Freddy.'

He'd never spoken to a scullery maid at home and if he had, none of them would have called him Freddy, but when in Rome… 'I'm afraid I've left towels on the floor in the bathroom.'

'I'll sort them after Sophie's bedroom. No worries.' The maid went into a nearby room.

Sophie sat at the kitchen table opposite Hugo, sipping coffee and half-watching the news on a wall-mounted TV. Oh, for a few more hours sleep… She yawned. 'Nearly ten. Freddy should be up soon.'

'He wasn't an early riser in Shorten,' said Hugo. 'Getting up at six was overkill.'

'Better safe than sorry.'

Charlotte pawed at the French windows. Sophie opened them and Charlotte ran out, braving drizzle and a sharp wind.

When Charlotte returned from the garden, George was hoovering dogfood from a bowl with labrador-thorough-ness, but she only glanced at him before sitting by the window and staring out at the lawn. Since they'd arrived at Hugo's house, she'd been waiting for Jack to turn up from Shorten, and Freddy's arrival had given her false hope.

'I can't bear to see her like this.' Sophie hurried over to Charlotte and closed the French windows. 'Once Freddy knows about us, I'll go back to Shorten to collect Jack.'

Hugo frowned. 'Hell of a risk. We still don't understand how the lift works.'

Sealed inside, the suffocating heat … but Sophie set her mouth. 'It's the only way they can be together.' She sat at the table again. 'Charlotte should have a treat — human break-fast food.'

'Absolutely.' Hugo strode to the bread bin and put a slice into a toaster.

Time with him was precious, to be savoured. His dark, unruly hair, his fringe askew on his forehead, those thick lashes, long for a boy, and his lips, firm and sensual—

'We need a plan.' Hugo spread butter on Charlotte's toast.

'For today or life generally?'

'Just today.' Hugo put the plate of toast beside Charlotte and, after a cautionary sniff, she ate it in one swallow.

'We could watch *Star Trek* in the drawing room?'

'Better in the games room,' said Hugo. 'Bigger TV.'

'You've got a games room?'

'And a virtual reality playstation.'

'Expensive toy.'

'It is, but everybody uses it, even Dad,' said Hugo. 'This morning, we tell Freddy the traveller cover story, so he won't be surprised if my family bring it up.'

'Including our "fictional" romance? Too near the bone.' Unease swirled, and she took a sip of coffee, hoping the feeling would fade.

'The most convincing lies contain a kernel of truth—'

'Good morning.' Freddy stood uncertainly in the doorway.

Sophie spilled her coffee. How long had he been there? He'd buttoned Hugo's shirt up to the neck, despite not wearing a tie.

Freddy felt his unshaved chin. 'I couldn't make head nor tail of your device. I plugged it in, but feared I'd cut my face.'

'I'll show you later,' said Hugo. 'Tea or coffee?'

'Tea, thank you. Why are you both in here?'

Hugo filled a kettle. 'Why wouldn't we be?'

'Shouldn't we adjourn to the dining room for breakfast?'

'It's not as cosy.' Hugo put a square muslin bag into a teapot.

'What's that?' Freddy peered at it.

'A tea bag,' said Sophie. 'You don't have to strain the leaves.'

'Does the bag taint the flavour?' asked Freddy.

'I guess it should, but it doesn't.' Sophie gestured at the chair beside her.

Freddy sat down and pointed at the fridge. 'What's that?'

'It does the same as an icebox but keeps cold without a gap to the outside.' Hugo pulled out a drawer. 'You freeze food so it lasts weeks, sometimes months.' He shut the drawer. 'And it makes ice.' He pushed a glass against the lever in the small recess. Ice popped into the glass, and he put in orange juice.

Freddy accepted the drink. 'Incredible.'

'You were smart to realise Lorna and Elliot didn't know about the lift.' Hugo added boiling water to the teapot. 'The theory of parallel universes might be respected, but most people don't believe in other worlds, any more than ghosts and gods and fairies.'

'I had no wish to be locked inside a lunatic asylum,' said Freddy.

'Same,' said Sophie. 'We've told everyone we joined a group of travellers who reject modern life.'

Hugo tipped milk into a mug in front of Freddy and poured tea. 'You convinced Elliot and Lorna that you'd grown up in a cult. Not that different.' He stirred in sugar.

'Lorna assumed my family was a cult thingy.' Freddy drank his tea.

'We also had to invent a reason why we left the university in the first place,' said Sophie.

'So, we embroidered the story,' said Hugo. 'We dropped out and joined the travellers because me and Sophie had a whirlwind romance.'

'A whirlwind romance.' Freddy chortled.

Sophie's stomach clenched. 'Yes, pretty lame.'

'We're stuck with it now,' said Hugo.

Sophie stood up and stashed her mug and Hugo's in the dishwasher.

'That does the washing up?' Freddy jumped to his feet, scurried over and looked inside.

'It works at a high temperature,' said Hugo, 'so crockery's cleaner than washing by hand.' He clicked the door closed.

Freddy perused the buttons and wash cycles. 'No need to pay these machines, or look after their families, and they don't require sleep.'

Hugo nodded.

'But who looks after the servants, and their families?' said Freddy.

'Nobody,' said Hugo. 'They look after themselves.'

'The descendants of the staff at Shorten here have machines in their homes, so in a way everyone has silent, efficient servants,' said Sophie. 'And I bet if we tracked down their descendants, some would be engineers and doctors, others would be running their own companies.'

'Why is everyone obsessed with betting?' said Freddy.

'It's only an expression,' said Sophie, resisting an urge to hug him. Maybe *not* telling Freddy straight away was crueller than putting it off—

'What's wrong with her?' Freddy pointed at the television.

A transwoman was advertising fitness equipment.

'Nothing's *wrong* with her,' said Sophie. 'Sometimes, people are born as a boy but in their brain, they're a girl. And vice versa. She may have started off male, but now she's female. You can have surgery to be what you really are.'

'When you say surgery,' said Freddy, 'you mean…'

'Yes.'

Freddy frowned. 'Would you rather be a boy?'

Very Freddy. Switching fast from the general to the Sophie-specific. 'No. I just enjoy doing boyly stuff.'

'Like your kickboxing,' said Freddy.

'Exactly.' She'd demonstrated her school hobby to Freddy in Shorten and he'd been baffled. Probably still was.

Hugo changed the TV channel. Grainy footage of soldiers running across a bleak landscape flickered, then dissolved into a static image. *'A hundred years on, we remember them.'*

'The First World War,' said Hugo. The picture switched to an aerial shot of white headstones and red poppies.

'Remind me,' said Freddy, 'when was your war?'

'1914 to 1918,' said Hugo.

'I was fourteen in 1918,' said Freddy, his eyes on the screen.

'Even if the Great War had happened in your universe,' said Hugo, 'you'd have been too young to fight.'

'On the first day on the Somme, over 57,000 British casualties…'

'That can't be right,' said Freddy. 'On the first day.' He swallowed.

'Hugo, turn it off,' said Sophie.

Freddy stared at the now blank screen. 'That can't be right,' he repeated.

'It is,' said Hugo. 'That's why it's called the Great War. The war to end all wars.'

'You told me about it, but I didn't appreciate the scale,' said Freddy. 'I hope before it finished, I would have volunteered, lied about my age.'

The poignant TV image lingered in Sophie's mind. 'I'm glad you never had the chance.'

Freddy put down his mug. 'I'm not a coward.'

'I'd rather you were the biggest coward in history,' said Sophie, 'than dead.'

'Junior officers' life expectancy was six weeks,' said Hugo. 'Even less than private soldiers.'

'It would have been the honourable thing to do,' said Freddy. 'My friends would have signed up—'

'Let's listen to Vaughan Williams,' said Sophie. 'Freddy's favourite.'

'I'm surprised you don't prefer Mozart,' Hugo said to him. 'Isn't it supposed to be perfect and beautiful, akin to high-level maths?'

'Mozart is beautiful but not relaxing,' said Freddy.

'Play *The Lark Ascending*,' said Hugo.

The glorious melody filled the kitchen and Freddy gasped. 'It's as if there's an orchestra hidden in the walls.'

'I'll add your voice to the machine,' said Hugo. 'There's almost every piece of music you can think of.'

Freddy took that in. 'This is a wonderful world.'

'Wait till you try out VR,' said Hugo. 'It'll blow your mind.'

'I'm not sure I want to "blow my mind,"' said Freddy.

Sophie smiled. 'In a good way.'

After lunch, while Hugo chatted with his parents, Sophie went downstairs with Freddy to the games room. She sat in a squishy chair, reading a book on her phone, and Freddy battled a Bond-villain. Hugo had lent him his credit card to purchase a powerful weapon which might vanquish evil forever.

When Freddy finally removed the VR headset, he looked tired but triumphant. 'I won,' he said, wiping his brow with his sleeve. 'I *love* the future.'

His cheekbones were perfectly symmetrical. As fit as Hugo, but with fair hair—

Freddy's phone pinged. 'It's Ziggy. How far is Soho?'

'Not far.'

'*Come late for the best vibes. Every night till Friday,*' read Freddy. 'Let's go. It'll be wizard fun.'

An all-nighter. Sleeping with Hugo held far more appeal. 'That bug's knocked me out. Go in a few days?'

Freddy nodded. He pointed at Sophie's sky-blue short-sleeved shirt. 'That's pretty.'

'One of the tops I ordered.'

He pulled her gently out of her chair and his lips covered hers. Sophie's body reacted like a flame imbued with petrol. Her senses were revved during the day, maybe due to them being hammered at night.

Cheating bitch sounded in her brain, but it was a while before she could draw back without it seeming a rebuff.

'Your kisses are different,' said Freddy, 'more intense.' He reached out for her again.

'I've got to tell you—'

Freddy kissed her with increased urgency, his arms around her as unyielding as iron bands. While Sophie's skin heated, her head considered the ethics of stamping on his foot.

Someone cleared their throat.

Hugo was in the doorway, his expression carefully neutral. Freddy stepped back, his face flushed with desire or embarrassment, or both.

That evening, after midnight, Hugo came into his room and Sophie sat up in bed. Charlotte barely stirred, briefly opening one eye.

'Do we have an odd relationship?' said Sophie. 'You and me, I mean.'

'No.'

'This afternoon, with Freddy... If we were normal, you'd be angry, and I'd be mortified. But I'm not and you're not. That's odd.'

'It's an odd situation. Doesn't make *us* odd.' Hugo sat on

the bed and pulled off his trainers. 'You shouldn't have waited up.'

'I couldn't sleep.' She shut the book app and put her phone aside. 'Let me guess. Freddy wouldn't stop playing VR.'

'He's addicted.' Hugo undressed and slid into bed.

Sophie lay on her side, facing him. She pushed an errant blonde hair from her eyes.

'Look, this afternoon when you were smiling at Freddy, you need to stop.' Hugo plumped his pillow.

'I can't just go all dour on him.'

'In Shorten, I thought of it as your microwave smile.'

'Doesn't sound nice.'

'It isn't,' said Hugo. 'I know what that smile's doing to his insides.'

She frowned. 'Oh.'

'Subconsciously, he realises something's wrong. After he stopped playing the new game, he insisted on Googling World War 1. All the bad stuff, mustard gas, chemical weapons … traumatising himself, and for no reason. It never happened in his universe. I don't understand where his head is.' Hugo drew her into his arms. 'But I've had it with deceiving him.'

'He'll be *so* hurt,' said Sophie.

'I downloaded that friends app onto his phone. If he bolts, we can keep an eye on him.'

'You think he might … hurt himself?' Apprehension closed her throat.

Hugo held her closer, but the unease didn't abate, only forgotten in sleep.

~

Piercing ringing wrenched Sophie awake. She cast about in the dark for her phone on Hugo's bedside table. She squinted at it. *04:17.* And an unfamiliar number. She pressed the green button. 'Who is this?'

'It's Ziggy. I got your number from Freddy's phone. He's collapsed.'

'*What?* Where is he?'

'In hospital. Someone spiked his drink.'

CHAPTER 12

Freddy floated on his back in the river on the Shorten estate. The water was pure and cool, and the sun was radiant in a flawless sky.

Sophie was floating beside him. She kissed him on the cheek, the touch of her lips like gossamer.

Bleep. Bleep.

Peculiar noise. The bleeping was mechanical.

'How's party boy doing?' said a woman with a foreign, sing-song accent.

'Hanging in there,' said a man's voice.

Sophie hadn't reacted to the strange voices. Couldn't she hear them?

Whispering in the air. 'You need to wake up.' Sophie's voice, but her face above the water was still, her lips not moving.

A flicker on his forehead. He brushed off an insect.

The next instant, he was in the lift, his heart pounding. Freddy ran his fingers over the wall panelling. Wood-swirls but no texture. Not real.

Bleep. Bleep. What *was* that noise?

Sophie came into the lift, sobbing as she walked. 'If you don't wake up, you can't have your Happy Ever After.' She sniffed. 'You deserve that.' She squeezed his hand, but he couldn't respond.

The Lark Ascending. Wondrous and perfect.

Sophie's voice cut off the music. *'There was a table set out under a tree in front of the house, and the March Hare and the Hatter were having tea at it; a Dormouse was sitting between them, fast asleep...'*

He loved *Alice in Wonderland*, but Sophie couldn't be reading it. Where was she?

The trace of lips on his.

Bleep.

'I'm sorry the magic kiss didn't work, but the brain scan was clear,' said Hugo's voice. 'He's in there.'

Freddy's chest ached. He wanted to double over but couldn't.

Sophie's voice again. *'Please* wake up.'

But Freddy's eyelids were iron shutters, welded shut.

He pictured pulling at a rusting portcullis, marshalling every ounce of will. A brilliant light bored into his eyeballs, and he screwed his eyes shut.

After a moment, he opened them a fraction, then a fraction more. Hugo was standing a few feet away, his arm around Sophie.

Freddy blinked.

'He's awake.' Sophie ran forwards and there was a different bleep. 'Freddy, can you hear me?' She waved her hand in front of him.

Was this part of the dream? Something hard and sharp was inside his nose and throat, preventing him swallowing. Freddy tried to scream but no sound came out.

'He's conscious.' Sophie gestured frantically at a woman in a short blue dress.

'I'll get the consultant.'

The light was far too bright...

'Come on, time to face the world.'

Freddy hauled up his eyelids. Sophie and Hugo had vanished. Had he imagined them?

'Let's take this off.' The lady in the blue dress pulled a long tube from out of his head.

Freddy drew a shaky breath. His throat was burning from whatever had been shoved down it, but he could swallow.

The woman helped him sit up, arranging pillows behind his shoulders. She offered him a flimsy white beaker and he sipped.

Water. He finished it. 'Hello.' The word came out as a croak. 'Could I trouble you for a cup of tea?'

The woman nodded. 'But we should wait for Ms Laycross. Ah, here she is.'

A slim lady in dark trousers and a white shirt strode through a swinging door. 'Hello,' she said. 'Do you know your name?'

'Of course,' said Freddy.

'What is it?' she said patiently.

'Mr Frederick Lacey. My chest hurts.'

'He's already on maximum co-codamol,' said the woman in the blue dress.

'Switch him onto Zapain,' said Ms Laycross. 'They broke two ribs bringing you back. It happens. You'll be sore for a few days.'

A tube was embedded in his left hand. It hurt, though not as badly as his ribs.

Someone was crying. The same sobbing as in his dream. Freddy turned his head, his neck stiff and aching.

Sophie was there, wiping her eyes, Hugo beside her. As they came towards him, Ms Laycross left, the door to the ward swaying behind her.

'Where am I?' said Freddy. The air smelled of carbolic soap.

Sophie held his right hand. 'In hospital.'

He'd seen pictures of huge dormitories in a book on Florence Nightingale, but this room was tiny.

'Someone at Ziggy's gig spiked your drink,' said Hugo.

Music that was terribly loud. Speaking to a man with a wispy beard then … nothing.

'A drug called ecstasy,' said Sophie.

'I've been dreaming. A ghastly confused mess. *Not* ecstatic.'

'You're talking.' Hugo grinned.

'Why wouldn't I be?'

'The consultant said you could have brain damage,' said Sophie.

Freddy felt his clammy forehead. 'How long have I been here?'

Sophie's grip on his hand tightened. 'Fifteen days.'

'Why did you tell the people in the hospital you were my brother?' Freddy asked the following day as Hugo drove him to his house.

'If they'd thought we weren't family,' said Hugo, 'they wouldn't have let us see you.'

Sitting by Freddy on the back seat, Sophie squeezed his arm. 'We told them Ziggy was your brother too.'

'How would *anyone* believe that Ziggy's my brother?' said Freddy.

'Half-brother,' said Sophie. 'Only next of kin are allowed in intensive care.'

'Intensive care. That sounds nice. Lots of care.'

'No,' said Hugo. '*Not* nice.'

'You nearly died.' Sophie hesitated. 'Actually, you *did* die. They had to resuscitate you. That's how they broke your ribs, pounding on your heart.'

'I was *dead*?' said Freddy.

'Only for a few minutes,' said Sophie. 'Don't think about it.'

He'd been resurrected, like Christ. 'How can they do that?'

'They use a machine,' said Sophie. 'It's not creepy or anything.'

'I dreamed I was in Shorten. You were there, but it was a mix of memories and fears.' Would that happen again when he died — properly? Freddy shuddered.

'The nurses were fantastic,' said Sophie.

'They were, but over-familiar. They called me Freddy.'

'That's your name,' said Sophie.

'My family call me that,' said Freddy, 'and close friends. I was Master Freddy to the servants and Mr Lacey to everyone else.'

'I've always called you Freddy,' said Sophie, 'so has Hugo.'

'As I said, close friends.' In the hospital, he'd been affronted, then annoyed, and finally resigned to how the staff behaved. 'My bedgown was all open at the back.'

'Undignified,' said Sophie, 'but I guess that makes it easier for the nurses.'

'They served me tea in a normal cup and saucer, and the food was outstanding.'

'Really?' said Sophie.

'The vegetables I've eaten here before were undercooked,' said Freddy.

'Al dente,' said Hugo. 'Cooking to the point that food has some bite.'

Sophie rolled her eyes and gave Freddy a familiar look. It meant, 'Humour Hugo. You know how he is.'

Mrs Beeching was waiting for them on the doorstep and enveloped Freddy in a heartfelt hug. As she disappeared off towards the kitchen, Sophie said, 'It was Pamela's daughter who revived you. She works in the resus unit.'

Freddy briefly closed his eyes. He couldn't bear to think of it.

In the basement, he was too tired to play the game, and his chest ached whenever he moved, so he sat as still as he could on the squishy chair.

Hugo flicked through television channels.

'The police have arrested Spiking Guy,' said Sophie. 'He was caught on CCTV.'

'Can I see it?' Freddy looked at the television.

'The police need it as evidence.' Sophie patted his shoulder. 'The main thing is you're in one piece, and all is well.'

But all wasn't well. A dreadful suspicion had come to Freddy, and it wouldn't go away.

Before Hugo and Sophie had arrived to take him from the hospital, the nurse had given him glossy periodicals, apologising they only had women's magazines. He'd read them with growing disbelief: advice to women on how to *please their man*, advertisements for scanty, erotic underwear, and a groom boasting how he'd proposed to his mistress in bed.

Everything Hugo had told him in Shorten about this world's immorality was true. One photograph was particularly memorable, though on the surface innocuous. A couple posing before their wedding, the man's arm draped about the woman's shoulders, the gesture resonating with affection — and intimacy.

In the hospital, Hugo's arm had been around Sophie.

Never, in all their time in Shorten, had he seen Hugo touch Sophie in that way.

It could be innocent. After all, Freddy Lacey had *died*. That must have brought Hugo and Sophie closer? And cheating death had affected his own mind: his ability to concentrate, his thoughts flitting from the past to the present, without meaning or purpose.

Sophie was engrossed in a novel — on her telephone, although there were many fine books upstairs in the drawing room.

Hugo's attention was on the television and people cooking, the meal on the screen so perfect, it didn't appear to be real.

Deceptive, like a magician's trick.

CHAPTER 13

*B*uzz. *Buzz.*

Sophie turned on the bedside light, switched off her phone alarm and forced herself to sit up. *05:56.* She'd become lazy while Freddy was in hospital. Yesterday, she hadn't left Hugo's room till nine.

When Freddy had been so ill, making love with Hugo had been a guilt-ridden release. Now Freddy was alive and well, making out felt more normal, but there wasn't much time for sleeping.

Next to her, Hugo groaned and sat up.

Sophie hauled herself out of bed, slipped on Isobel's pink dressing gown and secured the tie about her waist. 'A few more hours' kip in the guest room, then I'll cook Freddy a slap-up breakfast. He's still not himself.'

'I feel as knackered as if *I'd* been in a coma.'

Charlotte was determinedly asleep, prostrate on the floor. Sophie yawned. 'Get more sleep, then bring Charlotte down.'

She unlocked and opened the door. Once in the corridor, she closed it behind her, turned around — and yelped in shock.

A shadowy figure stood right in front of her. Sophie switched on the light. 'Freddy.' She caught her breath. 'You scared me half to death.'

In the pre-dawn, wearing his Shorten suit, his pale face gaunt, Freddy looked like a spectre.

Charlotte barked behind Hugo's door and Sophie rubbed her eyes. Think.

Freddy folded his arms, covering the red sauce stain on his jacket. 'I've been waiting for you.'

Play for time. 'Why?'

Freddy laughed, the mirthless, bitter noise sending shivers down her spine.

'I know you regard me as a naïve fool.' His voice was flat.

'I don't—'

'He'll never marry you. He already has what he wants.' Freddy pushed by her. 'Hugo, open up.'

'It's not locked.' Sophie fought to gather her wits.

Freddy strode inside and she followed, her insides churning.

Charlotte stopped barking and sensing tension, leaned against Sophie's legs. Sophie reached down to reassure her, even though her own heart was pounding in her ears.

Hugo closed his dressing gown. 'Calm down. We can explain.'

'I am calm,' said Freddy.

And he was. Sort of. But he was spitting out every word. Freddy gave her a dismissive glance. 'This doesn't concern you. Go to your room.'

Sophie gaped.

'Are you not curious how I found out?' Freddy stepped forward, toe-to-toe with Hugo.

Hugo swallowed.

'When I opened my eyes in hospital, you had your arm around her shoulders. So unlike you. Then I remembered what Sophie had said to me. Wake up to get *your* Happy Ever After.'

Sophie's brain stalled, paralysed with panic.

'Not *our* Happy Ever After.' Freddy's tone was emphatic. 'I rose early and went to Sophie's bedroom. Of course, she wasn't there.'

'How were you sure it was Sophie's?' Hugo was hemmed in against a fitted wardrobe, his eyes wide.

'Your maid told me she would clean the bathroom after Sophie's room, as it was next door.' Freddy paused, as if remembering a rehearsed speech. 'And Mrs Beeching mentioned this bedroom used to be the nursery, on the top floor by her rooms.'

Hugo tightened the tie on his dressing gown. 'We were going to tell you—'

'You are a *despicable* man,' said Freddy, his voice unapologetically loud.

'We should talk in a civilised way,' said Sophie, at a normal volume. 'Sort this out in the Stables.'

Freddy didn't move. Neither did Hugo.

'You've ruined her, for your own perverted ends. *That* was why she was reluctant to marry me. She was already in your bed.' Freddy balled his fists.

Hugo didn't react, had evidently decided to take whatever Freddy was about to dish out.

Sophie jumped between them and blocked Freddy's fist. It was a standard kickboxing defence, but Freddy froze.

'Please stop, Freddy.' She lowered her arm.

Freddy looked down at her, no longer calm. Shaking. 'I could have hurt you. Remove yourself.'

'No.'

'When you have all the facts,' said Hugo, 'you'll understand. On my honour.'

'On your *honour*.' Freddy drew a slow, tortured

breath. 'You ruined her in *my* home.' His voice broke. 'And you wanted to return here so you could *keep hurting her.*'

'I would appreciate the courtesy of hearing us out,' said Hugo. 'In the drawing room?'

Freddy hesitated, maybe wrong-footed by Hugo's formality.

They trooped downstairs.

Hugo's father was in the hall, about to leave for work. 'Have a good day.'

'You too,' said Hugo.

A mad impulse to run away came over Sophie, but she gritted her teeth. Freddy was owed a full explanation and an apology.

In the drawing room, the boys paced, opponents in a boxing ring, and Sophie shut the door.

'When you tire of her, she'll end up destitute,' said Freddy, 'selling herself in a whore house.'

Sophie winced. 'Can you *please* keep your voice down?'

Freddy ignored her. 'As God is my witness, Hugo, I'll make you regret you were ever born.'

'Freddy, sit down.' Sophie sat on the sofa, Charlotte at her feet.

Hugo sat opposite, his game face on, but Freddy kept pacing, eyeballing Hugo.

'If you have any decency at all, let her marry,' said Freddy. 'I'm prepared to have her.'

'You can't marry Sophie, or anyone,' said Hugo. 'You need ID, official documents.'

'I'll take her to Shorten.' Freddy set his mouth. 'We'll marry there.'

When Hugo said nothing, Freddy added, 'There's time to save her reputation. If we set off now, we could leave your families in ignorance, prevent a scandal.'

It was like she wasn't in the room. Sophie cradled her head in her hands.

'My parents are aware we're sleeping together,' said Hugo quietly. 'They're happy for us.'

Freddy stopped pacing.

'We knew you'd be gutted,' said Hugo, 'so we put off telling you.'

Freddy resumed pacing.

'I haven't hurt Sophie, any more than she's hurt me,' said Hugo. 'We're in a normal relationship.'

'You're not in a *relationship*,' said Freddy. 'She's your mistress.'

'Sophie's my girlfriend, Freddy, and I'm her boyfriend, not her … fancy man.' Hugo's measured tone was failing.

She'd had enough. 'Freddy, you need to listen.'

He faced her, his lips pressed in a tight line.

'Hugo did *not* seduce me at the Manor. All through Shorten, we were only friends. I didn't know how Hugo felt, so I was set on you.'

Freddy's eyes were on her but unfocused, maybe remembering.

Sophie glanced at Hugo. 'We're equal partners.' She took a calming breath. 'I'm master of my own destiny.'

'I think you mean mistress,' said Freddy, his expression sullen.

She'd let that go. 'Hugo didn't seduce me. We *both* wanted to get together. And I'm not disgraced or ruined, any more than Hugo is. I could marry, but I might not. I'll earn my own living, make my own choices.'

Freddy flopped into a chair, all his anger wrung out.

'I didn't mean to come back here,' said Sophie. 'On my … I meant to be with you for the rest of my life. When I ended up in the lift and got home, I planned to return to Shorten the next day.'

'You've made up these lies between you,' said Freddy. 'It was all a game.'

'It was *never* a game.' Sophie dearly wished she could reach out and hug him. No. That would comfort her, not Freddy. 'You're a dear friend and I love you. But I'm not *in* love with you.'

'Clever words.' Freddy jumped up. 'I can no longer accept your hospitality.'

Sophie leaped to her feet too and put her hand tentatively on his arm. 'Where are you going?'

'Away.' He shrugged her off.

'Please don't do this,' said Sophie. 'It's not a good idea to—'

'Goodbye.' Freddy marched into the hall, removed his coat and scarf from the rack and left, slamming the front door behind him.

CHAPTER 14

When Sophie believed Hugo didn't feel as she did, she'd been desperate to get away from him, to hide somewhere she was loved and cherished.

Five minutes after Freddy's traumatic departure, that memory resurfaced. She sat down abruptly on the sofa in the drawing room, hunched over, and put her head in her hands. Freddy was going through that now.

Hugo sat beside her and patted her arm. 'He just needs time.'

She looked up and met his eyes. 'He'll try to go home, back through the lift.'

Dawning horror crept over Hugo's face. 'In the state he's in, he won't be able to focus.'

'He'll land … who knows where. We have to stop him.'

'How? Knock him out and lock him in the basement?'

'We could,' said Sophie. 'Somehow—'

'Mrs B and my parents would notice,' said Hugo. 'It's not practical.'

'Okay, we remind Freddy how we think it works.' Sophie's voice rose in panic. 'Tell him he could die in there.'

'He won't listen.'

'Even when he calms down?'

Hugo frowned. 'He won't wait to calm down.'

'We can't let him get in. If necessary, we...' She drew a calming breath.

'What?'

'Go with him.'

Hugo's eyes widened. 'No way.'

'If we don't, he could end up in a hell world—'

'Yes,' said Hugo. 'And so would we.'

Two hours later, Sophie tapped her phone for the nth time. 'Freddy's still close by. He's in Cannizaro House. What's that?'

Hugo paced in front of the drawing room fireplace. 'Swanky hotel. I wonder why he's gone there?'

'Pulling himself together before setting off?' Sophie couldn't pace. She was trapped on the sofa, Charlotte resting her furry head on her lap.

'Or planning something, so I'll *regret I was ever born.*'

'Better than throwing himself under a car.' She shuddered.

'Likely, he's using my credit card from the VR game,' said Hugo. 'The pin's easy to guess.'

'23rd June. Your birthday.'

Hugo's lips tightened. 'And his.'

Now that coincidence tasted bitter. 'Freddy prides himself on behaving properly. He'll feel uncomfortable using your card. Stealing.'

'But he'll justify it.' Hugo stopped pacing. 'From his perspective, I've stolen you.'

Sophie looked at her feet.

'He's missed breakfast,' said Hugo, briskly, 'and it's too early for lunch. He must be in the hotel lounge.'

Charlotte jumped off the sofa and leaned insistently against Sophie's legs. 'I know, I need to get a grip.' She sat up straight. 'He could have got himself a room. I can check.' She called the hotel and reception picked up. 'A friend of ours, Freddy Lacey, is staying with you. We're meeting up for breakfast tomorrow. Should I book two extra places in advance?' She put it on speaker.

'He's pre-paid for breakfast, madam. No problem. You're booked in.'

'Thank you.' Sophie ended the call, relieved. If Freddy had been contemplating harming himself, he wouldn't have pre-booked breakfast. 'Hopefully, he'll have a good night's sleep, and in the morning, we ambush him, go to the lift and cross.'

Hugo sat down heavily next to her. 'Twenty-four hours won't lessen the risk, and believing the crossing could kill him, and *us*, could be a perverse incentive.'

Despite the central heating being on full blast, a chill ran down Sophie's arms and she hugged herself. 'Me and Charlotte, double gene-power, should counter Freddy's … lack of focus.'

'You're in bits.'

'I can get past that.'

'If you can't, going with him would be suicide.' Hugo's eyes hardened. 'Freddy understands the risks.'

'He doesn't. He crossed safely, and he won't believe a word we say, about the lift or anything else. And he can't make a rational decision, not after what *we* did to him. If we do nothing, we'll never know what happens to him, and it will nag at us — forever.' Sophie squared her shoulders. 'This is on me. Without the gene, you can't guide the lift to Shorten.'

'You can't be certain of that.'

'It's a fair assumption, Hugo.' He'd only seen the lift when she'd said his name. Her resolve strengthened, and she kissed him on the cheek. '*I have to cross with Freddy.*'

'You win.'

'What do you mean?'

Hugo held her gaze. 'I won't let you do this on your own.'

Rebuff him, say whatever it takes. Keep him safe.

The words danced on the tip of her tongue, but she bit them back, and she repeated what Hugo had said to her in Shorten. 'We're in this together.'

CHAPTER 15

At eight thirty the next morning, Sophie opened the drawing room curtains, blinking and bleary-eyed.

Hugo had fallen asleep on the sofa in the early hours and was out for the count. Telling his parents and Pamela they were returning to the 'travellers' had worn him out more than the packing.

Sophie had already said her goodbyes, and she'd no need to lie to her parents. They'd died years before, in a car accident.

On the floor were three bulging backpacks. Packing camping and survival gear had taken all the previous day and half the night. Hugo had stashed a pistol with six bullets in a side pocket — his great-great-grandfather's personal weapon from the Great War. It had been locked away in a safe in the study for decades, but Hugo knew the combination. He'd also packed souvenir gold sovereigns he'd found in a drawer, and three knives from the kitchen.

The other gear was 'just in case' supplies, including hiking boots for Freddy, a waterproof cigarette lighter, a regular lighter, and ski clothing good to minus thirty — as well as a jacket for Charlotte that promised *expedition-standard, cold-climate protection.*

Charlotte was dozing next to the bags, and Sophie tiptoed around her.

Sophie emptied a packet of tampons, knelt, and stuffed each one individually into her backpack. The bag strained closed.

She got stiffly to her feet, walked over to the sofa, and nudged Hugo awake. 'It's time.'

When they arrived at the Cannizaro hotel, breakfast in the dining room was in full swing, families and couples eating and chatting. Many had brought their dogs, who lay under or beside their tables.

The glorious scent of freshly roasted coffee in the spacious conservatory soothed Sophie's sleep-deprived brain and further stiffened her resolve.

Freddy was sitting alone by the windows, a half-eaten cooked breakfast and a newspaper on his table. As they approached, he saw them and paled.

Hugo set down his holdall and the bag they'd packed for Freddy. 'Do you mind if we join you?' he asked, not waiting for an answer, and sat down. He slipped off his ski jacket.

Sophie put her backpack on the floor, tugged open the Velcro fastenings on Charlotte's ski jacket and took it off her. Charlotte settled under the table.

'Coffee for two.' Hugo addressed the waitress.

'How did you find me?' Freddy stared at his remaining breakfast, looked as if he was about to be sick.

'Your phone,' said Sophie, taking off her jacket. 'The friends app.' She felt for him, but said evenly, 'Hear us out.'

Freddy kept his eyes on his plate. 'Please leave.'

The waitress arrived with coffee and Hugo studied a menu. 'I've had one slice of toast since … you left.'

Freddy made a scoffing noise. 'Why are you hounding me?'

'You're intent on going to Shorten,' said Hugo.

'What if I am?' Freddy gazed out at the hotel gardens. 'It is nothing whatsoever to do with you.'

'I was in a bad way after Parkes nearly killed me,' said Sophie, 'and though I concentrated as hard as I could in the lift, we were lucky to land here.'

'If it does rely on focused thoughts, you could end up anywhere.' Hugo looked straight at him. 'Or dead. Do you want to take the risk?'

Freddy rolled his eyes. 'Yet somehow you arrived safely. Perhaps there are only two universes, and your scientists are wrong?'

Sophie looked down at her place setting. 'I hope so.'

'I've done the trip once,' said Freddy. 'This will be no different.'

Sophie drank her coffee, the caffeine bucking her up, and Hugo ordered identical cooked breakfasts.

'Have you decided to eat meat now?' Freddy asked her, his lips curling in a sneer.

'Of course not. I'll give the bacon and sausages to Charlotte.' Sophie blinked hard.

'With how you're feeling, you won't be able to focus,' said Hugo flatly.

Freddy shrugged.

Sophie opened her mouth but couldn't find the right words. Finally, she said, 'We can't let you go on your own.'

'I hate it when you do that.' Freddy took a bite of toast, chewing as if it were cardboard.

'What?'

Freddy pushed his main plate aside. 'Treat me like a child.'

'I'm not,' said Sophie. 'To survive this, we *all* need to go.'

Freddy added more toast to his side plate. 'If you truly

believed the crossing's so dangerous, you wouldn't consider travelling.' He spread butter, then marmalade on the toast. 'I'll travel alone.'

The waitress brought their breakfasts, and Hugo and Sophie ate their meals in minutes, Sophie only pausing to feed Charlotte.

She was still knackered, though her eyelids felt less scratchy. 'We can't prevent you hitchhiking to the university, but we'll be waiting for you in the students' union.'

Freddy frowned. 'I'd be grateful if you'd allow me to pay for a train ticket with your card.'

'The card's not an issue.' Hugo scanned the dining room. 'And as for this place, you were in no state to sleep on a park bench.'

Was anybody? Sophie finished her coffee. 'At the university, we should call the lift after midnight when the students' union's empty.'

'That man will stop you,' said Freddy.

Hugo put down his cup. 'What man?'

'Who showed me to Lorna's flat.'

'We can distract one security guard,' said Hugo, reaching for some toast.

'And we should tell Elliot and Lorna about the lift,' said Sophie. 'If … this doesn't work out, they'll know we've gone forever, and the police can't help.'

Freddy shrugged again. 'They won't believe you.'

'They will if they see it for themselves,' said Sophie.

'It's statistically improbable that Elliot has the gene.' Freddy gave Hugo a patronising glance. 'He's ordinary, like you.'

Hugo ignored the dig and finished his coffee.

'When I said Hugo's name, he saw the lift,' said Sophie, 'so if I say Elliot and Lorna's names out loud, they *will* see it.'

'Lorna won't,' said Freddy. 'She's blind.'

'I forgot,' said Sophie, embarrassed. 'What's Lorna's guide dog called?'

'Fudge.' Freddy busied himself moving his napkin from his lap to the table. 'I have no choice but to put up with your company. I only hope it's for the shortest possible time.'

'I've packed you basic shaving stuff, not electric,' said Hugo. 'You could shave.'

Freddy rubbed his stubbly chin. 'Very well.'

They followed him upstairs and into his room. Freddy accepted a razor and shaving cream and shut the closet door.

He came out dabbing at his chin with a tissue where he'd nicked himself.

'This is yours.' Sophie pointed at the holdall.

Freddy lifted the bag strap but then dropped it with a thump. 'What on earth is in it?'

Sophie hauled hers onto her back. 'The food cans weigh a lot.'

They trooped downstairs, and in the lobby, Freddy checked the bill — and rechecked it. 'Outrageous. More than my annual allowance.'

Hugo smiled at the lady behind the desk. 'This is fine. Thank you.'

Outside, the chilly wind had picked up.

'Tube's this way,' said Hugo, setting off down the road.

Keeping Charlotte close, Sophie kept pace with him, the straps of the bag digging into her shoulders. Freddy morosely followed, and Sophie mentally crossed her fingers, relieved he hadn't made a scene or bolted.

In the tube train, Freddy sat next to her and Hugo, the rattling carriage whining through tunnels like a wounded animal.

'Look,' said Sophie, 'I know this is horrible, but we're trying our best.'

Freddy studied the bag between his knees. 'Some deeds can never be forgiven.'

'I thought you were a Christian?' said Hugo.

'Only saints forgive those who trespass against them,' said Freddy. 'That's why they're saints.'

A fresh stab of guilt ran through Sophie, and she distracted herself by stroking Charlotte who'd rested her head on her lap.

Freddy leaned forward, his face too pale.

'He's going to be sick,' said Sophie, instinctively putting her hand on his shoulder.

Freddy stiffened. 'Leave me be.'

When they reached Saint Pancras station, Freddy seemed disorientated, staring at people dragging wheeled suitcases. He tilted his face towards the roof. Recently renovated, an entire upper floor had been erected, and the chatter in shops and restaurants filled what had once been an echo-vast space.

A youth hurried past them, pushing a buggy.

'What's in that?' asked Freddy.

'They're for babies,' said Sophie.

'But where's the mother or nurse?' said Freddy. 'A young man with a perambulator. This world is quite upside down.' He wiped his eyes and turned his back on her, and Sophie bit her lip.

'Try not to dwell on how Freddy's feeling,' whispered Hugo. 'Conserve your energy for the crossing.'

Sophie had left her observations and lift sketches in Shorten, so she bought a new notebook with an attached pencil, and as they waited on uncomfortable chairs for the train, she drew the pictures and symbols she'd seen on the doors. 'If I forget the details, it might somehow stop me calling it.'

'The doors were open in the lane, so I saw no pictures,'

said Freddy. 'And in the students' union, dealing with that man, I paid no mind to them. Anyway, it was dark.' He shook his head. 'You're wasting your time with this play-acting. The lift will take us to Shorten, just as it carried me here.'

'Sorry, I should have returned this.' Sophie pulled off her ring and held it out to him.

'Sell it.' Freddy's lips twisted. 'Or give it away.'

∼

Four hours later, they got off the train at a tiny Derbyshire station.

Sophie closed her jacket collar against the rain dripping through the roof of a graffiti-splattered shelter. Hugo huddled beside her, and Charlotte kept close. Freddy perched at the far edge of the bench.

'Ziggy should be here soon.' Hugo checked his watch.

'Freddy, I'm completely knackered,' said Sophie. 'Why don't we find a cheap hotel, brave the lift tomorrow?'

'No.'

Ziggy's car drew up in a flurry of exhaust smoke and loud music. 'Meant to get here sooner. Tutorial overran.'

Freddy climbed into the passenger seat and Sophie and Hugo got into the back, Sophie hauling Charlotte onto her lap.

As they sped off, Freddy said to Ziggy, 'Good to see you.'

'Likewise.' Ziggy turned off his music. 'I'm so sorry about what happened at the gig, Freddy, and that … things haven't worked out.' He glanced over at Hugo and Sophie, then at Freddy. 'You all look terrible.'

'We're okay,' said Sophie.

'If you're okay,' said Ziggy, 'I'm a walrus.'

In the early hours of the morning, the only light in the students' union came from phone screens, angular pockets of brightness. The heating wasn't on, but Sophie was too hot. She took off her jacket and Charlotte's.

Freddy was carrying his formal coat. Somehow, he'd squeezed his ski jacket into his bag.

He'd insisted on telling Ziggy about the lift, and Ziggy half-sat on a table, swinging his long legs. Elliot was beside Lorna, his arm through hers, and Fudge, in his fluorescent coat, stood to attention by Lorna. Charlotte was keen to explore, so Sophie had shortened her lead.

Ziggy checked his phone. 'The security guard's investigating a power cut on the other side of campus.'

'We appreciate that,' said Sophie.

'If you value your life chances and reputations,' said Hugo, 'I advise you to keep what happens tonight to yourselves.'

'We didn't drop out of Uni and join a cult,' said Sophie. 'And Freddy isn't a traveller. Well, he is, but not the regular sort.'

'Last September, Sophie and her dog got into *that* lift on

the right.' Hugo pointed to the two nondescript lifts. 'I went in at the same time. When the doors opened, we found ourselves in a parallel universe, similar to ours, but a century ago. We stayed at Shorten Manor, the mirror equivalent of a house not far from this campus. The other version of Freddy here, his descendants live in the same property.'

Elliot's grip on Lorna's arm tightened. 'The stately home.'

Hugo nodded.

'Whatever stuff you're smoking, I think I'll pass.' Ziggy uncoiled himself from his half-seat on the table.

Nervous laughter.

Sophie handed Elliot a bulging plastic bag. 'Freddy's smart shoes.' They'd made Freddy wear the new hiking boots, and his ring was stashed in Hugo's wallet inside the shoes. 'And our phones and cards.'

'Freddy wants to return home, and we're going with him,' said Hugo. 'The lift's a transport vehicle that crosses between universes, using travellers' emotions and thoughts. If a traveller's upset or distracted, they could land in the wrong place, or never land. It requires calm and focus.' Hugo put his hand through his hair. 'I don't want to do this, but I owe it to Freddy—'

'*We* owe it,' said Sophie.

Freddy frowned.

'To get him back in one piece,' added Hugo.

'If it's so dangerous,' said Ziggy, 'why go at all?'

'His family protected us in the other universe,' said Hugo. 'We're returning the favour.'

'If you could prove multi-verse theory,' said Lorna, 'it would be the biggest discovery since DNA.'

'DNA determines who can travel,' said Hugo. 'A gene passed on by the beings who built the lift. I don't have it, but Freddy, Sophie and Charlotte do.'

Ziggy raised his eyebrows. '*Charlotte*?' At the sound of her name, Charlotte turned her head and stared at him.

'I know it sounds crazy,' said Hugo, 'but we believe Charlotte called the lift in the first place. She's our best hope.'

'Your "best hope" is a labradoodle,' said Ziggy. 'Mental.'

'*If* the lift appears, you should film and take photos,' said Lorna.

'That might record it,' said Sophie, 'but once we've gone, please delete it all.'

'I saw Dynamo live last year,' said Ziggy. 'I couldn't believe my eyes. How will we know it's not a trick?'

'Once you see it,' said Sophie, 'you can touch it.'

'Assuming all this is true,' said Ziggy, glancing at Freddy, 'if safe travel relies on calm, focused thoughts, you have a problem.'

'Which is why we're crossing together,' said Sophie.

'If this isn't a reality show joke,' said Elliot, 'have I got this right? You might die?'

'Yes,' said Hugo.

'You seem to believe what you're saying,' said Ziggy, 'but either you're insane which is sad, or this is a date with trash TV, which is worse.'

'No TV,' said Hugo. 'And if I'm insane, so are Sophie and Freddy.'

Ziggy shook his head, sceptical.

'What does it look like?' said Lorna.

'A fancy lift,' said Sophie. 'When it first appeared in the lane in Shorten, you could make out the exterior shape, but then it changes to merge in with its surroundings. Here, it replaced the regular lift, so I only saw the front. Painted gold, with pictures.'

'What kind of pictures?' said Lorna.

'Travellers see different ones,' said Sophie. 'They're destinations, or they symbolise the choices travellers make. And there are maths symbols.'

'A sort of code?' asked Lorna.

'We don't know,' said Hugo.

'You'll describe it all?' Lorna said to Elliot.

'Of course, love. If there's anything to describe.'

'If scientists ID people with the gene,' said Hugo, 'they'll start messing with how the lift works. Another reason to keep schtum. It's complicated enough.'

'Let's do this.' Sophie started moving chairs into a semi-circle before the lift. 'Might take a while.'

Hugo set out more chairs and everybody settled themselves.

'Ready?' Hugo asked Freddy.

'I can't wait.' Freddy's eyes shone with malice.

Sophie's brain screamed, *Don't* call it, but she whispered to Charlotte, 'Think about Jack,' and Charlotte stilled.

'Jack,' Sophie repeated, picturing the black retriever dozing beside Charlotte in the Manor library. The tall bookcases, dust motes dancing in the air, Freddy kissing her... A lurch of regret interrupted her train of thought.

But the next moment, one of the grey lifts flashed gold. A blast of icy air, and Sophie shivered and put on her jacket.

Charlotte pulled towards it, but Sophie kept a firm hold on her lead. 'It's here.' She stood up. 'Hugo, Lorna,' she said loudly, again forgetting Lorna was blind. 'Ziggy, Elliot, Fudge.'

Ziggy and Elliot gaped, but Lorna gasped and jumped out of her chair. 'I can *see* it.' Her face shone with surprise and joy.

Was the lift somehow channelling the image into Lorna's brain?

Fudge gave a single bark, and everyone was on their feet.

'Okay, I'm impressed,' said Elliot. 'But there are no pictures on the doors.'

'Hell of a stunt, though,' said Ziggy. '3D hologram?'

'No,' said Sophie. 'It's real.' She could see pictures, but they'd changed. No mansion or cottage on fire. The girl with the hefty sword was there, so was the man rocking a cot. The dark strokes outlining the images were more defined. Thicker. And there were new pictures: people on horseback racing along a deserted beach with a huge wolf, and a plainer sketch: a wavy line that forked.

The Pi and infinity symbols were still there, and the two others Sophie didn't recognise. She pulled out her notebook and quickly sketched: a five-sided shape and another one, criss-crossing lines within a rectangle.

'It's *beautiful*,' said Lorna.

Rattling.

The lift doors scraped open, and the chandelier shone light into the hall as bright as a film projector.

Freddy put on his coat, picked up his holdall and strode into the lift, his mouth set in a resolute line. Ziggy approached the threshold and cautiously touched the door frame.

Hugo zipped his jacket closed and chucked his bag inside.

Gripping Charlotte's lead, Sophie walked through the doorway, every neurone in her brain shouting louder than ever. *Don't Do This.*

Charlotte sat down near the rear interior wall, surprisingly calm given how she'd nearly died during the last crossing. Horrible she couldn't leave her in Pamela's care, but Charlotte was crucial to reaching Shorten. Sophie stood close to her, hoping canine serenity would rub off on her mistress.

Hugo came into the lift and Freddy shoved him violently in the chest. Taken by surprise, Hugo fell backwards and slid along the students' union floor. Sophie gasped and moved forward, but Freddy blocked her way, clenching his fists at Hugo like a cartoon boxer.

Ziggy helped Hugo up, and Freddy tensed, ready for battle. Before Freddy could land a blow, Sophie punched Freddy on the chin, so lightly it was almost a tap, but he crumpled, his legs sprawling over the door tracks.

Hugo stepped over him and Sophie dragged Freddy completely into the lift. She took in Hugo's reproachful expression.

'A stage punch,' said Sophie. 'Honestly.'

As if in response, Freddy groaned.

'Fell on my elbow.' Hugo rubbed his arm and grimaced. 'No good deed goes unpunished.'

The doors began to clatter shut. Just beyond them, Elliot clung to Lorna, who was holding on tight to Fudge, and Ziggy moved his head from side to side, searching for hidden wires or cameras.

Inside the lift, as Freddy staggered to his feet, the gap between the doors vanished, sealing them in.

As soon as the lift doors closed, Sophie fastened Charlotte's jacket on her, and tied the lead around Charlotte's middle and onto the rail near the front. Sophie gripped the bar. Any minute, they'd be spinning like clothes in a washing machine.

Freddy rubbed his jaw and glared at her. 'You *hit* me.'

'I wasn't going to allow you to start a fight—'

'It was never going to be that,' said Hugo.

'It was going to be something,' said Sophie, 'and if you'd started scrapping outside, I could have gone to who knows where. And so could Charlotte.'

Charlotte seemed relaxed but Sophie gave her a comforting pat before addressing Freddy. 'What were you *thinking?*'

'Without Hugo, back at the Manor, you wouldn't have called the lift again. My will against yours.'

Sophie shook her head, surprised. He didn't mean that, was still in bits.

'We need to focus on Shorten,' said Hugo.

Freddy sat on the floor, his hand on the rail opposite Sophie.

She curled over Charlotte. 'Jack.'

'Make sure you've a tight hold on your bag,' said Hugo, pushing Freddy's towards him.

Freddy looped one strap over his shoulder. 'I hate you.'

'I suspect most people would have let you take your chances.' Hugo grasped the rail. 'But here I am.'

Freddy stared at Hugo with a visceral intensity that made Sophie shudder.

'Concentrate, Freddy.' She kept her voice quiet, reasonable. 'Remember home.' She shut her eyes and pictured the Manor: the crenelated gables, the mullion windows, the tended gardens. But the images wavered, replaced by the footmen in the dining room, laughing and gossiping, revelling in Freddy's broken engagement.

Charlotte yawned and lay down. Sophie nudged her and whispered desperately, 'Jack.' Could Charlotte not focus either?

'Why isn't the lift doing anything?' said Hugo. *Please,* Freddy, if you don't long for home, we'll die in here.'

Freddy rested his head on the wall. 'So be it.'

Sophie's heart sank, and she curled closer around Charlotte.

The lift tilted, turned over, and corkscrewed up, faster and faster until the interior was a psychedelic blur.

Finally, it slowed, and Sophie slumped in relief.

The lift gently tipped, and Freddy got to his feet, watching Hugo like a swaying snake.

Sophie uncurled herself from Charlotte who settled on the floor, her golden eyes fixed on Freddy. Hopefully, remembering Jack.

The oppressive, air-tight silence intensified, and the

temperature climbed. Hugo and Sophie hauled off their ski jackets. Sophie tied the sleeves about her waist, took Charlotte's jacket off her, and held onto the holdall. Her mouth had dried with fear. 'It's no good. My mind's all over the place.'

'You called it entirely by yourself before,' said Hugo, 'and steered us safely. Keep going.'

'I don't want to die. Freddy, we *both* need to long for Shorten.'

He removed his formal coat and loosened his tie. 'You can't manipulate me.'

'If you make no effort to concentrate,' said Hugo, desperation edging his voice, 'your parents will never know what's happened to you, and nobody will find your body.'

'The mechanism for getting rid of waste in here includes corpses,' said Sophie. 'Vaporising us or throwing us out into space.'

Freddy shot her a horrified glance. 'Do not talk to me.' His eyes were red-rimmed.

'Okay,' said Sophie. 'I understand.'

'You'll *never* understand.' Freddy turned his face from her, but only a moment later, slid to the floor, his breathing slow and even.

Hugo lay down with a sigh and Charlotte stretched. It was the last thing Sophie saw before she gave in to sleep.

Sophie blinked in the bright light cast by the lift's chandelier. No movement. Must have landed.

The humid air smelled of ... nothing, and steady breathing, soft and close, was comforting in the deep silence. Hugo's arm was stretched away from him, his half-curled hand a few inches from Freddy. Reaching out in his sleep.

Sophie frowned. A dream about Freddy's mother still

lingered. Explaining this mess to her would be near unbearable.

Charlotte made her morning greeting noise, a cross between a happy whine and a yawn, and Sophie untied her lead from the rail. On the previous crossing, they'd all woken up just before the doors opened.

The candelabra flickered. If the light-fitting was an illusion, maybe the panelled walls were as well. Sophie stepped over the boys and traced a swirling wood grain with her finger, remembering a similar pattern from the Hubble telescope.

She wiped sweat from her brow with her shirt sleeve and bent down to pat Hugo's shoulder. 'Wake up.'

Hugo stared at her, puzzled.

If this was the same as before, his dazed state would only last a few minutes, but missing the gene, he'd remember little of the crossing.

Charlotte bounded over to Freddy and licked his face. 'Ugh.' He gently pushed her aside.

Sophie put Charlotte's jacket on her, closed the fastenings, and slipped on her own. It was winter in Shorten.

Hugo put on his hat, scarf, and jacket in a sleepy daze, then looked around, as if registering his surroundings for the first time. Freddy pulled on his coat.

Sophie sat by her holdall and checked her watch. Stuck on twenty past midnight. She wound it and the second hand moved.

'When did you wake up?' Hugo asked Sophie, winding his ancient watch.

'Ten minutes ago.'

'Why isn't it opening?' said Hugo.

'I don't know.' Not the slightest flaw in the wall. No crack that could become a gap between doors.

More minutes ticked by, and with the temperature still

tropical, the boys removed their cold-weather gear, and Sophie slipped off her jacket and Charlotte's. 'Freddy, what pictures did you see on the doors?'

'Nonsensical.' Freddy sat on his coat. 'A road that split.'

'I saw that,' said Sophie.

Freddy fidgeted and crossed his legs. 'And there was a baby swing cot.'

'I saw a cot,' said Sophie, 'but there was a man beside it. And there was another new sketch.' She described the galloping horse riders and the wolf.

'I wish I could see them,' said Hugo.

Freddy gave him a patronising smile.

Sophie frowned at Freddy and hugged Charlotte. 'Shame you can't describe *your* pictures.'

'These images are travellers' destinations, or symbolic of where they'll end up,' said Hugo. 'So, it's logical that individuals without the gene wouldn't be able to choose where they go.' He bit his lip. 'If neither of you saw the mansion this time and that represented the Manor…'

Sophie swallowed. 'Shorten was never our destination.'

An hour later, fighting against panic, Sophie pressed the chunky wooden button to open the lift doors.

'Repeating an action, hoping to produce a different result, is pointless,' said Freddy.

He could be right. Just an ornamental button, a stage prop. Sophie forced herself to take deep, calming breaths.

Hugo fished out a pocket-size book from his holdall.

'You said no novels.' Sophie sat beside him. 'Too heavy.'

'This isn't a novel.' Hugo read the title out loud. '*SAS Survival Guide*.'

'What does SAS stand for?' asked Freddy.

'Special Air Service.' Hugo unfolded the book to where he'd turned down a page. 'Elite soldiers. This gives survival tips.'

Charlotte laid her head on Sophie's lap. 'Any tips about escaping from an alien spaceship?' Ingrained at school, banter helped with setbacks, but didn't help with *really* bad situations… Focus on practical stuff. 'Now we're awake, how long before the water runs out?'

'We've three travel mugs' worth,' said Hugo, 'plus Charlotte's bottle.' They'd packed a plastic dog-travel device that poured into an attached shallow bowl. 'Once that's gone, a few days.' He glanced at the wall that should have been the doors. 'After that, we drink our own urine. Over time, it'll get thicker and more disgusting.'

Freddy wrinkled his nose. 'No.'

'The process is straightforward for us,' said Hugo, addressing Freddy. 'We return the fluid to the mugs.' He looked at Sophie. 'More of a performance for you, and as for Charlotte, you'll need to catch it under her. If she refuses to drink it, you'll have to tip it down her throat.'

Sophie gulped.

Hugo fitted the book into his bag.

'I'd rather die,' said Freddy.

Hugo's lips tightened.

Rattling.

A crack appeared. A trickle of liquid pooled on the floor, the doors opened, and in roared a towering wall of water.

CHAPTER 18

When something will kill you any moment, you need time to process what's happening *before* you react. Except time is running out.

Thoughts skitter, slowing and stretching the moment … possibilities, options. Surprise, despair, desperation—

Iron-cold water slammed Sophie against the lift's rear wall. She struggled to stand, but her head was still under water. Frantically, she swam upwards and broke the surface, gasping for breath.

The chandelier in front of her dimmed and failed.

In the pitch black, close by, Charlotte barked, and Sophie reached out and found her, swimming.

Sophie's sight adjusted. Feet away were Hugo and Freddy, their faces pale and shaken above heaving water. She glimpsed a sliver of light outside the lift, high up... Sunlight? 'Look.' She gestured at it and the boys saw it.

The water around them swirled and shifted, and a rip tide pulled at Sophie's legs. She put a cold, wet finger in her mouth. Salt.

A wave crashed in, and Sophie crammed her face against

the ceiling to find a layer of air. She grabbed the candelabra chain. Solid, and rough as concrete.

The water level briefly receded, before a fresh wave thundered over them.

'If this is tidal, it could be coming in,' shouted Hugo, over the roar of water. 'We have to swim out.'

Don't. Panic. Think this through. Charlotte weighed fifty-five pounds. Four stone. Giving thanks she'd untied her from the rail before the doors opened, Sophie double-tied the end of Charlotte's lead around her wrist. Would Charlotte know to hold her breath?

'No,' Hugo yelled. He untied the lead and closed Sophie's fingers over it. 'Trust Charlotte.'

A holdall dashed against them. 'Leave the bags,' said Hugo. 'They'll weigh us down.'

Another wave knocked the stuffing out of Sophie, but she held onto the chandelier again and drew deep breaths like the boys.

'We go together,' said Hugo. '*Now.*'

Keeping her eyes open, Sophie dived in, dragging Charlotte behind her.

Beyond the lift, to her right, a black shape loomed up and she swam sideways to avoid it.

Go, go to the light. But her boots were weights, weighing her down… Her lungs burned and she kicked harder. Keep. Going.

Her face met air, and she took a shuddering, thankful breath. She yanked the lead taut, but Charlotte was already beside her.

Sophie hadn't thought a dog could look shocked. Charlotte did, her golden eyes prominent and staring.

They were in a sea with a hefty swell. Waves pounded a nearby beach.

'Here.' Hugo's voice.

Only yards away. Sophie desperately scanned the surface of the water. *Freddy.*

There he was. Swimming towards the shore.

Ten minutes later, Sophie sat on the sand, her legs drawn up to her chest. A bitter wind scraped at her skin, and her clothes clung to her, clammy and heavy. She was uncontrollably shivering, her teeth were chattering, and she'd lost all feeling in her feet and hands.

Next to her, Charlotte heaved, trying to catch her breath.

Her collar must have shrunk in the sea, was choking her. Sophie fumbled to let it out to the furthest notch, but then stood back and stared.

Freddy stared too.

'Charlotte's … enormous,' said Hugo.

The collar hadn't shrunk. Charlotte was *much* bigger, the size of a Great Dane. And her head was broader.

Charlotte shook herself, droplets flying off her fur in all directions, drenching them more.

'She seems okay though,' said Sophie, 'apart from that.'

The sky was brittle-clear, and Sophie shielded her eyes from the sun, taking in their surroundings.

The lift had opened inside a cave, under a grey slate cliff. Rocks stuck out around the cave entrance, random and irregular, the sea sliding and smashing over them. That black shape under the water had been a rock. She'd been lucky to avoid it. Lucky too that the beach had been close by.

'We should fetch the bags and jackets while we're wet.' Hugo pulled off his boots.

Sophie unlaced hers.

'No, stay with Charlotte.' Hugo set his jaw. 'Come on, Freddy.'

Freddy removed his boots and sullenly followed Hugo into the waves.

Sophie kept Charlotte's lead short. Not a good idea for the new, huge Charlotte to explore new scents when they had no idea where — or when — they were.

The sun looked like the regular sun, and birds circled the promontory, their cries harsh and familiar. But the salty air tasted different: intense and sour.

The boys' heads, tiny bobs in the sea, had disappeared and Sophie ran on the spot, her boots squelching on the sand. *Please* keep safe.

She'd just resolved to go with Charlotte to search for them, when she saw their heads near the cliff, and soon afterwards, Freddy waded out of the surf with his backpack and dropped it by his feet.

Hugo took longer to reach the beach with the other bags. He was wearing his ski jacket, with hers half-stuffed into a holdall.

'We had to dive for the bags.' Hugo extracted Charlotte's jacket from a backpack.

'Is the lift still there?' asked Sophie.

'Yes, but there's no point trying to direct it to Shorten.' Hugo flicked his eyes towards Freddy, who was scowling at them.

The sea had slicked their hair as smooth as seals, and their sodden clothes stuck to them, dripping and plopping on the sand.

'Let's find shelter,' said Hugo. 'Get dry.'

Freddy pulled his ski jacket from his backpack and slipped it on.

'Where's your long coat?' said Sophie, fastening up her jacket.

'Ruined. Shrunk.'

Sophie put Charlotte's jacket on her, but it wouldn't

fasten. She returned the dog-coat to the bag and shrugged the holdall onto her shoulders. Soaking wet, it should have been heavier, yet seemed lighter.

Keeping Charlotte on the lead, Sophie clambered after the boys, worry curdling in her stomach. Where and when were they?

Undulating dunes covered a steep bank, dotted with tall, waving grass and the occasional hunched tree. At the top of the bank was a dirt road.

Charlotte made a beeline towards some poo, and Sophie pulled her away, relieved Charlotte wasn't stronger as well as bigger.

'Horse,' said Hugo. 'A few days old.'

'Domesticated horses could mean people,' said Sophie.

'That could be good,' said Hugo. 'Or not.'

Over the road was a strip of scrubland and beyond that, forest.

'Into the woods,' said Hugo.

Freddy hesitated, as if he wanted to argue, but then set off towards the trees.

Charlotte trotted beside Sophie, her wider brown face fixed in a familiar expression: resolute, curious.

In the forest, they left behind the bitter wind, and the sound of the surf faded, replaced by the cracking of foul-smelling leaves underfoot.

Hugo extracted a compass from his bag. '*Not* waterproof.' He pocketed it.

From deep in the bag, he pulled out a small paint can and sprayed a blob of green paint on a tree trunk and on others at intervals as they walked.

'I didn't see you pack that,' said Sophie.

Hugo glanced at her. 'I thought it could work as a weapon.'

'Really?' She frowned.

'Not too heavy,' said Hugo, 'and squirted in someone's face could have given us time to run away, but we should use it now. Stop us getting lost.'

'Theseus' string in the labyrinth,' said Freddy.

'Ariadne's string,' said Hugo. 'It was her idea.'

'What *are* you talking about?' asked Sophie.

'The Greek myth,' said Hugo, spraying another paint blob. 'You know, escaping the Minotaur's lair.'

Minutes later, they came to a clearing.

'Stop here?' said Sophie.

'Still too near the road,' said Hugo. 'We don't want Charlotte hearing a noise and barking, drawing attention.'

They trudged on.

Charlotte pulled on her lead towards denser trees.

'We should check out what she can smell,' said Sophie.

The trunks were so close together, their bags only just squeezed through the gaps.

On the other side was a sunken gully bisecting the forest floor. Shrouded in green moss, the slopes were as tall as a railway siding. At the end of the gully was a massive fir, perfectly proportioned, like an idealised Christmas tree. Charlotte veered towards it.

Behind the fir was a rocky wall, half covered in vines. Charlotte sniffed and pawed at it.

Sophie found the kitchen knife in her holdall and cut off a vine. 'There's a hole here.'

Hugo joined her in cutting the greenery. 'What do you know? A cave.'

A dark enclosed space. Sophie paused.

Hugo peered inside, went in, and quickly came out. 'Empty.'

The interior was predictably gloomy, but at the back, fresh water slid down smooth stone into a natural trench.

Charlotte slurped the water. 'Well done.' Sophie hugged

herself. She was bone-cold, but also hyper-aware: the subtle, contrasting shades of the cave stone, every crack and angle, were HD sharp, and the scent from water-worn rock and sweet moss mingled with saltwater on her clothes, layered, yet distinct—

'First priority, sort a fire,' said Hugo.

'How?' said Freddy. 'Everything's soaked.'

'We can use twigs and detritus,' said Sophie. Underfoot, the leaves had been dry.

Hugo found the cigarette lighter they'd bought, but it was too wet to work. He dug out the camping cigarette lighter. Resembling a vanity mirror, it had a metal coil attached. 'Now we discover if this is waterproof, and if the few hours in the garden were enough.'

'What on earth do you mean?' said Freddy, his voice irritated.

'Straight after we bought it, we left it outside to charge.' Sophie set down her bag. 'It works on solar power.'

Hugo touched a button on the disc. The tip of the coil glowed, and he exhaled in relief. 'But at dusk, we should bank the fire.'

Sophie nodded. Who knew what a light in the dark would attract?

CHAPTER 19

A few minutes later, Sophie staggered dejectedly out of the cave in her wet clothes. Along the top of the gully, she squatted behind an oak tree.

Stay in the cave, boys.

Edgy sunlight danced on the natural clearing, bright but not warm, reminding her of a long-ago holiday in Scotland: bracing autumnal walks featuring bulky jackets and bobble hats. She adjusted her sodden clothing and straightened.

On the far side of the gully something moved, pale against the dark trees. Sophie held her breath.

A white deer, as startled as her.

Then it was gone, swallowed up by the forest.

Sophie hurriedly gathered up twigs, returned to the cave, and told the boys what she'd seen.

'I like venison,' said Hugo.

Sophie grimaced and tried to stop shivering. 'Don't go there.'

The fire finally caught. Set at the cave entrance, most of the smoke stayed outside.

Freddy sat cross-legged near the spluttering flames, his

face shuttered. Around him, emptied out to dry, were the contents of his holdall. Survival gadgets and food cans lay scattered where he'd dropped them.

Hugo carefully spaced out his kit. 'Are the colours here the same as home?' he asked Sophie.

She nodded and sat down beside him by the fire.

'For me, they're brighter, stronger,' said Hugo. 'Your ski jacket's almost glowing.'

He'd wanted her to choose a less in-your-face colour, but the shiny red was pretty.

'I'm not really seeing colours.' Hugo pushed his hat and gloves closer to the flames. 'Neither are you.'

'Come again?' Sophie emptied her holdall.

'Our brain makes them up to see easier,' said Hugo. '530 million years ago, the first fish developed eyes. Those that did, turned into better predators and ate the others.'

'Evolution's a bit depressing,' said Sophie.

'My perception of all the contrasting shades isn't the same as Shorten,' said Hugo, 'so we're not in Freddy's parallel universe, in a different country or time. Nor are we somewhere off the beaten track in our own world.'

'Assuming the sun's similar to home, it's after midday. The sun was high in the sky when we left the beach.' Sophie separated out her stuff to help it dry.

'I'm so cold,' said Hugo. 'Why couldn't we have landed in California?'

'You knew we'd come here.' Freddy stared at Hugo. 'You packed for the winter.'

Was Freddy angling for another fight?

'I assumed a worst-case scenario,' said Hugo, evenly. 'Cold weather, no shelter, no food, no water.'

'Did you think about Shorten in the lift at all, Freddy?' Sophie flexed her fingers to return some feeling.

'I prayed,' said Freddy. 'To be anywhere, far away from both of you.'

'You didn't think of a particular place?' said Hugo.

'I asked God to choose.' Freddy gazed at the flames. 'I thought, over and over…'

'What?' said Sophie.

'Do your worst.'

The sentiment repeated in Sophie's head, and she was lost for words.

'We should eat,' said Hugo, his brisk face on.

'Did you pack plates?' Freddy scanned the gear on the ground.

'Just spoons.' Hugo reached for a plastic packet. 'This is a self-heating ration pack, left over from my Combined Cadet Force exercises at school.' He peered at the label. 'Use-by date's only recently expired.'

Sophie took it and read the ingredients aloud. '*Aluminium powder, sodium carbonate, calcium oxide, sodium hydroxide.* We can't eat this.'

'That's the heating element.' Hugo extracted a small square packet. 'You add water to heat it, sealed off from the rations.'

Sophie sniffed. 'Smells like chlorine.'

Hugo inserted it back into the bigger plastic packet and pointed to another bag inside. 'The food's in there.' He poured in cave water from his travel mug. 'Up to this line. Then you fold the outer packet in half and seal it, but not completely. You want a little steam to escape, or it could explode.' He laid it down.

'Now what?' said Sophie.

'We wait.'

Eventually, popping sounds erupted from the bag and steam hissed out.

'A chemical reaction,' said Freddy.

Hugo cautiously opened it. 'Too hot to hold.' He stirred it with a spoon. 'Needs to be mixed up or you get lukewarm lumps and scalding lumps.' He bit into a sausage. 'Not bad.'

Sophie dug out beans with her spoon. 'Yum.'

Charlotte sat to attention, deploying her, 'Give me your food' stare, and Hugo gave her the rest of his sausage. 'I wish I'd had time to buy more online.'

Freddy found his spoon, dipped it in the bag, and warily tasted it.

Between them, they finished every morsel.

Beyond the cave, the shadow cast by the fir tree had darkened, and the sky was dusky.

Sophie helped Hugo stamp on the fire, though she craved its warmth. Their kit was still wet, but they repacked and retreated inside.

After filling their travel mugs with fresh water, Hugo and Sophie set out their sleeping bags. They'd bought four, each packing away to the size of a cabbage, but they were an eye-popping, lurid orange, designed to attract the attention of emergency services. Less garish sleeping bags had been too bulky.

'Waterproof, and you zip it shut to keep snug.' Hugo climbed into his and pulled up the black zip. 'You could fit two or three people in here.'

'You look ridiculous,' said Freddy.

Hugo's lips thinned. 'You'll be glad of yours tonight.' He partially opened the zip and sipped his water.

Sophie tried to coax Charlotte into a sleeping bag, but Charlotte lay on top of it.

Giving up, Sophie went to the back of the cave and topped up her mug. 'I could kill for hot tea.' A moment later, she jumped and almost dropped the mug. She poked inside it with her forefinger. 'It's mad, but this water has heated up.' She ran over to Hugo.

He did a double take. 'It's boiling.'

'I just wished for a cup of steaming tea,' said Sophie. 'Can you do it too?'

Hugo stared into his own mug. 'Nothing.'

Freddy frowned at his. 'No.'

'Physics, biology, and chemistry must be *very* different here,' said Hugo. 'Somehow linked to gender?'

Sophie rummaged in her holdall for tea bags and smiled. 'How cool is that?'

Just after dawn the next day, at the edge of the forest, Hugo lay on his stomach on the cold ground. He'd heard the army on the coastal road long before he'd seen it. The chink, chink of jangling metal, the rhythmic thud of feet.

The men marched four abreast. Weak sunlight glinted on black chain mail which covered the soldiers' chests and hips and enclosed their arms to their elbows. Under the armour, they wore dark woollen jerkins and red skirts, like kilts.

Scarlet cloaks swirled at their backs, and below pointed iron helmets, sable scarves protected their necks. On their feet were buff knee-high boots, and they carried swords or spears and round, crimson shields. In the centre of each shield was a circular white motif: an eight-sided snowflake.

The men were Caucasian, chatting among themselves in what could have been Russian. Hugo had studied the language at school, but the cadence was so strange, he couldn't understand a word.

Assuming the sun rose in the east, the army was heading north, up to where the road curved behind the headland. But his assumptions about this parallel world could be wrong. On Venus, the sun rose on the opposite side of the planet and Venus spun backwards.

A single horseman rode at intervals between the foot soldiers. Beyond them, Hugo could see the beach. The tide was out, the cave an easy walk across the sand.

Hugo checked his trusty old watch. The mechanism had dried out, and at sunrise, he'd adjusted the minute hand to seven, guessing the time.

Yesterday, dusk had arrived in the late afternoon. A short winter's day like at home. But the moon had looked odd. Bloated.

Hugo waited for an hour, but with no sign of the rear of the army, he crawled deeper into the forest, then stood up and followed his paint splodges.

Sophie was by the cave entrance. 'We were getting worried.' Their kit was laid out in neat rows around the fire.

The soldiers might notice the smoke. Hugo stamped out the flames, extinguishing them as fast as he could. 'No more fires.' He summarised what he'd seen and heard.

'Are we in Russia?' said Sophie.

'I don't know. The accent was weird.'

They tramped inside the cave.

Freddy was sitting on top of his sleeping bag, his knees folded close to his chest. Despite the temperature dropping to well below freezing at night, he'd refused to huddle together to keep warm, curling up in a solitary, orange ball.

'He hasn't tried to get past me,' said Sophie.

'My turn to stand guard.' Hugo settled himself at the cave entrance. Freddy going AWOL bothered him more than the army.

'Were the soldiers human?' asked Sophie.

'Yes. No orcs or demons or vampires.'

'That's good,' said Sophie.

Hugo frowned. 'I guess.'

'I've dismantled the revolver, dried it with the spectacle cloth and put back all the pieces.' Sophie handed it to him. The narrow, 1918 extended barrel gleamed. 'It's not that different from the pistol I learned to use in Shorten.'

'We should practice until it's instinctive, even in the dark,' said Hugo. '*Especially* in the dark.' He shivered. 'The tide's low at the moment, but until the army's gone, we can't reach the lift.'

'Okay, but we should return as soon as we can.' Sophie chewed her lip. 'Though we might be running out of luck with it.'

'I think the lift was protecting us,' said Freddy.

'How do you make that out?' said Hugo, surveying their wet possessions.

'It landed in that cave because eons ago the location wasn't near the sea, but registered it was under water and we wouldn't be able to breathe,' said Freddy. 'It waited until the tide turned before opening the doors.'

'But if the lift assesses its surroundings,' said Sophie, 'why not wait until the tide was completely out?'

'Because if Janus is somehow part of the software, personality must come into it.' Hugo shuddered.

CHAPTER 21

It took two whole days for the army to pass by, but on the third morning the road was empty, and the tide was out.

Sophie scurried along the beach with Charlotte, pulling her damp ski hat further over her ears. Though the sharp coastal wind had dropped, it was freezing. Hugo and Freddy followed behind.

Once in the cave, Sophie stuffed the hat into her jacket pocket. The sound of dripping water evoked carefree memories of seaside day trips, and she breathed in a familiar, soothing smell: old earth and salty-clean moisture.

The stone walls had dramatic, irregular fissures and high above her was a sea-worn, jagged ceiling.

Charlotte strained on her lead to explore, but Sophie kept her close. Seaweed-streaked boulders and little pools were too enticing, and they carried on deep into the cave.

'Here, and safe,' said Hugo, smiling.

Sophie returned the smile. She had no wish to meet the locals. Finding intelligent life in parallel worlds should have been exciting, but the thought filled her with dread.

She pulled Charlotte away from where the lift would appear and stood with her near the entrance. 'Remember Jack.' Charlotte stared straight ahead.

'Please help,' said Hugo to Freddy, who was hanging back. 'The army could turn around.'

'I think you invented those soldiers to make me so miserable in the woods that I'd long for Shorten.'

'I don't care what you think,' said Hugo. 'Get on with it.'

Sophie briefly closed her eyes, exhausted by their bickering and the trials of camping. It had been too cold to sleep properly, and they'd spent the days fruitlessly foraging. The SAS book listed numerous edible forest plants, but they hadn't found a single one.

Freddy rubbed his chin stubble.

'Not a good look, both of you not shaving,' said Sophie.

'Too much hassle in the great outdoors.' Hugo sat on his holdall. 'Let's leave.'

Freddy knelt and shut his eyes.

Sophie patted Charlotte on the head, repeated, 'Jack,' and concentrated, picturing the Manor: walking in the gardens, the air summer-hushed and sweet with flowers, curled up on the sofa with Charlotte in the small drawing room, all cosy while rain rattled the windows, waltzing with Hugo at the grandest of balls…

After half an hour, Freddy frowned at the space where the lift should have been. 'I want to go to Shorten, I do.'

'I believe you,' said Sophie. 'No idea why this isn't working.' Charlotte was quiet, appeared to be concentrating.

Hugo glanced over at the beach. 'The tide will turn soon.'

Sophie swung her holdall onto her shoulders. 'Try tomorrow?'

'Until we know why we can't call it, there's no point,' said Hugo. 'We need to find a town before we run out of food. That army must have billeted somewhere.'

They hurried from the cave and crossed the sand. On the road, as they walked south, away from the army, Sophie wondered again about her bag. Yes, it was nearly dry, and she'd eaten four cans of food, but how come it weighed hardly anything?

She checked in both directions. 'Shouldn't we keep off the highway? Travel through the woods?'

'The going would be really slow,' said Hugo.

'Or maybe travel by night?' said Sophie. Something felt wrong.

'Only if we have to,' said Hugo. 'Unfamiliar terrain, we'd be more vulnerable.'

Reluctantly, Sophie agreed.

An hour passed, Sophie still feeling twitchy, but the way remained deserted.

They topped up their mugs with clear water from a stream, and the road curved with the terrain, climbing steadily to the top of the sea cliff.

The path cut inland, and they spotted a column of faint smoke hanging in the air like a limp flag. Smoke meant chimneys and roaring fires and, hopefully, a hot meal. Sophie's ability to heat water hadn't worked with food.

They followed a narrow, meandering path towards it.

Negotiating a sharp bend, flanked by wind-battered trees, Hugo stopped so abruptly that Sophie slammed into his back.

She gaped at the destruction ahead of them.

Square, squat buildings and looming towers were built into a defensive wall. Part of the wall had collapsed, and the rubble was scarred and black.

Charlotte kept near to Sophie as she and Hugo inched forward. Freddy stayed behind them.

'Could be injured people,' said Sophie. They had first aid

kits. Helping someone might dispel the unease that twisted in her guts here.

They stepped over the rubble.

A sweet, sickly stench assaulted her nostrils. 'What is that *smell?*' Sophie spread her scarf over her nose and mouth. Behind her, Freddy did the same.

'I can't smell anything,' said Hugo. 'Perhaps because it's so cold.'

Charlotte gave a single bark and Sophie spun round to see what she'd spotted.

A man with a dark beard was sprawled in front of a door-way, one arm outstretched as if pleading. Another man lay close by, his eyes glazed. Each wore a short coat, and trousers tucked into socks that were crisscrossed with laces from flat black shoes.

'A disease,' said Sophie, tightening the scarf on her face.

Hugo approached the nearest body. 'He's been stabbed in the neck.' He averted his gaze. 'This happened a while ago. Decomposition's setting in.'

Sophie grimaced. 'How do you know?'

'GCSE biology.' Hugo paused before a building with its door hanging off its hinges and peered inside. 'Both dead,' he blurted, then threw up. He wiped his mouth with his gloved hand.

Sophie steeled herself and went to the doorway. Inside were a woman and a baby, slumped on the floor, streaked in blood. The stench from the room was overpowering, and she staggered, nausea souring her throat. No, no … this couldn't be happening. She had to get away.

She whirled around and bumped into Freddy. He mustn't see this. He'd freak out. She grabbed his arm and pulled him through the gap in the wall.

Freddy threw off her arm and strode down the path.

Sophie and Hugo skidded together after him, Charlotte straining against her lead, wanting to run.

'Evil, horrible…' Sophie's insides churned. Those men had been stabbed. Likely that poor woman and her child had been too. She tripped, but Hugo steadied her, his face tense and pale.

When they reached the road by the shore, they all slumped down on a grass verge and Charlotte put her large head on Sophie's lap.

This was vile. Worse than vile. What had Freddy prayed for? *Do your worst.*

On the sea, sunlight twinkled: tiny white stars, beautiful and indifferent. Freddy hadn't condemned them to exile in a hell world. There were streams and forests and air to breathe. The hell part was down to humans.

She met Hugo's eyes. 'Turn around or go on?' Her capacity to take charge, to be decisive, had deserted her.

'Travel as far as we can from the army.' Hugo watched the waves breaking on the beach, a muscle flexing in his jaw. 'They must have done that.'

'What do you think, Freddy?' asked Sophie. He'd not said a word since the lift cave.

Freddy shrugged.

His indifference to their survival made her want to weep, but she forced herself to stand up — and get moving.

Much later, well into the afternoon and miles down the coast, they saw smoke in the distance.

'Avoid or investigate?' said Hugo.

Sophie hesitated. 'Investigate.'

The curling plumes were from chimneys, set at the ends of a two-storey building with a red-tiled roof. In the twilight, the swollen moon hung low in the sky above it, giving the structure an eerie glow. Amber light, shining from ground-floor windows, looked hazy through the sea mist.

Someone in a dark cloak led a horse into another building, presumably stables, and a sign on the verge creaked to and fro. On it was a simple image of a tankard and strange, loopy writing — like elvish.

'An inn?' said Sophie. Hot food and an actual bed… Her clothes had finally dried as she'd walked, but she was chilled to the bone.

'Not Russian. I can't read it,' said Hugo. 'We should camp in the woods. Return in daylight.'

Charlotte hauled on the lead to go in. Her canine instincts had been right before. 'If it's dodgy inside,' said Sophie, 'we'll leave.'

Hugo sighed. 'Okay.' He rummaged in his bag and found one of the gold sovereigns.

'That might be worth this entire building,' said Sophie, 'not a night's stay.'

'Agreed.' Hugo put the sovereign back and selected a chunky necklace. They'd brought jewellery to barter. The stones were costume, but the chains were gold-plated.

'I'll wear it,' said Sophie, 'pretend it's mine.'

Hugo nodded. 'Presuming women wear necklaces here.'

Sophie took off her own necklace and secured it in a zipped compartment in the holdall. A gift from her mother before she'd died in the car accident with Sophie's father, the blue opal wasn't worth much, but to her it was priceless.

She slipped the other necklace over her head and Hugo checked the pistol on his belt.

The door of the inn opened into a room filled with sturdy tables and benches, half-obscured by jumping shadows cast by a candle on the wall.

Two people sat at a table by the candle. The guy's cloak

hood was down, but his bristling black beard and moustache concealed most of his face. His companion also wore a cloak, her long brown hair loose over her shoulders. A few feet from them, a strong fire blazed in a rustic fireplace.

Sophie inhaled a pleasing smell of beer and cooking and headed to a table on the other side of the fireplace. She sat on a bench with Hugo, and after a moment's hesitation, Freddy sat opposite.

Charlotte lay down by Sophie's feet, her bulk filling the aisle between their table and the next. Her fur appeared lighter in the firelight, streaked through with silver. More a wolf than a dog.

The couple stared. Beside their wooden bowls were a lit candle and a curved hunting knife. The man closed his fist around the hilt.

A door at the rear of the room opened, and a burly man strode towards them. His brow was sweaty, and he wore a dark apron over lighter trousers and a jerkin.

Sophie smiled at him, and the man gawped. After a moment, he said something incomprehensible.

Hugo spoke in careful Russian.

'Da,' said the man.

'The innkeeper speaks an unknown language, but he also speaks Russian,' said Hugo. 'Well, a sort of Russian.'

'Brilliant, you can understand some words,' said Sophie. 'What's the other language?'

Hugo talked slowly, the innkeeper replied, and Hugo said, 'Georgian.'

'So, we're in Georgia,' said Sophie.

The innkeeper spoke again, his gaze on Sophie.

'You've come from the forest?' translated Hugo. He nodded at the innkeeper.

Sophie removed the necklace and offered it, but the innkeeper backed away. He threw a nervous glance at the couple on the other table before addressing Sophie and talk-ing, spreading his arms wide.

'That,' said Hugo, 'I did not expect. He said we can stay and eat for free.'

The innkeeper hastily pushed through the door he'd come through, the open doorway revealing a bubbling caul-dron on a rough stove.

'He's in a state.' Sophie unzipped her red ski jacket.

Hugo frowned. 'Particularly when you offered him the necklace.'

The couple kept their heads down, eating fast.

'Maybe it's because of our clothes,' said Sophie. Their jackets and hats shouted twenty-first century.

The innkeeper returned, warily eyeing Charlotte who was watching him. He poured red wine into a tankard and set a jug on the table, before hurrying through the kitchen door.

Sophie tried a cautious sip. The wine was deep and fruity and smooth. Her shoulders relaxed, the stress of the last few days lifting.

The innkeeper brought a tray of steaming bowls and spoons, and a pile of flat bread.

Hugo tasted the bread topped with cheese. 'Fabulous.'

They all tucked in.

Beer was brought and Hugo poured himself some.

'We should order water,' said Sophie.

'No,' said Hugo. 'Where there's people, it's often polluted with sewage and other nasty stuff.'

'But if the inn has some,' said Sophie, 'I can boil it.'

'We keep that to ourselves.' Hugo sipped his beer. 'We've no idea what's normal here — or what would get us locked up.' He took another sip. 'I think this is "small beer" with a low alcohol content. Beer's brewed so it's safe, and wine's … wine.'

Freddy drained his tankard and Sophie savoured the wine, but when she tried the stew, she spat the lump she'd tasted into her hand. 'Meat?'

'Pork,' said Hugo. 'Spicy and nutty.' At the bottom of his bowl was thick corn bread. He wiped the bowl with it.

Freddy soon demolished his.

The innkeeper brought more bowls for the boys, and Sophie put down the dog-travel container she'd filled with stream water for Charlotte, and her own meaty stew. Charlotte lapped it all up.

Sophie put the empty bowl on the table and ate cheesy bread.

The innkeeper approached, his face strained. He pointed to Sophie's empty bowl and said something in a rush.

'He's worried that you didn't eat the stew. I'll ask about a veggie meal.' Hugo spoke in halting Russian.

The innkeeper frowned, maybe not understanding.

'You should compromise,' Hugo said to Sophie. 'I'll ask if he has any fish.'

The innkeeper produced a dead fish laid on leaves of green cabbage. The fish lay prone on its side, one eye staring.

Sophie's stomach roiled. 'Could you ask for more bread?'

CHAPTER 22

The following morning, Sophie's eyelids fluttered open, and she groaned. The light was too bright, her parched mouth tasted of dust, and her head throbbed. 'That wine was *too* good.'

Something prickly itched under her back. She was wearing her ski jacket, had slept on a low straw cot with no sheets or blanket.

Freddy lay on another cot, fast asleep. Charlotte was asleep too. Stretched out, she took up half the room.

'Here,' said Hugo. He handed her a packet of ibuprofen. The growth on his chin was more than stubble, but not yet a beard.

Sophie swallowed a couple of pills with a swig of water from her travel mug and scratched an itch on her hip. Only two cots. She'd not noticed that before falling into tipsy-oblivion. She glanced over at Hugo. 'Where did you sleep?'

'On the floor.'

'I'm sorry.'

'Don't be. I was snug in my sleeping bag, and the cots could have bedbugs.'

Sophie leapt off the cot and knocked over a worn chamber pot with a clang.

'I'm indisposed.' Freddy's shaky voice was a whisper.

'Freddy, we can sort our … ablutions outside,' said Hugo. 'We'll take Charlotte.'

At the sound of her name, Charlotte yawned and stood up.

Freddy held his head and grumbled but staggered out with Hugo and Charlotte.

When Sophie went downstairs, there was no sign of the couple from the previous night or anyone else. In daylight, the dining room looked basic but welcoming, the fire freshly lit.

Within moments of her sitting on a bench, the innkeeper appeared with jugs of wine and beer.

She scratched her hip again, and her ankle, before reluctantly sipping beer. She'd never tried 'hair of the dog' but needs must.

By the time the boys and Charlotte came in, cheesy bread and hot stew had been set out.

High on a wall by their table was an alcove and inside, a painted statue. Sophie pointed. 'Interesting.'

Hugo stepped closer to the recess. At six-foot three, his face was almost level with it. 'Blonde girl in a red dress with a gold necklace. A deer's beside her and on her other side, there's a wolf.'

'A hunting goddess?' said Sophie, feeding Charlotte bread and the last of the water.

'I need to figure out this weird Russian accent,' said Hugo, as he sat next to Sophie. 'And let's see what the innkeeper knows about the army.'

Freddy seated himself opposite Sophie, scratched his thigh, and took a tiny sip of beer.

When the innkeeper brought more bread, Hugo invited him to join them. The innkeeper hesitated but sat down.

Hugo practised his Russian and the innkeeper gradually gave longer replies, at one point violently gesticulating.

The innkeeper returned to the kitchen and Hugo finished his stew, a line deepening between his eyebrows.

'Bad news?' asked Sophie.

'The army belongs to a queen called Rusa. It's headed for a fortress that's under attack by the Mongols.'

'Mongols?' said Sophie. 'As in … Genghis Khan?'

'Yes.'

Freddy shifted in his chair.

'If the Mongols take the fortress,' said Hugo, 'they'll turn south. Towards here.' He held her hand.

The scent of beer grew stronger and the crackle of the fire louder, and Sophie looked at Hugo in dismay. 'Warriors infamous for their cruelty.'

Freddy toyed with his bread. 'The medieval chronicler, Matthew Paris, called the Mongols *a detestable nation of Satan that poured out like devils from Tartarus.*' His tone was flat and preachy, as if he were reciting from a textbook. 'We're in the Caucasus, and this is the thirteenth-century.'

'So, we landed by the Black Sea,' said Hugo. 'But the Black Sea isn't salty or tidal.'

'The moon looks strange, could affect the tides,' said Sophie.

'Perhaps the Black Sea here really is a *sea*, not a lake. Seriously different geography.' Hugo looked thoughtful. 'I told the innkeeper about the village. He said the Mongols attacked it.'

'We should go back to the lift,' said Sophie, apprehension sliding down her spine.

'The lift won't appear until I've gone.' Freddy pushed his plate aside.

Sophie stared at him. '*Gone?*'

'Dead.' Freddy looked down.

Sophie had no idea what to say and Hugo flicked his eyes up, meaning, 'Let's go to the room.'

They went upstairs, and Freddy followed.

Hugo read his survival book while Sophie curled up in the too-bright sleeping bag and slept the day away. Freddy also chose the wooden floor over his flea-ridden cot and slept, Charlotte dozing nearby.

When Sophie woke up, it was dusk. Hugo was sitting in his sleeping bag, still reading the survival book by the light of his wind-up torch, Charlotte beside him.

With no fireplace for a fire, it was cold, and Sophie's feet and hands were numb.

Her brain jumped to Freddy and his state of mind. He was asleep, peacefully snoring, but guilt racked her anew.

She climbed out of her sleeping bag, stamped her feet, and attacked her hair with a detangler brush. She'd packed it as an 'essential,' though a comb would have taken less space.

'Your hair's thicker,' said Hugo. 'And wavier.'

'A matted nightmare.' She stretched her arms above her head and yawned. 'Must be the sea air.'

An hour later, they all trooped down for dinner. Despite a good fire in the grate, the dining room was chilly, and they kept on their jackets.

Three men with weathered faces and short greasy beards sat at a nearby table. After initially shooting curious glances at Sophie, the boys, and Charlotte, they focused on eating and drinking.

Sophie steered clear of the wine. As did Hugo and Freddy. There was no more water, so Charlotte had to drink weak beer.

'They're talking in both Georgian and Russian,' said

Hugo. 'Said they'd brought rabbits. I'm guessing this is rabbit stew.' He stirred his broth with a spoon.

Sophie fed hers to Charlotte. Fortunately, there was an endless supply of warm-fresh cheesy bread and a loaf stuffed with walnuts. She'd glimpsed a woman and a girl working in the kitchen, presumably the innkeeper's family.

The innkeeper was run off his feet, the men banging knife hilts on the table when they wanted service, but after they'd eaten and drunk their fill, the innkeeper sat with them, talking and laughing.

'Most of it's incomprehensible,' said Hugo, 'but they caught sight of a bear in the woods.'

'A *real* bear?' said Sophie.

Hugo nodded. 'And they're saying the innkeeper drinks too much. Banter between friends.'

Freddy finished his beer. 'Goodbye.'

Hugo put down his tankard with a clank. 'What do you mean?'

Freddy stood up, his expression resolute. He walked over to the group at the nearby table, and before Sophie or Hugo could stop him, he punched the nearest man.

The man's mates leapt up and launched themselves at Freddy, shouting and laying into him. Freddy staggered, but then lashed out again.

'Hugo, hold on to Charlotte,' yelled Sophie, giving him the lead, and dashed over to extract Freddy.

Somehow, Freddy was holding his own, and he ignored her when she grabbed his shoulders to pull him away.

Charlotte strained on her lead and barked. 'Stay,' shouted Sophie. This fight needed to peter out, not rev up. To her relief, Charlotte moved closer to Hugo and just barked.

The innkeeper was gabbling, his face red with agitation, and Sophie tried afresh to drag Freddy out. As she did, the tallest man, who was lean and muscled, tapped his own wrist. Strapped there was a knife. Warning her off?

Sophie executed a targeted kick to his arm. The man swayed, grimacing in pain. Even allowing for the element of surprise, she could only have delivered a glancing blow. Another guy threw a punch at her, connecting with her chin, but she hardly felt it. What the hell?

The tall man reached for something behind a chair and Sophie kicked him in the back, slamming him to the floor. Beside him was a sword and she picked it up, pulling off the sheath. The weapon was huge. Russell Crowe could have wielded it in *Gladiator*.

Freddy was still fighting like a madman. He sent two guys sprawling, one after the other.

Hugo shouted in Russian and waved his pistol. The men — *and* Freddy — stopped brawling.

Sophie breathed a sigh of relief, pointed the sharp end of the blade downwards and rested her hands on the hilt. The weapon was half as tall as her.

The man she'd kicked was on his feet, holding his right arm, and he and his friends stared at her. The next moment, they fell over each other to sprint out of the inn.

Hugo lowered the pistol and dropped Charlotte's lead, flexing his fingers.

Sophie carefully laid down the sword, shut the inn door and leaned against it, bewildered. What just happened?

Freddy flopped onto a bench and put his head in his hands, and the innkeeper sat on a different bench, breathing heavily and muttering.

'Please return to the forest,' translated Hugo. 'Or nobody will come here. I'll be ruined.' He frowned. 'I don't get it.'

'One thing's clear,' said Sophie. 'We're frightening away his customers.'

Half an hour after leaving the inn, Sophie stood in a winter-silent forest by a chilly stream. But thanks to her modern ski clothing, she wasn't cold.

She turned around and frosty leaves gave way under her boots. 'Ugh.' Sophie wrinkled her nose.

'What can you smell?' Hugo asked her, laying out his sleeping bag.

'These leaves stink of dirt and mildew.'

'Missing out on weird smells must be down to me not having the gene.' Hugo rummaged in his holdall and fished out his pistol and wind-up torch.

'And the sap in this tree, it's *gurgling*,' said Sophie. 'That punch did something to my head.'

'He hit your chin,' said Hugo, climbing into his sleeping bag.

Freddy was already inside his. Charlotte settled next to him.

'I know you're not asleep, Freddy.' Sophie wriggled into her sleeping bag and closed it up to her neck. 'Whatever happens, we'll always have your back.'

Freddy pulled his hat further over his ears. '*Never* assist me again.'

A keen wind rustled nearby branches, and inside her sleeping bag, Sophie brought her knees up to her chest. 'Do you think there really are bears?' she whispered to Hugo.

'Yes.' He patted the pistol on the ground beside him.

'I'm glad you didn't have to use that on the hunters,' said Sophie.

'I'm glad too,' said Hugo. 'We only have six bullets.'

Freddy was lying motionless. Could be asleep.

'We should go further south,' said Hugo. 'Away from the Mongols.'

Sophie nodded. 'What did you shout in the inn?'

'We're armed.' Hugo took a shiny metal flask from his pocket. He'd asked the innkeeper for it. 'If you boil water in this, we can warm our hands.' He wrapped it in a thin towel.

Sophie jumped out of her sleeping bag, went over to the stream, dragged the flask through it and boiled the water. She held it tight. 'Fabulous.'

After Hugo warmed his hands, she strode over to Freddy who wasn't asleep and accepted the flask. Charlotte didn't stir.

'We got lucky in that fight.' Sophie made tea.

Hugo glanced over at Freddy. 'No more picking fights. And if someone picks a fight with us, we run away.'

'Run, hide, call,' said Sophie. 'What to do in a terrorist incident.'

'Except there's no one to call.' Still in his sleeping bag, Hugo examined the sword on the ground with the torch. 'This workmanship is exquisite.'

Curiosity was evidently stronger than Freddy's need for solitude. He crawled out of his sleeping bag, picked it up, and climbed into it next to Hugo.

The three of them peered at the sword. The horizontal

guard was gilded and engraved with an eight-sided snowflake. Another snowflake was carved into the round brass bauble at the top of the hilt.

'The queen's army had this symbol on their shields.' Hugo studied the bauble. 'Cool pommel. Those fencing lessons at school might yet come in handy.'

'You know how to use this?' said Sophie.

'I was joking,' said Hugo. 'I practised with a fencing foil. Light, with blunt tips. This is a very different beast.'

'I did fencing at school.' Freddy glared at Hugo. 'Sophie could have been hurt in the inn. *We* should do the fighting.'

'Good luck with that.' Hugo shot her a resigned smile.

Sophie leaned down to feel the grip. Wrapped in dark leather strips, it had a firm hold.

The sword's scabbard was plain, made from the same leather that covered the handle, but a few inches below the guard, inlaid within the iron blade, was latticework, repeating the snowflake.

'Those men didn't look wealthy enough to have this,' said Freddy. 'Might have stolen it.'

Hugo touched the flat edge of the burnished steel blade. 'When Sophie snatched it, perhaps they worried they'd get done for stealing.'

'Doesn't explain why they bolted.' Sophie sat on her sleeping bag and enjoyed her tea, relishing its heat. 'This place is pre-firearms, right? Your gun wouldn't have scared them off. They couldn't have known what it was.'

Hugo slapped his brow with his hand. 'The hunting goddess. What if the innkeeper thought *you* were her?'

Sophie guffawed. 'That's mad.'

'Think about it. The red ski jacket, your wavy hair, Charlotte looking like a scary wolf.' Hugo drank his tea. 'And when we first walked in, the innkeeper said, *You've come from the forest.'* I assumed that was a ritual, conventional greeting, but perhaps it wasn't.'

'Would explain the free food and accommodation,' said Sophie, 'but not why the men were so frightened.'

'The shepherds were frightened when the angel told them about Jesus being born,' said Freddy. 'Could be the same with a goddess.'

'Was the statuette good or evil?' Sophie asked Hugo. The alcove had been too high to study it up close.

'Neither.' Hugo finished his tea. 'All we need now is for the deer you saw to appear.' His tone was flippant, maybe trying to lighten up.

Sophie gripped the sword hilt and lifted the weapon slightly. 'This might be a magic sword.' Except she didn't believe in magic. 'Why isn't it heavy?' She laid it down.

Hugo hauled the sword up with a groan and sank the tip into the ground. 'It *is* heavy.'

Why was he play-acting? Sophie stood up, picked up the sword, and waved it above her head. 'This is fun.'

Hugo shuffled out from his sleeping bag and knelt beside a flat-topped rock. 'Sophie, arm wrestle.'

'What? No.'

'Humour me.'

'Okay.' Sophie put aside the sword, knelt, and they locked hands. He hardly resisted and she pushed down his arm. 'Why aren't you trying?'

'I *was* trying. The sword isn't miraculously light, Sophie. *You* are miraculously strong. This has to be the gene.' Hugo got to his feet. 'And I'm weaker. My holdall feels *much* heavier here. We can prove it. Freddy, pick up the sword.'

Freddy lifted it with ease and held it in the air. 'You can't do this?' Freddy asked Hugo.

'No.'

Freddy stood straighter, pleased to be one up on Hugo. He rested his hands on the guard. The weapon was as tall as his hips.

A memory stirred. Sophie took the sword from Freddy and laid her hands on the guard, her thick hair tumbling over her shoulders. The pommel reached her waist.

She put down the sword and hunted in her bag for the notebook she'd bought in Saint Pancras station. Flicking through her lift sketches, she paused when she reached the girl with the sword. The figure's face was generic, as on the lift, but other details were distinctive: the hip-length jacket with a hood, the long curly hair, and the sword, half the height of the girl. Though the notion was absurd, she showed the image to the boys. 'Could this be *me*?'

'Disturbing idea,' said Hugo. He stepped closer to Freddy. 'Your hair's thicker too, and you're taller. We're now the same height.'

Sophie found the baby cot drawing. 'Freddy, you said the only way we could call the lift was if you … died. But you saw a cot. A symbol of birth, not death.'

Freddy said nothing.

Sophie turned another page. 'The wavy line that splits in two directions.' She pointed. 'Could symbolise our choices?'

'About what?' said Freddy.

'If we make the wrong choices,' said Sophie, 'maybe the lift won't appear?'

'The lift's a machine,' said Freddy. 'It can't reason and has no knowledge of my choices.'

'It uses thoughts and emotions as fuel, and to guide it,' said Hugo, 'and travellers see different images on the doors. It must somehow access your minds.'

'Your opinion is worthless,' said Freddy, 'given you're unable to see the pictures and never will.'

Sophie frowned. 'That's mean, Freddy. Unworthy of you.'

'The *old* me.' Freddy set his mouth. 'Before you cast me off like an unwanted toy.'

CHAPTER 24

The next morning, the coastal road was obscured by heavy snowflakes, tossed by the wind.

Charlotte stopped to sniff at a tree. A wooden plaque, the size of a large hand, was nailed to the trunk just above Sophie's eye level. On it was a crude carving of a long-haired figure with a sword. Underneath were Cyrillic letters.

'Death for something … the red goddess,' said Hugo. 'Oh, *impersonating* the red goddess.'

'The statuette's dress was red, hence the red goddess.' The unease was back, sharpened by a dart of panic. Sophie unzipped her scarlet jacket, hauled it off, pulled it inside out and put it on again, the dark lining now on the outside.

'If those hunters believed Sophie was a goddess,' said Freddy, 'why would they have attached this to a tree?'

'Perhaps they didn't,' said Hugo. 'I'm guessing word has spread.'

Sophie zipped the jacket to the top and arranged her scarf snug about her neck. 'Cool that you spotted the sign,' she said to Charlotte, patting her impressive, white-flecked head. 'We'd have missed it in all this snow—'

Charlotte barked.

A wagon appeared out of nowhere, the horse and the wood of the cart a solid, frightening shock. Then it was gone, lost to sight.

'Must be going to a farm or a settlement,' said Hugo. 'Close enough to reach before dark.'

Before she'd crossed universes, Sophie had never travelled anywhere without the certainty of a destination. She pictured a hot meal and a cheery fire and gave the boys a determined smile. Hugo nodded, but Freddy blanked her.

They trudged on, keeping to the side of the road. The snow had not only concealed the wagon but deadened the sound of its approach.

At midday, it stopped snowing, and an hour after that, a town came into view. Fortified like the village, it was thankfully intact.

But a few steps further on, another plaque was nailed to a tree, identical to the previous one.

'We shouldn't go in there,' said Sophie. 'Better to wait for a wagon. Ask for food in exchange for jewellery.'

'Word would get to the town,' said Hugo, 'and now the weather's cleared, finding you on the road wouldn't be difficult. You've ditched the red jacket, so we might blend into a crowd.'

'The sword is rather conspicuous,' said Freddy.

Sophie frowned. 'Let's wrap it in towels.'

They searched in their bags, Sophie covered the hilt and the bottom of the blade with towels, but the middle was still exposed.

'I should carry it,' said Freddy.

She reluctantly handed it over. In most medieval societies at home, women didn't go for a stroll openly armed.

A low rumble signalled another wagon, half-filled with

furniture. A skinny couple sat at the front, behind a mangy, tired-looking horse.

'Time to blend in.' Hugo rifled through his holdall and took out a bracelet. 'We're hitching a ride.' He approached the wagon and it stopped, and he spoke with the driver. Hugo held up the bracelet, and there was more conversation, slowed by Hugo's ponderous delivery.

The woman accepted the bracelet and the man gestured to the rear of the wagon. They climbed in and sat between a spindle and wooden boxes. Sophie pulled Charlotte half onto her lap.

'This stuff is their possessions,' said Hugo. 'They've come from near Anacopia.'

'Where?' asked Sophie.

'North of where we landed. The fortress that's been attacked by the Mongols.' Hugo adjusted his hat to cover his ears. 'They assumed we're refugees. We should go with that.'

The wagon rolled towards the town gates, paused at the entrance, and a guard looked them over. His dark woollen cloak was belted at the waist and on his head was a round green hat. A short knife hung from the belt, and he held a spear.

After a brief exchange the guard waved them on, and the wagon clattered into a busy street. Horses stabled on a long stall whinnied and snickered while people hurried about their business swathed in grey and brown cloaks, scarfs pulled up against the cold. All wore cloth hats, each a different vibrant colour: orange, green, or blue.

The smell of greasy meat and fresh bread mingled with horse manure, and Sophie gripped the edge of the wagon, breathing through her mouth under her scarf. If this was the smell-fest in winter, what was it like in summer?

They passed a warehouse where women tended to vats of black sludge hung over open fires, their contents steaming.

Apprehension was lined into the women's faces as they worked, their skin slick with sweat.

The stench from the vats scratched the back of Sophie's throat, bitter and hot. 'Cooking oil?' She wrinkled her nose.

'It may not be for cooking,' said Freddy. 'If the Mongols besiege the town, they'll pour that over the ramparts.'

'Medieval napalm,' said Hugo. 'Burns skin to the bone.'

Sophie winced.

'We shouldn't stick around,' said Hugo. 'Buy food and go south.'

A child in a dirty jerkin cut across the path of their wagon and disappeared between wooden stalls lining the road. Hawkers' sing-song chants competed with rhythmic banging, metal on metal, from a blacksmith's workshop.

The wagon jerked to a halt, and they climbed out.

'This is quite something,' said Freddy, heading to a stall with bowls of hot dumplings stuffed with who knew what.

Sophie put her arm through Freddy's, and he flinched. 'Stay close,' she said. 'Don't do anything stupid.' *Not* being in love with him didn't stop her feeling protective.

'We're getting curious looks,' said Hugo. 'Let's fit in better.' He made his way to a different stall selling grey cloaks. He haggled, more confident with the language, and the stallholder accepted a gaudy necklace as payment.

They wore the cloaks over their jackets and drew the hoods up, hiding their hats. Georgian style, they wrapped their scarfs to just under their eyes.

After buying bread and cheese, they walked into a packed square. The buzz of conversation suggested excitement, anticipation. Sophie stood on tip toes. 'A festival?'

Hugo gripped her elbow. 'Not a festival. Someone's tied to a stake and the wood at the base is burning.'

'I can't watch,' said Freddy.

Sophie gulped, consumed with revulsion. Maybe this was

a 'choices' moment? Doing the right thing could help them call the lift. 'Freddy, we're mega-strong and these people think I'm a goddess. We can stop this.'

'You said not to do anything stupid.' Freddy tightened his grip on the sword.

'*You* said you'd have enlisted in the Great War, fought for your country,' said Sophie. 'Saving this person is what a … gentleman would do.'

Freddy nodded. 'An awfully big adventure.'

Sophie searched her brain. Peter Pan. *To die will be an awfully big adventure.* 'A rescue. Not a suicide mission. Give me the sword.'

'No. I should have it.'

Sophie sighed. 'I'm the *goddess*, remember? *Me* having the sword will be more awesome.'

Freddy hesitated but let her take it.

'This is a bad idea.' Hugo grabbed Sophie's arm.

She shrugged him off. 'We stay together.' She shoved the towels and the leather scabbard into her holdall, peeled off her cloak, reversed the jacket to red, and secured the bag over her shoulders. She gave Hugo her cloak and hat.

'Will you *listen*.' Hugo thrust the cloak and hat back at her. 'Do Not Do This. If the crowd turn on us, *we*'ll end up on that pyre.'

'It's a risk,' said Sophie, 'but I can do this. Well, the "goddess" can.'

The crowd was chanting. 'What are they saying?' Sophie asked Hugo.

'Coward.' Hugo grabbed her arm again. 'We need to leave.'

'No. We brazen it out,' said Sophie. 'And it'll soon be too late. Shout, "Make way," or something.'

Hugo's lips twisted in frustration, but he yelled in Russian.

No one took the slightest notice.

With one hand, Sophie lifted the sword above her head, stepped forward, and the crowd parted like startled birds. Keeping the weapon high, she marched with the boys to the centre of the square. Charlotte paced with them, snarling.

Tied to the stake was a teenager, shaved bald and dressed only in a white shift. He was coughing, inhaling smoke.

The cloaked man who'd lit the pyre was grinning, admiring his work. A long dagger hung from his belt. He saw Sophie and stood stock still. A human statue of liberty with a flaming torch.

'Tell Fire Man to untie the prisoner,' Sophie said to Hugo, 'or I'll kill him.'

'This is bloody mad,' said Hugo, but he shouted in Russian.

The crowd fell silent, collectively holding their breath.

Flames eating the wood sparked red and yellow, and woodsmoke, sweet and musty, filled Sophie's nostrils and mouth. She pressed her lips together. Don't cough. Goddesses don't cough.

Fire Man yelled at Hugo, and the crowd whispered, uneasy.

'A deserter from the queen's army should die by flame, not by blade,' translated Hugo.

Without warning, Charlotte produced a tremendous bark, so loud that everyone in the square put their hands over their ears. But Freddy didn't. Neither did Sophie.

Charlotte seemed unfazed and Sophie continued with her plan. She advanced towards the pyre, her mother's gilt-chained necklace bouncing against her red jacket. 'Tell him again, that I'll kill him. Right now.'

Fire Man gulped at Hugo's words, clambered up the smoking wood and hacked at the prisoner's ropes. They fell away, but the boy didn't move, watching Sophie with hooded, shadowed eyes.

Fire Man was hopping from foot to foot to avoid the flames, his eyes darting and panicked.

'Bring the prisoner to me,' said Sophie.

Hugo translated her words as an order.

Despite his trepidation, he was playing his part. But how long would the crowd keep out of this? They'd been baying for blood.

Fire Man stumbled off the pyre, gripping the boy's arm.

'Drop the dagger,' said Sophie, and Hugo gave the order.

Fire Man threw it down.

Hugo shouted, gesturing for the crowd to disperse.

A sudden yelling and screaming, and people near the front pivoted and ran, keen to exit the square. More raced away, and Fire Man bolted, was soon lost in the throng.

'Freddy, grab Prisoner Boy,' said Sophie. 'This is where we do an awesome exit and hide in the woods.'

Keen to acquire another weapon, Sophie grabbed Fire Man's dagger and gave it to Hugo, handle first. The two-sided blade looked nasty-sharp.

Freddy had a firm grip on Prisoner Boy who was squirming and gabbling and blue with cold. Hugo wrapped Sophie's cloak around him.

Nerves were threatening to deplete precious adrenaline, but Sophie sashayed out of the square. Hold your nerve.

She stopped mid-sashay. Someone was moaning. She cut down an alley.

The sound was coming from a cage, barely holding a large light-brown bear, its fur scabbed and dotted with sores.

As she drew closer, the bear bellowed and scraped at the bars with pale claws.

'For God's sake,' said Hugo. '*No.*'

'Releasing this animal is unwise,' said Freddy.

'In for a penny, in for a pound.' Sophie looked back

towards the main street. 'Hugo, throw bread up the alley. That should encourage it to run to the town gate.'

'Why would that work?' Hugo's voice cracked. 'You've lost it.'

Sophie glared at him. She'd thought this through. 'We can shelter in that doorway behind the cage.'

Freddy and Prisoner Boy huddled in a recess in front of a wide doorway partly blocked by the cage, and Freddy hauled Charlotte to him, squeezing her into the bay.

At the top of the alley, Hugo threw down loaves, quickly returned and scrambled into the recess. He fumbled for his pistol.

'Right, here goes.' Sophie whacked the sword down on a rusty lock on the cage door and with a loud creak, the door swung open. But like Prisoner Boy on the pyre, the bear stayed put.

Sophie shrank into the doorway. 'Hugo, shout at it. Tell it to escape.'

'Why would it understand Russian?' But Hugo yelled, his voice husky from shouting.

The bear turned its enormous head in their direction. It climbed out and stood on its hind legs.

Nine feet tall.

The bear roared, and a spike of primaeval terror tore through Sophie.

Hugo raised his pistol.

The bear dropped to all fours and lumbered towards the bread. It thrust the loaves into its mouth but then looked straight at them.

Sophie gasped in terror. The cage wouldn't protect them. That bear could toss it aside in a heartbeat.

'Don't move,' said Hugo. 'If it charges, I'll shoot it.'

Sophie held her breath.

The bear sniffed the air and bounded off to the main street, as fast as a car.

'*No* idea bears could move so quickly,' said Sophie, stumbling over her words.

'Goodness.' Freddy stepped from the doorway, holding Prisoner Boy who swayed on his feet.

'*Please*,' said Hugo, 'we need to get out of here.'

Sophie drew a deep breath, held the sword high, and walked up the alley at a stately pace. Keep it together. Goddesses don't run.

Up ahead, the bear had emptied the road. People were crouching at the rear of stalls, others cowered in doorways. The bear reached the town gate and loped through it.

'I'll get us horses,' said Freddy, going to the stabling line. He sounded surprisingly calm.

The tethered horses were *not* calm, alarmed by the bolting bear and panicked citizens.

Freddy made confident, reassuring noises to them as they hung their holdalls from three horses' saddles. He lifted Prisoner Boy up, and in a trice mounted behind him.

Hugo seated himself and Sophie somehow mounted while holding the sword upright, her heart hammering against her ribs.

As they approached the deserted open gate, Charlotte prowled at their side, her wide head turning left and right, deterring anyone from approaching, never mind stopping them.

Once they were through, Sophie urged the horse into a trot, then a gallop until she reached the forest, Hugo and Freddy following. Charlotte kept up with ease.

Sophie stashed the sword in its scabbard, and Hugo took the compass from his bag. They rode into the woods, heading east.

Traces of the adrenaline that had buoyed Sophie up in the

town lingered, empowering as a swig of rum. The wind whistled cold and harsh through the trees and with no noise of pursuit, she wanted to punch the air and shout, 'yes,' but the boys were quiet, so she stayed quiet too.

Charlotte found a stream, and they paused for a quick bite to eat.

Hugo looped his horse's reins over a branch, then gripped his pistol. 'I hope that bear isn't tracking us.'

'It's long gone,' said Sophie. Rustling from the forest floor suggested scurrying mammals — nothing as big as a bear. She trusted her senses now. Sharper. Quicker.

Securing her horse, she glanced over at Freddy. 'Is your hearing more acute, your sense of smell improved?'

'I think so.' He exhaled. 'I can't believe we did that.'

Cowering next to Freddy, Prisoner Boy eyed Sophie as if she would eat him.

'Hugo, can you ask him his name?' she asked.

Hugo spoke softly, trying to reassure, and Prisoner Boy mumbled a response, his attention still on Sophie.

'He says he's called No One,' said Hugo.

No One spoke again.

'He says your sword is his commander's,' said Hugo, 'taken by bandits.'

'Angling for us to hand it over,' said Sophie. 'Not happening.'

Hugo unfolded his sleeping bag from his holdall. 'Let's get him warm.'

Prisoner boy jumped and stared at the orange bag.

'I know,' said Sophie. 'The colour's gross.'

Hugo set it out on the ground. 'I'll tell him he's safe.'

No One leapt forward, grabbed the dagger from where it lay on top of Hugo's holdall, and yelling something, plunged the knife into his own chest.

Sophie gaped in shock.

No One keeled sideways, seemed to collapse in slow motion, and his eyes turned glassy.

'Good God,' said Freddy.

Sophie knelt beside the boy and gently closed his lids.

'Hugo, what did he say?' asked Freddy, his voice trembling.

'*Take me, not family*, but some of it was Georgian, so I don't know.' Hugo sighed. 'In any event, we've risked our lives for someone who didn't want to live.'

With a grimace, Hugo pulled the dagger from the body and wiped the blade on a clump of moss. He wrapped it carefully in a towel and slid it into his holdall, point first.

Sophie cradled No One on her lap, though he was beyond comforting.

Reluctantly, with a hard lump in her throat, she stood up, dragged her blood-streaked cloak off him, and put it on over her jacket.

In death, No One looked younger, and with his pale skin and his white shift smeared with red, he lay on the dull, fallen leaves like an abandoned, kitschy statue. Undignified. Un-mourned.

Melancholy came over Sophie, hollow and draining. 'We can't just leave him here.'

'We've no spade to dig a grave,' said Freddy.

They laid brushwood over him, until he was hidden under a sylvan blanket.

Charlotte lay down facing the makeshift grave and Sophie cleared her throat. 'We're sorry you're gone. We hope you're somewhere nice.'

'Rest in peace,' said Freddy.

Hugo turned around and opened his holdall. 'We should eat, then go south.'

They moved to a respectful distance from No One,

Sophie made tea, and they ate their bread and cheese in silence. Snow fell, deepening the quiet.

'What's going on with you?' said Hugo. 'This idiotic saviour complex will get us killed.'

Sophie hesitated. 'Rescuing No One didn't go so well, but we freed the bear.'

'How many other people and animals here need rescuing?' said Hugo. 'Hundreds, probably thousands. Better to mind our own business and work on why we couldn't call the lift.'

Sophie got to her feet and dragged her travel mug through the stream. 'Helping No One and the bear *was* about calling the lift. If the pictures on the doors represent our choices, we made the right ones.'

'Perhaps there's a much simpler reason it failed to appear,' said Hugo. 'Freddy's longing to travel wasn't strong enough, or his state of mind negated you and Charlotte.'

'I did *try* longing for home,' said Freddy, 'but I also thought how it would be, telling my parents how you and Sophie…' He filled his mug from the stream and handed it to Sophie. 'May I have another cup of tea, please?'

Even now, Freddy's manners were intact.

A brief Sophie-stare and the water boiled. 'Much quicker than a kettle.'

Hugo chewed his lip. 'How you're different here, how Freddy and Charlotte are as well … it creeps me out.'

'It is weird.' Sophie took his mug. 'Top up?'

CHAPTER 25

In the afternoon, fortified by hot tea and full stomachs, they rode a few miles south through the woods, but it was slow going and eventually they headed west to check out the coastal road.

Sophie scanned the snowy highway. 'Deserted.' She'd half expected soldiers or townspeople with pitchforks.

'They won't follow us,' said Freddy. 'Who in their right mind pursues a terrifying hunting goddess?' For the first time since London, he managed a genuine smile.

'But in case they do…' Sophie dismounted and stretched, her legs aching from riding. She threw off her cloak, turned her jacket inside out and, over it, put on the cloak again.

Hugo dismounted and scraped handfuls of dirt from under snowy bushes by the roadside. 'I've always had a thing about filthy brown hair.' He pushed mud onto Sophie's scalp.

She trailed the grime through to the ends and added a dollop on her brow.

On horseback, Freddy watched her. 'You could be an earth goddess.'

Sophie smeared some over Charlotte. It didn't make her

look any less wolf-like or detract from her size, or the teeth that had grown with the rest of her, but it dulled her distinctive silver fur.

Sophie and Hugo remounted, and they cantered off, Charlotte running beside them. They galloped and Charlotte sped up and moved faster than the horses. Surreal.

Conscious of tiring the horses, they slowed, and so did Charlotte.

'I'm calling you Black Beauty,' announced Sophie, patting her horse's neck.

'Original,' said Hugo. 'So, what do I call mine?' His horse was also black.

'Handsome?' said Sophie.

'If you're serious,' said Freddy, 'giving them new names might confuse them—'

A toddler ran out from a bush and fell over in front of Sophie's horse. Sophie only just managed to pull up.

Charlotte sniffed at the child, who screamed, and they all dismounted.

The little girl wore a grey, knee-length cloak, the hood stretched tight over a tangle of brown hair. Sophie knelt next to her. 'She's injured.' She pointed at a deep cut on the child's leg.

'Our towels are too thin,' said Hugo. 'Tampons would stop the bleeding.'

Sophie fished out three from her holdall and Hugo laid them over the gash and applied pressure. The toddler screamed louder, screwing up her face.

'We need something to keep the wound closed.' With a kitchen knife, Sophie cut a ragged strip off the bottom of her cloak.

Hugo removed the tampons and tied the material firmly around the child's leg.

Sophie returned the knife to her bag and shoved the

trashed tampons out of sight under a bush. She sat on the road. 'We won't hurt you. You're safe.'

'Tempting fate.' Freddy made a face.

A man, shouting and gesticulating, sprinted out of the forest. He carried a bow, the arrow nocked and ready to shoot. Behind him trudged men, women, and children, weighed down with bags and parcels. Two donkeys were overloaded with sacks and boxes, and a strapping boy held a dog on a chain. The dog was almost as big as Charlotte.

'Caucasian mountain dog.' Sophie gripped Charlotte's collar. '*Not* good with strangers.'

Hugo raised his arms in a placating gesture and Freddy did the same.

Sophie turned to Freddy. 'Hold Charlotte.' If Charlotte leapt at the mountain dog, Hugo wouldn't have the strength to stop her. 'They'll feel less threatened by a girl.'

Once Freddy had Charlotte, Sophie picked up the toddler, cautiously walked towards the group and set the child by the archer's feet. The man shook his head, looking confused.

A woman examined the little girl's leg and rattled off a stream of words to the archer.

The man lowered his bow and addressed Hugo.

'What's he saying?' said Sophie.

'I may have misunderstood.' Hugo kept his hands in the air.

'What do you think he said?' asked Freddy.

Hugo swallowed. 'Why didn't we kill her?'

The archer spoke again.

'He's asking if we're with the Mongols,' said Hugo. 'Niet.' He frowned in concentration as the man continued talking. 'They're refugees, like the couple in the wagon.' Hugo spoke in halting Russian. 'I told them the wound needs cleaning.'

Women buzzed around the toddler, tending to the injury, and the archer talked to Hugo.

'He's the child's father. He says we can travel with them to the queen's stronghold.'

'Good idea,' said Sophie. 'Lower our profile.'

They remounted but kept the pace slow, in line with the families. Sophie held Charlotte on a firm lead.

'What are tampons?' Freddy asked her.

'Once we're on the road, I'll explain,' said Sophie.

'We're *on* the road,' said Freddy.

Whatever the physiological or other changes he'd gone through, Freddy was still Freddy. Sophie was saved from replying by Charlotte lurching forward, straining to attack the other dog. *Not* like herself.

The child's father walked beside Hugo's horse, talking in Russian. 'His name's Bacha,' said Hugo. 'They have relatives in Kajet. We'll get there in two days.'

Hugo pointed to the man's curved bow, and the snowflake symbol on it, and Bacha nodded and spoke.

'That white symbol isn't a snowflake, it's a star,' said Hugo. 'Associated with the red goddess — and queen Rusa.'

'So, the queen uses the goddess myth to bolster her image,' said Sophie. 'Might explain the placards on the trees.'

'She's put out by the real one making mayhem,' said Freddy.

Sophie shot Freddy a droll look.

Bacha said something else.

'By his account, Rusa's adored by her subjects,' said Hugo, 'and her army will see off the Mongols.'

'I wonder why we've not seen them,' said Sophie. 'Mongols...'

'The people in that village died at least a week before we landed,' said Hugo. 'I'm guessing that since then, the Mongols have been preoccupied with attacking Anacopia.' Hugo's breath rose in white spirals into the air. 'Let's hope Rusa's army sees them off.' He patted his horse. 'Or the Mongols will move south and control all of this road.'

Sophie glanced at him in alarm. 'Between us and the lift.'

CHAPTER 26

Kajet, the queen's coastal stronghold, graced a snow-covered hill resembling a tiered wedding cake. Along six encircling paths, at regular intervals, were flaming torches. On top of the hill, beyond a crenelated wall, was an elegant cluster of red-roofed towers, shrouded in mist.

Near Kajet, the road widened. Flanking it, suspended on poles, were cages enclosing human skeletons. Strips of ragged clothing fluttered from their bones like macabre welcoming flags.

Sophie moved her horse closer to Hugo's. 'What is it with cages here?' she muttered.

Hugo stared ahead at the palace. 'I'm guessing those people didn't adore Rusa.'

'I never thought I'd say this,' said Sophie. 'Camping in the woods was mighty fine.'

'Are those skeletons real people?' Freddy whispered to Hugo.

'They were.'

Freddy screwed up his eyes.

Black Beauty whinnied, jittery, and Sophie whispered, 'It's all right.' Padding beside them, Charlotte was wired, her head cocked, hearing sounds even beyond her mistress's enhanced hearing.

Bacha shrugged and said something.

'He says they were all traitors.' Hugo paused. 'Presumably, including that one.'

They passed a baby-sized skeleton and Sophie's fingers tightened on her reins.

As they approached an iron portcullis entrance, cages gave way to skulls on spikes.

On both sides of the road and around the fortress were rows of trenches, with more being dug. Groups of men laboured in silence, sweating in the cold.

At the city gate, Sophie and the boys dismounted, and Bacha spoke to a guard wearing a black greatcoat and a scarlet cloak. A short, gleaming sword dangled from his belt and he wore a pointed metal helmet. Another four guards stood behind him.

Sophie held her breath as the guard assessed them, but he gestured them through into a noisy, bustling street. The stalls were sturdier than in the previous town, with permanent roofs. The scent of roasting meat rose from the nearest and Sophie tightened her scarf over her nose. Super-senses had a downside.

Timber buildings with smoking chimneys fronted the lane, their ground floors displaying food and clothing, and signs in swirling Georgian script. Down the centre of the street was a line of covered vats. Going by the fumes, they contained military-grade oil.

Amongst shoppers wrapped in their cloaks, guards strode around, some pausing to eat snacks from stalls. High up on the city wall were more guards.

'Kajet's obviously defendable, but if the Mongols attack,

we could be trapped here for months, perhaps years,' said Hugo. 'We should only stay for one night.'

'By ourselves, we're vulnerable,' said Sophie.

Hugo leaned closer to her. 'Sieges are too horrible, in any time. Think World War Two and Stalingrad.'

Sophie nodded. 'One night it is.'

Bacha made an open gesture with his hands and chatted.

'He says we're welcome to stay with his relatives,' said Hugo.

'But given my goddess profile, and the queen's ... control issues,' said Sophie, 'that might place them in danger.'

'I'll say we don't want to impose and ask if there's an inn.'

In reply, Bacha nodded and pointed to a three-storey stone building with tall windows.

'That's the best,' said Hugo.

Bacha said farewell, and he and his family hurried down the street. Charlotte watched them leave, her gaze lingering on the mountain dog. The animal had hunted every day, bringing back a variety of unfortunate creatures, including a fawn.

'Our ski hats stand out, even under our hoods.' Sophie walked up to a stall. Hats in Kajet were mostly wool, with a few made of dark leather or grey fur, and there were plenty on the counter to choose from.

Hugo haggled and handed over jewellery. 'Just a necklace and bracelet left.' He shoved his ski hat in his holdall and put on an orange hat. Freddy chose a blue hat, pulled low over his ears, and Sophie selected a green one.

In a stable block behind the inn, the grooms seemed pleased with the last bracelet, and led the horses away to be fed and watered.

The inn had a porticoed entrance and a reception hall with embroidered hangings on the walls, interspersed with candles in sconces that flickered in the draught as they came in.

'Fingers crossed,' said Sophie. 'No bed bugs.'

A stout woman in a long blue dress approached like a bouncer, her brown eyes assessing.

Hugo greeted her in Russian and the woman replied.

'She wants to see our coin.' Hugo found the last cheap necklace.

The lady shook her head. 'Niet.'

Hugo searched in his bag and grudgingly offered a gold sovereign.

The woman lifted it to her mouth and bit down hard. She smiled, her grin almost as wide as her broad face as she reeled off a torrent of words.

'We can stay forever,' said Hugo.

They'd paid way too much.

Their room had four straw cots and a faded rug covered most of the timber boards. The rug was red and black, diamond-shaped repeating patterns, and within each diamond was the queen's symbol, rendered in pearly white.

The walls and ceiling displayed wooden beams and the air smelled clean, if damp. Kindling and wood in a stone fireplace had already been laid, and the innkeeper lit it with a taper.

Near the fireplace was a round wooden structure, the size of a large chair. It was open at the top and had round sides, similar to a wine barrel. Girls carrying iron buckets filed in and emptied water into it. More came in carrying water and in ten minutes, the bath was three quarters full.

A woman handed Sophie a pile of folded sheets and a hard piece of … bacon fat. Soap? Charlotte sniffed at it suspiciously.

After the innkeeper and the girls had left, Hugo closed the door. 'This isn't so bad.'

Sophie tested the water. Pleasantly warm.

Freddy sat on the floor, facing away from the tub. 'Sophie should bathe first.'

Sophie stripped as fast as she could and climbed in. 'This is amazing.'

She made herself wash with the bacon-soap, though keen to keep an ungoddessy appearance, she resisted rinsing her mud-stained hair. She got out, dried herself with basically a sheet, and slipped on her undies.

'You go next, Freddy,' said Hugo. 'You really stink.'

Freddy grimaced, but Sophie shot Hugo an impressed smile. Most men would have fought for the next bath. She wiggled into her trousers and merino shirt, and her jacket. Despite the blazing fire, it was chilly. She determinedly studied the wall.

Freddy bathed quickly and Hugo put on a brave face, washing last in lukewarm dirty water.

Once he was out, Sophie looked at Charlotte, then at the tub.

'She won't fit,' said Hugo.

'Luckily, she only needs a bath if she's rolled in something icky or splashed through a dirty puddle.' Sophie planted a kiss on Charlotte's head. She mysteriously smelled of honey and nutmeg, just as she did at home.

Sophie dipped her cloak in the bath and scrubbed with the stinky soap at No One's blood stains. Eventually the marks faded. 'This should dry in front of the fire.'

Outside, a snowy wind blew hard, and the windows rattled. Freddy closed red shutters.

'I said we were siblings,' said Hugo, sitting on a bench by the fire. 'We've no idea how this society works. Two men sharing a room with a woman might be beyond the pale. We could end up lynched.'

Freddy sat beside Hugo and warmed his hands. 'Or in a cage.'

~

That evening, in the inn's dining room, candlelight danced off heavy gold necklaces, set with emeralds and rubies, and sparkled on jewels sewn into the fabric of women's gowns: high-necked dresses with bell-shaped skirts. The men, in thick tunics with fur-lined collars, kept themselves apart from the women and earnestly conversed.

'Spices and wool,' said Hugo, when Sophie asked about the discussions. 'How war is disrupting trade.'

The merchants' dogs slept by the oak tables and benches, occasionally scrapping over discarded food. Hunting dogs, lean and muscled, though none as tall as Charlotte.

All the waiting staff were women. In contrast to the female guests, the waitresses' clothes were nondescript brown with revealing necklines. The innkeeper, still wearing the same blue gown, walked amongst her guests, listening and watching, her expression carefully blank.

With all the people, the hot meals, the candles, and the fire in an enormous grate, it wasn't cold. But conscious their ski clothes looked out of place, they kept on their cloaks.

Hugo and Freddy tucked into haunches of meat, while Sophie ate fragrant cheesy bread. Charlotte preferred the haunches, and they all enjoyed fried walnuts mixed with honey, served flat like pizza.

Nobody paid them any mind, and Sophie let herself relax. She smiled to herself, remembering explaining in a matter-of-fact way to Freddy how tampons worked. His face had been a picture: confusion, followed by appalled fascination.

As the innkeeper glided past their table, a man with a pointed beard engaged her in conversation. He put a finger to his lips and muttered something, then glanced over at Charlotte and Sophie.

A tremor of alarm. Sophie fixed her eyes on Hugo, who had a slight frown of concentration between his dark eyebrows. Freddy hadn't noticed the man's interest, and Sophie drank her beer with studied nonchalance.

The innkeeper clicked her fingers, and a barmaid gave the man a drink. He downed it and strode off, not glancing at them again. Who knew mud-coloured hair could be so useful?

'He was asking about a fair-haired woman with a wolf,' said Hugo. 'The innkeeper said, not around here, and when she asked him who wanted to know, he said, queen's business.'

Freddy's brow creased.

'Maybe I should go upstairs and take Charlotte?' said Sophie.

'No.' Hugo reached over the table and squeezed her hand. 'Keep acting unconcerned.'

On a raised stage was a skinny man with an upside-down navy hat at his feet. He played a lute, plucking out delicate notes.

His singing voice was deep and melodious, and the merchants listened. At the end of each song, the men banged their knife hilts on the tables in approval.

But at one point, his audience shifted uneasily in their seats.

'What's he singing about?' whispered Sophie in Hugo's ear.

'I'll tell you later.'

In their room, more wood had been added to the fire, and the bathtub was full of warm water. Freddy was already asleep on the floor, the rich wine gone to his head. Charlotte curled up next to him.

Sophie and Hugo bathed — brazenly, *not* averting their eyes — and after dressing, they lay on their sleeping bags, Charlotte-style.

'The goddess's real name is Dali,' said Hugo, 'and from the diners' reaction when her name was sung, I'm guessing saying it out loud is bad luck. She's known as the *red* goddess because she deals out bloody vengeance, smites invaders and kills with one look.'

'I thought she was a hunting goddess?' said Sophie.

'That too. According to the songs, she helps hunters *and* preys on them. If they accept her necklace as a gift, they can sleep only with her. If the hunters revert to sleeping with their wives, she lures the hunters up a mountain and throws them to their deaths.'

'Explains the "no-thank-you" reaction when I offered the necklace in the first inn,' said Sophie. 'But why bother luring men to a mountain if she can kill them just by looking?'

'Perhaps there were originally two goddesses, for hunting and for war,' said Hugo. 'Oh, and if Dali grants a human a favour, they have to pay an equivalent price, or their relatives must.'

Sophie slapped her hand to her mouth. *Take me, not family.* No One believed the goddess had saved his life, so a family member had to die in return. He took his own life instead.' She gazed into the fire, her mind back with the brave boy lying in the forest. 'Not a coward.'

'The musician sang about Dali's wolf, Q'ursha. How it runs faster than the wind and its bark echoes over mountains.'

Charlotte was asleep, her impressive face beside Freddy's. 'She's still the old Charlotte,' said Sophie, though she wasn't sure.

Hugo drew Sophie close, kissing her tenderly, and Sophie responded, relishing the distraction and comfort of his touch. He drew away and padded to his holdall, opening it as quietly as possible to find 'supplies' as they called them. They'd packed condoms more in hope than expectation.

Freddy stirred but didn't wake, his breathing slow and regular.

Sophie pulled Hugo down on top of her.

CHAPTER 27

The following morning, it had stopped snowing. Mindful of the queen's spy, Sophie had stayed with Charlotte in their room at the inn.

Freddy and Hugo stepped out onto the road, catching their breath as they inhaled the icy air. The place rang with the strident cries of hawkers, shouting over each other like crows, and guards stomped about in their greatcoats and scarlet cloaks, arrogance in every step.

Men and women haggled with stall owners, children with determined faces darted on errands with practised speed, and a slick stew smell, sweet and heavy, invaded Freddy's nostrils. He closed his mouth against it, and to ward off other scents: sickly, sour, and some he couldn't identify.

At the end of the street, soldiers with metal-tipped spears guarded flamboyant gold gates. The formidable lady innkeeper had explained to Hugo that just as she kept undesirables from the inn, the queen kept undesirables from the palace.

Towers were built into the palace wall, lined up in a row,

with rooms and windows jutting out near the top, their roof tiles as red as the guards' cloaks.

Freddy scratched his chin and he longed to shave, but none of the men here were clean-shaven.

With his beard, Hugo looked every inch the disreputable scoundrel that he was. Freddy pulled up his hood to counter the bitter wind, acutely aware that underneath his cloak was the kitchen knife he'd attached to his trouser belt. Hearing Hugo seducing Sophie last night had made him sick to his stomach, but he no longer wanted to die.

He wanted to kill Hugo.

'Look for a money-lender, or the equivalent of a pawnshop.'

A quick slash over Hugo's throat and he'd be gone. Or he could strangle him. Less bloody…

'There.' Hugo marched over to a stall.

A sharp-eyed, gaunt man sat behind a table, silver and copper coins arranged in different piles.

Freddy picked up a silver coin. One side had an image of a woman's head, on the other was Cyrillic writing.

Hugo peered at it. '*Queen of Queens, Glory of the World. Rusudan, daughter of Tamar.*'

Freddy selected a brown coin: a partial pentagram, and tiny writing on the flip side. More worn, of less value.

When Hugo presented the stallholder with a gold sovereign, the man stared at it, surprised. He gingerly accepted the sovereign, bit down on it, as the lady innkeeper had done, but then he shrugged, unsure of what was being asked of him.

Hugo did a scooping motion at the coins and indicated with a giving gesture that the man should have the sovereign. The man offered Hugo half the silver coins and all the coppers.

'Probably a bad bargain.' Hugo pocketed the coins. 'Let's get back to Sophie.'

'You can't keep your hands off her. Even here.' Freddy's lips contorted in disgust. 'I heard you last night.'

Hugo looked horrified. 'We were sure you were asleep, but it was a crass thing to do.' He glanced around. 'We're being watched. I can feel it between my shoulder blades.'

A pathetic attempt to distract him.

'We're taller than most men and more conspicuous together,' said Hugo. 'You return to the inn, and I'll follow in five minutes.'

'No, *you* go to the inn, and I'll follow.'

Hugo hesitated, perhaps thinking he'd start another fight, but to Freddy's surprise, Hugo gave a resigned nod and walked off.

Freddy strode behind the money stall and continued parallel to the palace wall towards the inn, screwing up his eyes against the cold. He was *so* much stronger than Hugo. Could easily kill him—

Rough hands slammed over his face and before he could react, he was dragged violently backwards. A door shut with a bang, plunging him into total darkness.

Freddy lashed out, his fists landing who knew where. He grabbed the knife from his belt, but it was snatched from him. An onslaught of punches and kicks rained down on him and he doubled over, straightened, and punched out again, hitting skin and bone.

His attackers' foreign curses echoed in the dark and Freddy's panic turned into grim determination. Left fist. Right fist. Take that, and *that*.

The blows against him increased in intensity, battering him like hammers. He could see them now in the dim light, surrounding him. Too many... Would he die here? '*Stop*,' he shouted. He raised his hands in surrender.

He was cornered in a narrow passage, lit by a single candle. His assailants wore thick jerkins and strange red skirts, akin to kilts. Were they soldiers? Hugo had said the queen's army wore kilts.

They snapped iron cuffs on his wrists and locked heavy shackles onto his ankles, cutting into his skin.

The men manhandled him along more corridors. As they moved, their shadows danced, grotesque puppets on the walls, and they talked and laughed.

Damn them. They were enjoying their power and his helplessness.

Who were they? Why had they kidnapped him? Where was he?

This couldn't be happening. Wasn't real. But the pain from his bleeding hands and feet told him it was.

Freddy closed his eyes and prayed.

When he opened them, he was looking down at himself from above. Was that prisoner in chains *him*? Would he be tortured? Murdered? Sophie wouldn't know what had happened to him. His parents would never know…

With a jolt he was back in his body, and he gasped at the searing pain in his ankles and wrists. He prayed again, drawing comfort from the familiar words.

Finally, he forced himself to look around. The passage curved to the right. A gigantic circle…

He was *within* the palace wall. These thugs were guards.

They hauled him through new corridors, empty store-rooms, and a room where men gabbled to each other, playing dice.

He was forced to stumble up uneven stone stairs.

At the top, something smelly and scratchy was rammed over his head, and he fought for breath.

CHAPTER 28

For three hours after Freddy vanished, Hugo and Charlotte searched the main street and every single alley. There was no trace of him.

Back at the inn, Hugo climbed the stairs to their room, wracked with guilt and worry. He was certain Freddy hadn't stormed off and left the city. His holdall was still here, and his horse was in the stables. More likely, Rusa's men had snatched him, hoping to lure out the 'red goddess' and kill her.

He and Sophie spent the rest of the day mulling over increasingly impractical rescue ideas, but at dinner, a chance remark by the innkeeper gave them a viable plan. Once a week, the common people were allowed into the palace to petition the queen — and Petitioning Day was tomorrow. Only desperate citizens took part, to beg for food, or for mercy for their imprisoned relatives. But new prisoners were paraded. Freddy could be among them.

The next morning, Sophie reluctantly stayed behind with Charlotte, and Hugo joined the crowd shuffling towards the palace, keeping his head down.

The stable muck Hugo had streaked on his cloak matched the pong of the people around him, but his cloak was otherwise too thick and tidy. Everyone else was dressed in rags. He shoved his orange felt hat into his trouser pocket, his arm brushing against the pistol on his belt. Despite the cold, he was sweating. If he were discovered and captured too… No, don't go there.

Hugo passed through the golden gates in the middle of the shabby group. Ignoring an imposing stone entrance, a guard led them to a rickety, wooden door and into a long, window-less corridor lit by candles. Many passages led off it, winding into the dark.

The corridor ended in stairs and a door that opened into a vast, high-ceilinged hall. The guard motioned them into a roped-off area and, conscious that he was conspicuously tall, Hugo dropped to his knees.

Winter sunlight streamed through arched stained-glass windows, and at the far end of the hall, the light shone ethereally on a woman on a raised dais. Rusa sat bolt upright on a gilded throne, regal in a red gown. Black and scarlet hangings adorned the dais, matching the rich tapestries on the walls.

On Rusa's dress, the white star symbol was outlined in pearls below her round collar, and square jewels on her skirt sparkled green and blue, edged with gold. Draped under her chin was a pale silk scarf, and another white star and more jewels sparkled on her gilded crown.

'Welcome,' said Rusa in Russian, her voice carrying easily across the huge room. No one spoke in response. The man beside him was shaking, and Hugo felt a rush of primeval fear. He laid his hand on his pistol. If this went bad, could he shoot his way out?

The guard grabbed an old lady roughly by the shoulders and pushed her forward to a spot behind the rope that fenced them in. She muttered, 'Bread,' and a word Hugo couldn't catch.

'Granted,' said Rusa.

The woman bowed, almost falling over, and was ushered back into the crowd.

A young man stepped up and asked for some sort of licence. After questioning him, Rusa again said, 'Granted.'

More people filed requests, most of which Hugo couldn't understand, and others whispered, less jittery. Still on his knees, Hugo shuffled to the rear of the throng to avoid being noticed and summoned.

Rattling like a cable car interrupted the serenity of the throne room, and the crowd fell silent.

A line of men and boys edged into the hall, shackled at the ankles, their hands locked in front of them. They were tied together on a cumbersome chain, held by a guard.

None of them were Freddy. Was that good or bad?

The prisoners were blinking, unused to the light. Jerky stick figures, barefoot and in rags, with grey, filthy skin. Hugo swallowed bile. If these were 'new' inmates, arrested in the last week, how had they been treated to look like this?

'Who should be spared?' said Rusa.

A man standing near Hugo spoke up. 'Gamkrelidze stole to eat. He won't again. I *swear* it.'

Another man spoke, his voice cracking. 'Losava. Only twelve summers. Show mercy.'

Hugo kept his face bowed, terrified he'd reveal the feelings that were flooding over him. Fear, but also disgust. Anger.

After many more pleas, Rusa said, 'Losava,' and the youngest prisoner's shackles were taken off. The child collapsed in a heap and the guard dragged him over to the crowd. The child's father repeatedly bowed, while the other petitioners stayed motionless and quiet. Numb with despair.

The other inmates shambled out of the hall.

'I grant one more mercy,' said Rusa. 'The goddess has outlawed death by fire, even for deserters.'

Hugo's heart missed a beat. Rusa had heard about them rescuing the boy from the stake—

A guard strode in and dropped something heavy. From where he was at the back, Hugo couldn't see what it was.

Rusa rose from her throne and glided through a doorway by the dais, and the crowd turned to leave.

Hugo got to his feet and saw what lay discarded on the floor. He clamped his hand over his mouth, horror holding him fixed to the spot. It was a body, the face so damaged as to be unrecognisable. Hugo exhaled. Not Freddy. Too short.

A skinny man from the crowd picked up the body and moved away.

Returning a body to his family… This was Rusa's *mercy*.

Hugo rushed into the gloomy corridor, catching up with the group. Keep going, get out.

But when he reached a passage leading off the corridor, he hesitated. Could that lead to the dungeons? Freddy was still missing. He couldn't leave now.

He slipped sideways, stepped as quietly as he could along the passage, and felt his way as it grew darker.

Worn stone steps twisted and steeply descended, and trepidation rose in his guts. His brain spiralled off into stupid, random thoughts. Dark and damp. Probably led to toilets.

He continued with care, his feet too large for the treads of the stairs. At the bottom was another corridor and a choice of direction. The air smelled stale.

A clinking noise came from his right. Lighter than the jangle made by shackles. More like crockery.

Hugo lifted the pistol from his belt. Up ahead was candlelight. Steady, with no breeze through any windows to disturb the flame.

He flattened himself against the wall. Two guards sat at a table, eating and drinking. Beyond them was a row of prison cells, fronted with iron bars. If there were prisoners inside, they were silent.

One of the guards noticed Hugo and leapt up. '*You*, stay where you are,' the guard shouted in Russian, and drew his sword, running towards him.

Hugo raised the gun, his hand trembling, and shot the guard in the chest. The weapon kicked back hard into his hand, taking him by surprise. The sound of the shot whined in the confined space as the man toppled, surprise and bafflement on his face.

The other guard stood, transfixed, before drawing his sword and launching himself at Hugo.

No. This couldn't be happening. No choice. Hugo pressed the trigger. Ended a second life.

His legs shaking, he checked the cells. Empty, except the last. A man was clutching at the bars, terrified. He was well-dressed, in a green velvet tunic, and his jowls were chubby. Either a *very* new inmate or not the common sort. Hugo slapped his head. This was the highest level. Freddy would be in a cell on a lower floor, in much worse conditions.

The prisoner's hands tightened on the bars, and Sophie's words before she freed the bear rang in his mind. *In for a penny, in for a pound.*

Hugo twisted on the spot, searching for the cell key. A string-tied purse hung from a nail. He grabbed it and pulled it open. Inside was an iron key.

It unlocked the barred door with a snap. 'Come quietly,' said Hugo in Russian.

The prisoner hesitated, but then stepped forward, and they both ran up the steps.

Hugo stumbled and swore. How long before the next guard shift turned up?

They made it along the corridor and into the open, and he savoured the fresh air in his lungs.

Outside the palace, the crowd was gone, and the golden gates were closed. Hugo hurried up to the guards, gestured at his companion, and said apologetically in Russian, 'Got lost.'

The nearest guard looked annoyed but opened the gate enough for them to pass through. From the corner of his mouth, Hugo whispered, 'Walk slowly.'

Once out of sight of the gate, the freed prisoner darted off into a side street and Hugo sprinted to the inn stables. They had to leave, and fast.

Sophie was there as they'd arranged, the horses saddled up. Her face fell when she saw Freddy wasn't with him.

Charlotte jumped to attention.

'Where is he?' said Sophie. 'You couldn't find him?'

'We need to go.' Hugo took a lead rope from a groom and tied the reins on Freddy's horse to his own. He mounted and clattered from the stables. Sophie rode behind him on Black Beauty, Charlotte trotting close by.

'Walking pace,' said Hugo. 'We don't want to draw attention—'

Screeching horns cut him off and Hugo gulped.

'An alarm?' said Sophie.

'Yes, change of plan.' He dug his heels into the flank of his horse and broke into a gallop. Sophie did the same and Charlotte ran ahead.

The alarm-shriek continued as they tore along the street, townsfolk and guards scattering as they went.

In front of them, the portcullis at the city gate slammed down, and Hugo brought his horse to an abrupt halt. The horse's breath coiled into the air as its breathing slowed.

Hugo's heart raced. Nowhere to hide.

Next to him, Sophie drew up on Black Beauty, her eyes wide with terror.

Charlotte glanced back at her mistress, then at the portcullis, and barked. The bark intensified, deepened, and expanded into a deep-throated roar.

Hugo's horse reared. Holding on for dear life, Hugo cried out as his eardrums popped, the pain cleaving his head in two.

Around him, horses and people screamed.

Charlotte's insane bellow rumbled on and on, deeper, louder, and as Hugo's horse trembled, Hugo kept hold of the reins and covered his ears.

Sophie was reassuring Black Beauty, making no effort to protect her eardrums. Seemed unaffected.

The noise lanced through Hugo like a scalpel, even with his ears covered. Please stop—

A different rumble, reverberating under Charlotte's roar, sounded from the city gate, and guards shouted.

Above the portcullis, the stones supporting the walkway swayed. Hugo blinked. What now? The whole structure was swaying ... an earthquake?

The portcullis splintered, thick pieces of wood stripping off, leaving ragged gaps. The pillars that flanked and supported it crumbled. Blocks of masonry slammed into the street, and dust rose in a cloud.

Charlotte stopped roaring.

A moment later, Sophie's mouth moved. Yelling? But Hugo couldn't hear her. The pain had gone, but his ears throbbed with a jarring ringing.

Sophie encouraged Black Beauty forward, gesturing for him to follow.

Hugo's horse picked its way over the debris while Charlotte effortlessly leapt over it.

Outside the shattered city wall, Charlotte raced towards

the forest, and Sophie on Black Beauty sped up. Hugo couldn't ride as quickly, hampered by leading Freddy's horse.

He reached the treeline and slowed, manoeuvring between ancient firs and fallen branches.

Sophie and Charlotte were waiting. Sophie said something.

'Charlotte's bark...' said Hugo. 'It's made me deaf.'

Sophie frowned and did a 'let's go' gesture.

Five minutes later, they came to a clearing as big as a football field.

The horses whinnied, and Charlotte stopped in her tracks. When horses and Charlotte were spooked, Hugo took notice. Should they keep to the edge, near the trees?

Sophie looked over her shoulder. 'They're coming.'

This time he heard her words over the ringing.

'But only one,' said Sophie, puzzled.

A horseman thundered towards them but galloped straight past. It was the prisoner from the palace, wearing a green cloak that flared behind him. As he rode away across the clearing, Charlotte slowly crept, her body low as if hunting prey.

Her head disappeared, followed by the rest of her, and Hugo nearly fell off his horse. What the—?

Sophie urged Black Beauty after her and also vanished. Swallowed up into thin air.

CHAPTER 29

Sophie followed Charlotte to the place where she'd disappeared, protective instinct eclipsing caution.

An intense tingling sensation prickled her skin. Tiny needles. Ouch.

Charlotte was in front of her, snuffling at a gap in a low, white wall. She looked fine, and not frightened. Which was odd, given the horses had been spooked.

Sophie sagged in relief and pulled up Black Beauty.

Behind the wall was a two-storey building with a grey flat roof and glass walls. A soft warm breeze caressed her face and she unwound her scarf. Was this real? 'Hugo, are you seeing this?'

She looked back. Hugo and the horses weren't there. And the forest was gone, replaced by a pale haze, like a blurred Zoom background.

Sophie dismounted, grabbed Charlotte by the collar and retraced her steps.

Her skin prickled, and there was Hugo, on foot by the horses, the forest behind him.

Hugo blinked at her, terrified. 'I went to where you disappeared. *Nothing.*'

Was this the same as the lift? She had to say Hugo's name so he could step through—

Flashes of red and metal by the treeline. Horsemen … palace guards.

They streaked into the clearing, bearing down on them.

'Hugo, grab the horses and run.' He took the reins, and she seized his other hand, frantically pulling him and Charlotte towards the barrier.

An instant later, her skin tingled, and the clearing and the guards were gone.

'Hurrrrr, an electric shock.' Hugo stared at the building. 'That's not Georgian.'

Presented with a concealed house in the woods, only Hugo would call out the architecture.

'It's warm,' said Sophie. 'If this place is empty and people without the gene can't get in, we should sleep here.'

Hugo gulped. 'It's not empty.'

Sophie spun around. A woman was strolling from the building. She was as tall as Hugo, her fair hair up in a braid, and her fawn trousers and shirt rippled in the pleasant breeze. Her face was stretched perfect, the sort of look achieved with plastic surgery, and she was sunless-pale, her age impossible to guess.

'Good afternoon,' she said in English. Her smile didn't reach her eyes.

Sophie paused, overwhelmed with déjà vu. This exact moment: the woman, the compound, Hugo, and Charlotte … had happened before. 'Hello. I'm Sophie and this is Hugo.'

'So glad you've found me.' Her English was faultless, if rather robotic, as if she'd rehearsed the greeting, and her mouth movements didn't quite match the words. 'Your horses will be cared for.'

'Who are you?' said Hugo. 'What is this place?'

'Of course, your ways are different. I expected them to be.' The woman turned towards the building and strode away, expecting them to follow.

'This is creepy,' whispered Hugo. 'We should leave.'

'I can't explain how, or why, but she's familiar, and if Charlotte sensed something bad, she wouldn't be skipping at her side.'

The woman spoke to Charlotte as they walked through the gap. 'You'll enjoy staying here. I have the tastiest cuts of meat.'

An oval glass door slid open and, as they approached it, Hugo held Sophie's hand.

Though the exterior of the structure appeared to be glass, the interior walls showed nothing of the outside: solid and white. They were in a double-height room that was empty, save for a utilitarian rectangular desk and an office-style chair. The air smelled sterile but of nothing. Reminded Sophie of the lift.

Two young men came in, carrying an oversized leather sofa. They were dressed in black and had dark hair, tied back in identical ponytails. Once they'd set down the pale couch, they nodded to the woman and left.

Their host gestured at the sofa. 'Be comfortable.'

'How come you speak English?' asked Sophie.

'I don't,' said the woman. 'You're just hearing the translation. The database picks up your thoughts, adapts itself. Please sit.'

Charlotte promptly jumped on the couch. 'I'm sorry,' said Sophie, moving to coax her off.

'Leave her be. Guests and pets should be at ease, and I haven't had guests in *such* a long time.'

The young men returned with side tables, a tray with three pewter goblets, and a water bowl for Charlotte.

'Why have you invited us into your house?' said Hugo, sitting down beside Sophie.

The woman rolled her eyes. 'I know I should be more tolerant of your customs but have you *no* control over your pet?'

Charlotte had settled herself on a cream cushion, resting her head on the sofa arm. Sophie grabbed her collar to pull her off.

'I mean *that*.' The woman glanced dismissively at Hugo. 'Asking questions, willy nilly.'

Sophie's jaw dropped. This woman thought Hugo was her *pet*? Why would she assume that? '*Oh*.'

Because Hugo didn't have the gene. He'd come through the prickly barrier because she'd said his name. But the horses had passed through and she didn't know their real names—

Hugo cleared his throat.

'He's not a lesser being,' said Sophie. 'He's my friend, my lover … my soulmate.'

The woman arched a too-shaped eyebrow. 'Unusual. Please call me Naga. It's the name I'm most fond of.' Naga gestured and a map of Georgia and the Black Sea appeared on the wall. 'You landed south of Anacopia.' As she spoke, a red dot marked the spot. 'The queen's palace at Kajet is in the south.' Another red dot appeared.

Hugo nodded. 'So "north" here is the same as home.'

'The merchant you released from the dungeon has been recaptured.' Naga gestured again and a projected video played in the air, showing the man who'd galloped past them marching through the forest, escorted by guards.

'He rode through this space,' said Hugo. 'We're not in the clearing, are we?'

Naga glanced at him and addressed Sophie. 'The barrier was originally placed close to Kajet for research, but we're located elsewhere.' She waved, and a new map materialised, showing a mountain range with three green dots.

'The green dots are us?' said Sophie. 'Individuals with the gene?'

'Indeed.' Both maps vanished.

'We're safe,' said Sophie, squeezing Hugo's hand.

'Queen Rusa was extorting money from the merchant's family.' Naga deleted the projection of the recaptured prisoner. 'To deter others from absconding, she may sever one of his limbs.'

Hugo's hand under Sophie's clenched.

Naga fixed her oval eyes on Sophie. *'The queen is cruel, but it's the cultural norm.'* Her voice whispered in Sophie's head.

'You can read my mind?' blurted Sophie.

'Just flashes,' said Naga, as if that made it less disturbing. 'You can learn to read mine. Charlotte already has.'

Charlotte's attention was fixed on Naga.

Consumed with protective love and worry, Sophie stroked Charlotte. 'Can Charlotte read my mind?'

'Possibly,' said Naga. 'The ability to listen and receive varies between individuals.'

'I see.' Hugo was right. Creepy.

Naga took a dainty sip from her goblet. 'Do have some tea.'

The liquid in Sophie's goblet looked like regular tea but she sniffed. Her super-sense told her it wasn't drugged or poisoned. She sipped, and the familiar taste made her smile.

'I gathered from the forest that you're fond of it,' said Naga.

Hugo's eyebrows shot up. 'You were in the forest?'

'Certainly not. I don't physically interact, and my staff and their families never leave the compound.' A cascade of different videos appeared: a coastline with waves crashing on a beach, the sacked village, the town where they'd rescued

No One and countless other scenes. 'You've been monitored since you arrived.' The projections switched off.

'All this … to spy on *us*?' said Sophie.

'Hardly,' said Naga.

'Satellite images,' said Hugo. 'You're conducting anthropological research.'

Naga nodded.

'I can boil water with my mind here,' said Sophie. 'Is that a girl thing?'

'I am aware,' said Naga. 'An anomaly in our Mitochondrial DNA. A barbaric and primitive ability, long since outlawed. You *must* suppress it. You can boil *any* liquid, including blood.'

Sophie clutched the arm of the sofa, the memory of boiling water in the woods playing in her head.

'When you focus on heating a liquid, when you picture it, every sentient creature in your line of sight burns.'

In the forest, there'd just been a mug or a flask in front of her, but only by chance. Sophie fixed her gaze on the floor, her heart hammering. Don't think about it. Think of something — *anything* — else.

'Historically, accidental burnings were common,' said Naga. 'But do not concern yourself. The initial trigger requires intent.'

Sophie shuddered. Good to know.

A young man returned with a tray of freshly baked fairy cakes, but Charlotte didn't react to the scent. She'd fallen asleep.

'Charlotte's bigger,' said Sophie. 'And her bark is *so* loud.'

'The temple bark is a call to action,' said Naga. 'However, the effort required is great. It cannot be repeated for many days, often weeks.'

Hugo touched his ears and gave Charlotte a rueful glance.

'Every parallel universe has its own chemical and biological processes, as well as physics,' said Naga. 'In this one, we have increased physical strength, and there are other differences.'

'My thicker hair,' said Sophie. 'The exact same colour as yours.'

'Please stop using the goddess myth for your own ends.' Naga put down her goblet. 'The mythology originates from a centuries-old culture-contamination.'

Hugo looked Naga in the eye. 'Is that why the images of the red goddess resemble Sophie and you? The locals believed your ancestors were gods?'

'They did. Personal contact was deemed crucial to the study of worship culture, but after the *Morning Star* mutiny, there were calls for it to be outlawed.'

'The *Morning Star*?' Sophie frowned. Why was that familiar…

'The name of the ship,' said Naga. 'It was on a mission to 666.'

Sophie's breath hitched. Her late father had been a pastor. She knew her bible. *If one is wise and has an understanding to count the number of the beast, which is also the number of a man, the number comes to 666. Revelation 13:18.* 'Theologically, 666 is associated with the antichrist, but also with a monstrous creature. A symbol of humanity's crapness—'

'It's a universe designation,' said Naga, 'for an anthropological mission.'

Sophie stared at her, speechless.

After a moment, Hugo said, 'So, over time, the original meaning was forgotten, became embroidered. But for the memory of 666 to persist for that long … why was it so important to the inhabitants?'

'Trusted locals were given a licence to trade and enrich themselves and, in return, they monitored their peers, dispensed justice with barbaric punishments, compatible with the culture. They carried a scroll, sealed with the number.'

Sophie shook her head, her brain spinning.

'The inhabitants' DNA was manipulated, some of our traits introduced and the results evaluated,' said Naga. 'There had been identical research conducted in other universes, but some of the *Morning Star* crew thought it unethical and they mutinied. Lucifer and the rest were banished to the planet.'

'Lucifer,' whispered Sophie. 'In our faith book, he's banished to hell.'

'He and his closest aides managed to leave 666, but they'd fallen out with the rest of the breakaway crew, so Lucifer abandoned them. They were retrieved in due course.'

'Lucifer's believed to be the devil,' said Sophie.

'His betrayed friends' stories lived on as oral history on 666 and other places, the remnants eventually preserved in religious texts,' said Naga. 'A revenge of sorts.'

Childhood memories played in Sophie's mind. Long afternoons at Sunday school, listening until she knew the passages by heart. She'd lost her faith when she'd lost her parents, but the bible stories had been a source of comfort, of hope for countless generations…

Hugo squeezed Sophie's hand. 'Different camps are mentioned in the bible. Stamps on foreheads…'

'My ancestors allocated inhabitants to a control group with no DNA manipulation and introduced changes in others.' Naga smiled politely at Sophie. 'As you're from 666, you're descended from the mutineers.'

Sophie rubbed her temples. 'I can't take this in.'

'When did the mutiny happen?' asked Hugo.

Naga ignored him and spoke to Sophie. 'By 666's time measurement, 40,000 years BC. The non-interacting policy didn't become mandatory until 541 AD.' Naga placed her empty goblet on the tray. 'Policy changes are beset by bureaucracy.'

Charlotte was awake and nuzzled into Sophie. 'How does Charlotte have the gene?'

'When we interacted, we used our own horses for transport, our dogs to guard our dwellings, and they mated with native species. The inhabitants here, and in your universe, called our dogs "temple dogs" because they thought us divine. Their descendants still sing about them, so the myth lives on.' With a feline grace, Naga stood up. 'Some of the artefacts my people used in their studies survive. They're kept in the legacy room. Come.'

Hugo, Sophie, and Charlotte followed Naga along a light, bare corridor into what looked like a museum. In wall-recesses and on stands were angular brass objects, none of them bigger than a small suitcase.

A column of scrolling data popped up, streams of coloured symbols.

'I don't recognise the characters,' said Hugo, 'but the format's familiar from school biology. DNA.'

Naga gave him a curt nod. 'Their methods were unethical.' The symbols disappeared, and Naga pointed to a chain and pendant on a blue velvet cushion. 'This Personal Obfuscation Device enabled the wearer to stay a nanosecond back in time, concealing them in order to collect data.'

'A time-turner!' Sophie stepped closer. The chain was burnished gold and its chunky red stone had spiralling depths and complexities.

'Worn for too long, the wearer became trapped in the near past,' said Naga. 'Condemned to watch forever.'

Of course, there'd be a downside.

They returned to the previous room.

'Have you records of parallel universes,' asked Hugo,

sitting on the sofa, 'including the rate that time passes in them?'

'We have.' Naga deigned to look at him. 'We use them to select locations and periods to research.'

'How did you come here?' Sophie sat beside Hugo.

'In my ship.'

'If you don't give a clear destination,' said Sophie, 'does your ship choose a random universe?' Hopefully, Freddy's *Do your worst* had been diluted by her and Charlotte's desire to land in Shorten.

'My vehicle can only act on my instructions.' Naga's slim lips twisted. 'The Janus ship you use is unreliable.'

Sophie caught Hugo's eye. Had any of his previous theories — guesses — about Janus been right? 'Why is it called Janus?'

'A variation on the previous model,' said Naga. 'Travellers in Juno didn't survive a crossing.'

Sophie leaned forward on the sofa. 'What happened?'

'Juno couldn't protect travellers from the passage of time. The longest recorded crossing was twenty days, so the travellers packed provisions accordingly. Unfortunately, that crossing lasted a hundred and forty days.' Naga's expression didn't change. 'Juno was called away by unknown travellers before she could be decommissioned. Hasn't been heard of since.'

'So, Janus shields travellers from that,' Hugo said to Sophie.

'And other modifications,' said Naga.

'Janus sees beyond linear time?' said Hugo.

'Apparently, but that final upgrade triggered his sentience, so wasn't used on subsequent ships.' Naga pursed her lips. 'Janus took himself off and now he shuttles between universes, collecting the unwary.'

'Can't you bring him back and dismantle him?' said Hugo.

'He cannot leave his ship. Why use finite resources on a trivial nuisance?' Naga made a delicate scoffing noise. 'A priority interest problem here is of far more concern.'

'Priority interest?' said Sophie.

'Our people.' An aerial view of the queen's palace materialised. Superimposed on it was a green dot.

'Is that Freddy?' said Sophie, her voice ending in a squeak.

'It is,' said Naga.

'In a dungeon.' Hugo's voice faltered.

'No.' Naga waved and a video came into focus, the view looking down, as if from a ceiling.

Freddy was lying in a luxurious bed with two stark-naked girls ... obviously enjoying himself. Sophie looked at the floor, half of her relieved Freddy was safe, the other half squirming with embarrassment. 'Please tell us what's going on. I mean, I can see what's going on with Freddy, but *why?*'

'The queen has records of my ancestor's ill-judged interactions. She's aware they had "god-like" strength. I would destroy the texts, but my contract forbids it. The queen understands that powerful stallions breed the best horses, so she's using Freddy to create an army, to drive back the Mongols.'

'Isn't that a good thing?' said Sophie.

'Freddy's progeny will subjugate everyone in Georgia, then the planet.' The film of Freddy vanished, and lines of data projected from the walls. 'If he's not stopped, he'll render this control world useless.'

'What would Rusa do if Freddy refused to carry on,' said Hugo, 'or couldn't...'

'He'd be executed.' Naga addressed Sophie. 'I'm bound by my contract not to extract him, but you're not.'

Sophie got to her feet and Charlotte jumped off the sofa.

'I cannot tell if the concubines have conceived,' said Naga. 'It's distasteful, but you must end them.'

CHAPTER 30

That evening, a misshapen moon hung low in the sky, most of its light lost behind heavy cloud. Snow danced in the air and sea mist curled in slow lazy strands around Kajet's red towers.

Beside the palace wall, Sophie dismounted from Black Beauty, drew a deep breath, and slipped the time-turner pendant over her head.

Hugo and Charlotte faded like an old photograph.

Against Sophie's chest, the ruby stone of the pendant glinted, an eye-catching tourmaline gem, but it was heavy and cold. The device worked for one DNA match at a time and wouldn't work at all for Hugo.

Naga had advised her to leave Hugo in the compound, saying his presence would lessen efficiency, but Sophie had ignored her. Hugo had his own divine fire.

'If you and Charlotte had been waiting with the horses nearer the palace,' Hugo had said, 'we'd have escaped with less drama.'

Sophie could make him out, faint as a ghost, stamping his feet against the cold, but there was no sound, and as Sophie moved towards a sluice gate in the wall, Hugo's eyes didn't follow her. Charlotte stayed by Hugo.

After Sophie had refused point blank to kill the girls, Naga had given her a small cylinder to press against their skin, to prevent conception. When Sophie had asked why she hadn't mentioned this before, Naga said the device was 99.98% reliable, while death was 100%.

Sophie pulled her cloak tight to her, ensured her scarf covered her nose and mouth, and waded under the sluice gate. Bent double, carrying Naga's contraceptive device in a canvas bag slung over her shoulder, she shuffled up the drain, wading through a half-frozen, slow-moving sludge that dropped into a channel to the sea.

The gate at the top of the drain wasn't locked and opened into an empty, communal loo. Holes in a bench. Just as she'd seen in Naga's projection. Sophie coughed. The sewage in the loo *wasn't* frozen and stank so bad she nearly gagged.

Sophie hurriedly climbed some stairs and, remembering the palace layout, ran along a corridor into a washroom. She knew the women by a tub couldn't see her, but still checked her belt. She'd attached Hugo's pistol and the dagger.

She passed through more corridors, up more stairs. Rough stone walls gave way to ornate tapestries, and her hiking boots moved in eerie silence over marble floors.

Beyond the last flight of stairs was Freddy's room. In front of the door, a guard in a scarlet kilt and cloak stood bolt upright, his hand on the hilt of a polished sword, but Sophie glided around him. The door was unlocked and once inside, she closed it and turned a key. Clever psychology … giving Freddy the option of locking a guarded room.

She recognised the bed from Naga's projected image of the room: a gaudy riot of black and crimson silk hangings draped on the bedposts, the colour scheme repeated with the bedding.

In its midst was Freddy, fast asleep and lying on his back. Naked.

Dear God.

A healthy fire burned in a grate and scented candles glimmered on the mantlepiece: rose, apple — and peonies, a calming aroma Sophie associated with her aunt's garden. Beside the fireplace on a long violet couch, four girls giggled and chatted. In various states of undress, they were half-wrapped in swathes of identical purple satin. Concubine uniform?

Only four. But there might be more who'd gone off shift.

Sophie crouched near the girls' couch, removed the pendant, placing it in the canvas bag. Wearing it made her invisible, but she couldn't interact. She leaned sideways and forward and laid the cylinder gently against the nearest girl's thigh, pressing the button as Naga had shown her. If a needle was involved, it was too small to see and left no mark. A blue light flashed on the device, confirming successful delivery.

The girl waved her arm as if to brush off a fly, saw Sophie, and screamed. The other girls screamed too.

One shouted something and pushed the others behind her. She grabbed a lit candle and threw it at Sophie's face, but it fell short.

Sophie pinched out the flame and glanced at the door in a panic, expecting the guard to start hammering.

Think.

Sophie forced herself to laugh. Loud and girlish. Hopefully, the guard would think the noise was rough play.

No noise from the guard. Sophie took the dagger from her belt, and the girls cowered, huddling together. Even the girl who'd thrown the candle looked frightened.

Freddy sat up. 'Sophie?'

'Get some clothes on.'

'What are you doing with my girls?'

'Stopping them falling pregnant.' Candle Girl's attention was on Freddy, and Sophie inoculated her.

The girl spat out a string of words: curses or threats. Sophie flourished her dagger, and she went quiet. 'Freddy, I'm getting you out of here.'

He yawned. 'No, thank you.'

'*What?*'

'Please leave. I'm perfectly all right.' He smiled at his reflection in a mirror opposite the bed. 'When they kidnapped me, I was treated roughly, but now there's not a mark on me.' He glanced down at his wrists. 'Not even a bruise.'

'A perk of the gene.'

The girls fidgeted and whispered between themselves as Sophie explained Rusa's agenda to him.

Freddy's eyes narrowed. 'How do you know all this?'

'Long story.' Sophie pressed the tube against a different girl, and she squeaked. One to go. 'You must have wondered what all this was about.' She gestured at the room with the dagger. 'Once you get worn out or fed up, the queen will lock you in a cage.' Sophie dropped to her knees by the bed and set the cylinder against the girl's calf.

Freddy wrinkled his nose and the girl she'd inoculated muttered.

'Natela said you smell,' said Freddy.

Sophie was impressed he'd learned some Russian. She hadn't got beyond yes and no. 'I got here through a drain. Get dressed, Freddy. *Please.*' She returned the tube to the bag.

'I was relieved they hadn't hurt me.' Freddy rubbed his eyes. 'But I thought it an outlandish custom.'

'The queen's using these girls, like she's using you. Do you stroll around the palace whenever you want?'

'No.' Freddy jumped off the bed, extravagantly naked.

A second too late, Sophie averted her gaze and looked at

the ceiling, coffered into squares. Nestled beside a white star, outlined in red and black, was a brown moth, its wings neatly folded.

Freddy pulled on a knee-length silk robe, tied it closed, and wiggled his feet into gold and silver slippers with a weird upward curl at the toes. Of course, they'd confiscated his clothes.

The girls were still whispering.

Sophie took a perfume bottle from her bag. 'This will knock out "your" girls for a few hours. Won't hurt them.' Sophie frowned. 'Are there others that you've...?'

Freddy looked affronted. '*I* chose these girls.'

'Good.' Sophie put her left hand over her own nose and mouth and sprayed. The girls slumped, one banging her head on a table. Sophie winced. She held up the pendant. 'This makes the wearer invisible.'

Freddy made a disbelieving face.

'Shifts the wearer slightly into the past.' She'd planned to wear it, but Freddy should instead. His theatrical slippers weren't fighting shoes.

Freddy folded his arms. 'A magic pendant. What rubbish.'

'It's a machine—'

Sophie put on the time-turner for a moment, then swiped it off.

Freddy gaped. 'All right, I believe you.' He looked about. 'Where's the sword?'

'It's huge and cumbersome, and I've never used a sword in my life.'

'You should have brought it for me.'

Sophie sighed. 'Let's go.'

She went to put the pendant on him, but Freddy stepped back. 'I don't know the way out. If I can't see you, I can't follow you.'

'You can still see people, but they're fuzzy.' She patted his arm. 'I'll knock out the guard with the spray. Follow me, don't stop for anything, and don't take the pendant off until we're clear of the palace.'

Freddy swallowed. 'Very well.' He bent his head for the time-turner and dissolved into nothingness.

Visible and vulnerable, Sophie secured her scarf over her face, unlocked and opened the door. The guard whirled round but she sprayed him, and he crumpled like the girls.

Sophie raced down the stairs. Two courtiers shouted as she passed but didn't chase. Once she reached the first servant corridor, she caught her breath.

Shouting rang out and panic rose in her throat. *Run.*

She sprinted through the washroom, into the loo. Hoping Freddy was close, she made a 'move' gesture at the gate. She flung it open, bent down, and splashed into the sewer. As he was taller, Freddy would have to bend lower.

The shouting grew louder, and the drain seemed never-ending, the exit a faint, mocking goal. She tried to run, but the sludge dragged at her legs.

Keep going.

Finally, she came up against the grate and threw herself under it.

She staggered into a moonlit night and a bitter wind. Hugo hugged her, and Charlotte leapt up.

'Where's Freddy?' said Hugo.

Sophie's insides turned over. 'I hope he's here.'

'He isn't,' said Hugo. '*Oh.*'

Freddy was next to Charlotte in the moonlight gloom, shivering in the exotic dressing gown.

Hugo took off his cloak and folded it around him—

The sluice gate crashed down. Guards fanned out and wielded their swords. Ten, maybe more.

Sophie touched the pistol. Four bullets...

Charlotte let out her thunderous bark and the soldiers

dropped their swords to cover their ears, but seconds later, her roar petered out, and they retrieved them.

Too soon after her mega-roaring. Charlotte could take some of them, but she'd be cut to pieces. Once the bullets were finished, it would only be Sophie Arundel and .the dagger. 'Freddy, hold Charlotte and get behind me. Hugo, stay behind Freddy. Do *not* get into my line of sight.'

'Trust us,' yelled Hugo to Freddy.

Freddy held Charlotte, but she snarled, straining to pull away. Freddy gripped her collar with both hands.

The guards swung their swords in a practised line and advanced.

These were living breathing men with families and plans... Don't think about it. Sophie focused on the men's faces, and as she'd longed for hot tea, she longed for their blood to boil.

The instant she pictured the heat and feel of their pulsing veins, the men stopped in their tracks.

A vision in Sophie's mind sharpened and danced, gloriously hot and thick, and blood streamed from the guards' eyes, noses, and mouths. As each life was extinguished, the shock of the void, of nothingness, was a kick in her guts.

Scarlet lines ran across the snow, and she stepped back to avoid them.

'Enough,' said Hugo, his voice harsh and edgy.

Sophie's knees buckled as she desperately tried to stop the blood lust, the thunderous vision in her brain. But the yearning and the imprint were too entangled, too strong.

The sea by the lift. The swell and the waves. Not enough. The sea crashing into the lift. The shock. The cold.

The intense imagery and her longing snapped off, like a door slamming shut. But her breathing was all over the place, quick and shallow, and darkness edged the corners of her vision.

Freddy picked her up, cradling her as if she weighed nothing, and sat her on Black Beauty. He untied the reins from the tree. 'Can you ride?'

She nodded. Riding was easier than walking.

Hugo and Freddy mounted their horses and galloped towards the forest with Charlotte, and Sophie urged Black Beauty forward.

Candle-bright palace windows dimmed behind them, the fat moon lit the way, and ahead of Sophie, Freddy sped up. The cloak flapped at his back and in his right hand was the time-turner, the dangling red stone swinging.

Sophie's legs trembled astride the horse, but the adrenaline high of escape was intoxicating. She encouraged Black Beauty on in the stinging wind, trying to ignore her parents' distraught voices in her mind: *you murdered them.*

Her family's faith had forbidden violence, even in self-defence, but her parents were beyond the veil of death, would never know...

In the woods, Charlotte darted between trees, keen to embrace Naga's warm sanctuary.

The sound of pursuing horses spurred Sophie on, and she reached the clearing. Hugo, Freddy, and Charlotte were just in front of her. She said Hugo's name aloud and vowed never to hurt another living soul.

Her friends passed through the barrier, and Sophie felt prickling on her skin.

By the compound, Charlotte, Freddy, and Hugo were sprawled, contorted, on the ground.

Naga raised her arm towards Sophie. There was something in her hand and it buzzed.

CHAPTER 31

aga's voice. 'It's for the best.'

Sophie lay on a bare single bed with no blanket, her head on a firm pillow. She squinted against harsh morning light and sat up. Freddy was sitting on the edge of an identical bed in his garish dressing gown, his legs dangling over the side.

Charlotte licked her hand and Sophie stroked her, her emotions echoing the ones flitting across Freddy's face: surprise, relief, bafflement.

The room's sterile air was edged with a sick sewage smell from the palace. 'Where's Hugo?'

'I used the lowest setting, but he's deeply unconscious — after twelve hours.' Naga gestured, and a video of Hugo materialised in the air. He was lying fully dressed, engulfed in transparent formulae symbols and blinking lights.

Freddy gasped.

'He'll wake eventually.' Naga's tone held the same odd, detached cadence whatever she said. She gestured again, and the video vanished.

'Freddy, this is Naga,' said Sophie. 'Her ancestors built the lift.'

He stared at Naga and swallowed.

'I cannot be associated with a blood criminal.' Naga's oval eyes swivelled to Sophie and hardened. 'I'd lose my funding and my reputation.'

'What's a blood criminal?' said Freddy.

'Those who kill by boiling blood.'

Sophie relived the guards dying in the snow while Freddy watched her, horrified.

'But my supervisors will soon see your supposed deaths,' said Naga. 'Consider the matter closed.'

Freddy scanned the room. 'Where are your supervisors?'

'On my home world,' said Naga.

'How can they possibly see us?' said Freddy.

'Our satellites record activity here and my ship crosses to my universe with the data.'

Freddy frowned. 'Are the … satellites filming us now?'

'No. Spy moths only monitor relevant indoor spaces.' Naga shot him a sharp glance and he jumped off the bed.

'A tiny machine resembling an insect.' Freddy shook his head as if he had water in his ears.

Sophie winced. Naga was planting images or memories into his mind. 'There was a moth in Freddy's room in the palace.'

'Some stay in situ,' said Naga. 'Others go where there's germane activity.'

Freddy flushed. 'Intolerable. You were *watching*—'

'How often is data transported to your supervisor in the other universe?' said Sophie, trying to distract Freddy. Naga's agenda wasn't clear. Arguing with her would be a bad idea. Sophie stroked Charlotte again.

'Every lunar month,' said Naga. 'The system also acts as a security protocol. If it doesn't arrive, a ticket is raised, and help sent.'

'Has that ever happened?' Freddy asked Naga, obviously keen to move the conversation on from the palace bedroom.

'Not to me.'

'Do your systems ever go wrong?' said Sophie.

'When I first arrived, there was a false priority interests alert, but that's rare.'

'Priority interests have the gene, like us,' Sophie said to Freddy.

Sophie brought her knees up to her chest. Light from a curtain-less window accentuated Naga's too-smooth skin. Unnerving. Yet she remained vaguely familiar, which was more unnerving. Sophie touched her shoulder where the projectile, or whatever it was, had hit her — painfully. 'I'm grateful you only *pretended* to murder us, but why wouldn't your supervisors report you?'

'Ending the lives of blood criminals and their associates is a duty, not a crime.' Naga's lips thinned. 'In any event, perpetrators don't long survive their victims. Enamoured of the curse, they succumb to exhaustion, or are mirrored.'

'Mirrored?' Sophie shrank from Naga's gaze.

'Forced to look into a vanity mirror,' said Naga, 'or, of their own accord, they seek out clear water or a burnished shield — to boil their own blood.'

Sophie put her head in her hands.

'Are there any other abilities we should know about?' said Freddy, his voice even.

'Turning creatures to stone also risks grisly consequences.' Naga rounded on him. 'But *your* boudoir activities could have ruined the project.'

Freddy shrank back. 'What project?'

'Ground-breaking cultural research,' said Naga.

Change the subject. 'If you don't mind me asking,' said Sophie, 'how old are you?' She seemed about thirty, but it was difficult to tell.

'Our lifespans are roughly seven times longer than yours,' said Naga, 'as Charlotte was to you.'

Sophie pulled Charlotte to her. '*Was?*'

'Charlotte regained consciousness hours ago. A useful opportunity to change her lifespan.' Naga gave Sophie a brief, tight smile. 'She'll live another seventy years, just as you do, barring accidents or disease.'

Shock, and a fierce rage surged up, and for a moment Sophie was speechless. 'How *dare* you make changes to her without my permission.'

Naga's eyes indicated surprise, but the rest of her face didn't move. '*Your* permission is not required. I asked Charlotte whether she wanted a human lifespan and she said she did. The procedure's routine. It would have been uncivilised *not* to offer.'

'There has to be a downside.' Sophie hugged Charlotte tighter.

'Charlotte is still Charlotte,' said Naga, 'though her linguistic understanding and reasoning ability has increased. A useful by-product is blood crime protection.'

'What's that?' said Sophie.

'Her blood cannot be boiled. Surely of value?'

Naga's conversation with Charlotte and the subsequent operation flashed as vibrant images in Sophie's mind. Charlotte had shared her consent in pictures, how she loved life: bouncing about as a puppy, greeting Sophie when she returned from school, cuddling up with Sophie at night. Naga's memory of the operation was more detailed. Mercifully, no surgery: injections and petri dishes.

'I also restored her ability to breed,' said Naga. 'Charlotte was adamant about that.'

Charlotte seemed the same, and unconcerned, but Sophie buried her face in her silver-brown fur.

A door slid open in the wall, revealing a wardrobe. 'New

clothes, Freddy. My staff used Hugo's as templates.'

Despite the rapidity and quantity of information thrown at him, Freddy seemed remarkably calm. 'Thank you.'

'There is also clothing for you, Sophie, while your garments are cleaned.' Naga sniffed. 'The air-circulation is efficient, but perhaps you'd both care to bathe?'

Sophie and Freddy nodded.

A bleep sounded.

'Finally,' said Naga. 'Hugo's awake.'

That evening, they ate dinner with Naga at a long table in the reception hall. Hugo and Freddy's steaks weren't real meat, but Sophie opted for veggie curry. Each meal was individually tailored by preference, including seasoning and spice, and the food was created when requested, like a *Star Trek* replicator, except it appeared directly on their plates.

'There are sensors in the table,' Naga explained. She cleared her throat. 'Apologies. I know you find our connection disturbing.'

Sophie ate her curry. Though Naga seemed to access her thoughts on a whim, Sophie only received random memories or emotions, maybe because Naga had chosen to share them: curiosity and interest when they'd arrived at the compound and, when she and Freddy had regained consciousness, mild pride she'd faked their deaths. But the flashes of concern about her project were intense.

A bleep, and an image materialised above the dining table. The aerial view showed a *Game of Thrones* fortress on a craggy outcrop, looming over a vast valley with snowy mountains in the distance.

'Why did this pop up?' said Sophie.

'Relevance to a priority interest,' said Naga. 'In this case, *you.'*

Sophie put down her fork, apprehension killing her appetite. 'What … where is that?'

'Atsq'uri,' said Naga. 'The Mongols have it now.'

The striking castle image changed to a stone room lit by torches. Three men with scruffy dark beards and shoulder-length jet-black hair stooped around a crude map, etched onto animal skin. The shape of their eyes suggested they were Mongols.

Their incomprehensible guttural conversation altered jarringly into posh British English. 'They rescued a deserter from execution,' said a gaunt man. 'And they released a bear.' Above him was a caption. *Foot soldier.*

'So?' said the oldest and shortest of the three. His caption read, *Subutai. Military Strategist to G. Khan.*

'The locals call her the red goddess,' said the gaunt man. 'She can kill with one look.'

'Superstition.' *Foot soldier two.* The man moved his lips, but no words were audible.

'Non-relevant profanities and crude humour are muted,' said Naga.

'Bring her, she could be useful,' said Subutai, 'and entertaining.'

The other men's responses were edited out, and Sophie felt a sharp stab of dread. Hugo held her hand under the dining table.

'If she resists capture,' said Subutai, 'kill her.'

'I can't leave this compound,' muttered Sophie. 'I'll never get back to the lift.'

'If you're monitoring the Mongols,' said Hugo to Naga, 'can't we plan a route around them?'

'Not without risk. They smear their arrow tips with wolfsbane poison. Until the end, the victim remains conscious and in agony.' Naga turned to Sophie and Freddy.

'You have too much empathy. You expend unnecessary energy processing information you cannot change.'

'I'm finding you sharing my thoughts difficult.' Sophie adjusted her merino top. Her laundered ski clothes had been returned in less than an hour, dry and stink-free.

Freddy said nothing, straightening the napkin on his knees. His replicated clothes were exact copies of Hugo's, down to a missing button.

'You can't read my mind?' Hugo asked Naga.

'I cannot.'

'Nor the minds of your servants?' said Freddy.

'No. Any issues are dealt with by my bands.' Naga grasped the arm of a young man who'd poured her wine from a decanter. Around his wrist was a thin, silver tattoo. 'If any of them stray too close to the barrier, they get a mild electric shock, but that doesn't happen often.' Naga smiled at Sophie. 'If you like, I can give a band to Hugo.'

Sophie shook her head. 'That would be … inappropriate.'

'Funny, though.' Freddy cast Hugo a 'take that' look.

Freddy seemed older with his beard, and his eyes had acquired a hard edge. 'You show me mental pictures and I feel you probing my thoughts from time to time,' he said to Naga. 'Why can't I read your mind or Sophie's?'

'Not everyone has the ability,' said Naga.

Sophie finished her curry, thankful for small mercies.

After dinner, Naga allocated Freddy a bedroom and a different room to Sophie and Hugo.

Sophie closed their door. Their room had an ensuite bathroom, an enormous dog bed and one regular bed. A narrow single.

Charlotte jumped on the human bed. When Sophie pushed her gently off, Charlotte graciously acquiesced.

'Great,' said Hugo. 'Naga presumes I sleep on the floor.'

'We'll fit. I'll lie on top of you.'

'Hmm.' Hugo sat on the bed and took off his boots.

Sophie tucked a blonde curl behind her ear. 'Feels weird, having clean hair.'

'On balance, I prefer it,' said Hugo. 'Naga's beautiful.'

'Hardly. Plastic surgery overload.'

'Why do you say that?'

'Her skin's so stretched, she can't move her facial muscles,' said Sophie, 'but that could be natural.'

'I don't think I'm seeing the real Naga. She's *gorgeous*. Reminds me of an older you.'

'Not a compliment, Hugo. When she talked about wolfsbane, I had a memory flash from her. She watched on a screen as Mongols attacked a village and recorded the shooting range of their arrows. *No* empathy.'

'She's witnessed so much brutality here, her detachment might be keeping her sane.' He grimaced. 'I can't get those dying soldiers out of my head.'

'I know.' Sophie sat beside him. 'But they'd have gutted us like fish.'

He winced.

Charlotte was curled up in her allotted bed, her face solemn. Did she understand everything they said? Sophie went over and snuggled her.

'Do you believe Charlotte really communicated her informed consent to a longer life?' said Hugo.

'She did. Naga shared her memory, but she was simply following protocol. It wasn't kindness.' Sophie sat next to him. 'And now I've got over the shock, I think her extended lifespan is a beautiful gift.'

'Whatever the alleged benefits, I wouldn't want Naga to operate on me,' said Hugo. 'Can you shut her out of your head?'

'No.' She pulled off her boots.

'But you're not afraid of her.'

'I'm not,' said Sophie. 'I don't know why.'

'You can boil blood, so perhaps Naga's scared of *you*.' Hugo frowned. 'To be honest, the way you are here … I'm scared.'

His words gave Sophie a cold jolt, but before she could reply there was a knock on the door.

Freddy stood in the doorway, holding his sleeping bag. 'May I sleep in here?'

Hugo got to his feet. 'Of course.'

'My room's too bare and quiet.' Freddy closed the door, laid his sleeping bag on the floor, and sat on it.

'What's happened?' said Sophie.

'I'm evil.' Freddy's voice cracked. 'I'm descended from the devil.'

Sophie felt his distress. She'd been where he was. Her parents dying had undermined every belief, every assumption she'd possessed. Her very sense of self had wobbled.

Freddy hugged his knees, the sleeping bag creasing under him, and Charlotte watched him from the dog bed like a solemn sphinx.

'I inherited the lift gene from Mummy, and she came from 666,' said Freddy. 'Your world.'

Sophie nodded. 'The number in the bible.'

'666's not in my bible at home,' said Freddy.

Mind-boggling. 'Does it have any number?' asked Sophie.

'422.' He sniffed.

'Other biblical details may be missing,' said Hugo, 'or changed…'

Freddy sighed. 'But our devil's called Lucifer.'

'Naga told us Lucifer's ex-friends trashed his reputation in 666 and *other places*,' said Hugo. 'So, in Shorten too.'

'I'm the devil's progeny,' said Freddy.

'We're probably related to one of Lucifer's mates,' said Sophie.

'Fallen angels,' muttered Freddy. 'Evil.'

'Look,' said Hugo, 'if you do have an ancestor who thought changing people's DNA without their consent was wrong, that doesn't make them, or you, *evil*.'

'But Naga's people created us in their image,' said Freddy. 'Not God. He doesn't love us—'

'This doesn't undermine the New Testament,' said Sophie. 'Christ could still be the son of God.'

'Only in some universes.' Freddy sniffed again. He climbed into his sleeping bag and frowned at Hugo. 'Why can't you see how terrible this is?'

'I'm not religious,' said Hugo, 'but when Naga laid it all out, it was a shock.'

'It's only one bit of the bible,' said Sophie, 'and, anyway, religion isn't about facts, it's about faith.' She tapped her chest over her heart.

'You're an atheist,' said Freddy.

'Wasn't always.'

'Scientists have identified a gene that makes some individuals more likely to believe in gods,' said Hugo, 'though I'm probably over simplifying.'

'That could be a legacy of the camps,' said Sophie. 'Manipulating genes in one camp and not in another.'

'The point is,' said Hugo, hastily, 'our bible has a lot of stuff that's not followed in mainstream Christianity anymore. Stoning adulterers...'

'*In my name shall they cast out devils*,' said Freddy. 'Jesus believed in devils.'

'We can imagine devils,' said Hugo, 'their appearance, how they act, and given there may be an infinite number of universes, perhaps devils or *the* devil exists ... somewhere.'

'Or conversely,' said Sophie, 'if he exists, that might be why we're able to imagine him?'

Freddy zipped up his sleeping bag. 'Too complicated.'

CHAPTER 32

The next morning when Hugo woke up, Sophie was in the bathroom, Charlotte was padding around, and Freddy was packing away his sleeping bag.

Hugo's first thoughts were of Naga's theological bombshell and Freddy's state of mind. 'How are you?'

Freddy's lips narrowed into a determined line. 'Better.'

Over breakfast, Freddy's concerns had evidently shifted to his life's passion: maths and science. He smiled at their host. 'I'd love to learn more about your technology.'

'I'll instruct you on how to use it, but I have limited knowledge of construction software.' Naga stirred her yoghurt, her same choice for every meal.

Hugo savoured the taste of a juicy slice of bacon. Incredible the way it had been replicated. But not all the food tasted real: the coffee smelled overly sweet and tasted bland.

'I'm looking forward to you assisting me,' said Naga, addressing Freddy and Sophie. 'You'll bring a fresh approach to the data, and the quality and quantity of analytics will improve.'

'How long would you like us to help for?' said Sophie.

'The project's end date is some way off, but I can extend your life spans.'

What she'd done to Charlotte… Live seven times longer than a normal human, but spend *centuries* here. Hugo met Sophie's eyes, alarmed.

Sophie turned to Naga. 'I don't want to do that.'

Naga did her small smile. 'Of course, it's up to you.'

Freddy cut in. 'I'd very much enjoy assisting you.' He hesitated. 'For a few months.'

Naga's expression didn't change, but Sophie looked taken aback.

Hugo frowned. What had she picked up from Naga?

Sophie fed Charlotte a sausage and explained how they'd tried calling the lift in the cave.

'Calling it by thought is unreliable,' said Naga.

'How should we call it?' said Freddy.

'Near the landing location, say, "Janus" aloud.'

Hugo mentally kicked himself. He should have thought of that. 'Would that work for me?'

'No,' said Naga.

'If Janus is sentient,' said Sophie, 'why would he appear, even if he's summoned by name?'

'The summons algorithm is a core one,' said Naga. 'It cannot be overridden.'

'To allow Hugo to see the lift, I have to say his name every time?' asked Sophie.

'Yes,' said Naga. 'It prevents unauthorised entry. The compound barrier's the same. However, Hugo has no need to *see* it. He is emotionally tied to you. If you touch him, he can travel.'

'That first time, when we stepped into the lift in the students' union, I didn't touch you,' Sophie said to Hugo.

'But Charlotte did. She barged into me, then sat by my

feet.' Hugo drank his too-sweet coffee. He loved Charlotte. He was emotionally bound to her too.

'What about the horses?' said Sophie. 'I didn't know their true names.'

'Domesticated animals only require indirect touch.'

'Got it,' said Sophie, giving Charlotte another sausage. 'Holding their reins is enough.'

'Does Janus sense evil intent?' said Hugo. 'Prevent bad people getting in, including those with the gene?'

'What a curious idea. No software can discern good from evil,' said Naga. 'If travellers already in the vehicle wish to exclude someone else, Janus will action their request, but the wish must be precise, like the requested destination. He uses ambiguity for his own ends.'

'For what purpose?' said Freddy.

'He seeks entertainment. Travellers and their struggles provide that.'

'There are drawings and statues of him in our universe,' said Hugo. 'Has he ever left the lift in corporeal form?'

Naga gave a curt nod. 'Field teams used walking staffs to summon the corporeal version for mythology research, or to reset the ship's software.'

'He's often portrayed with a staff,' said Hugo.

'To the inhabitants, it was simply a primitive walking aid. This is typical of their drawings.' A pencil sketch hovered in the air. The top of the staff was heart-shaped, its centre hollowed out except for a figure resembling the letter T. The three end points touched the round inner rim.

'What does the T symbol mean?' said Hugo.

'The end of the limbs within the circle represented the past, present, and future. Consistent with the mythology.' The drawing vanished. 'The item seemed to be fashioned from oak.'

'What was it made from?' said Freddy.

'A titanium alloy.'

'Is there a walking staff in the legacy room?' said Hugo. The symbol of a god. How wonderful to see it, touch it—

'Once interaction stopped, they were dismantled.'

'Janus became sentient after that?' Hugo asked her.

'Indeed.'

Hugo finished his coffee, surprised by a pang of sympathy for a Roman god, trapped in his own ship. 'Do you know what's happening with Rusa's army?'

An aerial picture of red and black vegetation appeared, stark and unmoving. The image zoomed down. Not vegetation. Hugo stared at it in horror. Rusa's army was strewn along the coastal road, slaughtered. How had the Mongols defeated all those soldiers?

Charlotte gave a single bark, her eyes on the screen.

'The battlefield is a few miles north of where you landed,' said Naga, as if describing a vaguely interesting painting.

The view panned up, showing the whole of Georgia. Smoke solidified in wavy lines: from the north to the middle of the country, another from the centre stretched west to the Black Sea, and one from Anapoli ran south, stopping halfway to the queen's palace.

'The smoke represents the Mongol forces on the ground,' said Naga.

'So, not real smoke,' said Hugo.

'Obviously.' Naga glanced at him indulgently. 'They're moving south.' She gestured again, and a concertina of scenes snapped up: men on horseback on narrow forest tracks, in villages — and countless riders on the coastal road.

Hugo caught Sophie's eye. Returning to the lift was only going to become more difficult.

'Your pendant would help us avoid the Mongols,' said Sophie. 'Invaluable. We'd only use it if we had to.'

A faint line marred Naga's brow. 'No, my supervisors

would realise you had it.'

'When I wore it, I could see people and objects,' said Sophie, 'but there was no sound.'

'Channelling sufficient energy to hold the wearer in the recent past *and* allowing them to see their surroundings was a feat of engineering in itself,' said Naga. 'Processing sound as well wasn't feasible.'

'I didn't enjoy wearing it,' said Sophie. 'I was there, but not there.'

'Okay, we keep off the roads.' Hugo stood up. 'We should get going.'

'You don't decide that,' said Freddy. 'We should wait until it's safe.'

'If we wait until it's *safe*,' said Hugo, 'we'll spend the rest of our lives in this compound.'

'A wiser choice than risking capture,' said Naga.

'You only want to go because you don't have the gene.' Freddy sat back in his chair. 'You're the odd one out.'

Hugo rolled his eyes and addressed Sophie. 'You've got the casting vote.'

'We go.' Charlotte leaned against Sophie's legs and Sophie patted her.

Freddy folded his arms. 'I'm staying.'

'Forever?' said Sophie. 'By yourself?'

'Good luck with that.' Hugo's words dripped with sarcasm.

Freddy's expression hardened.

Naga watched them, her flawless face inscrutable.

'Reconsider, Freddy,' said Sophie. 'We need to stick together.'

'I'll decide for myself.'

'Can you give us food and water?' Hugo asked Naga.

She hesitated. 'Yes.'

'And a physical map?' added Hugo.

'Manual map-making is my mindfulness activity.' Naga went over to a wall, tapped, and a drawer slid out. She handed Hugo a roll of paper and graced him with her tight smile.

After breakfast, Freddy reluctantly agreed to leave, and under Naga's humourless supervision, he began replicating food supplies. He also made short ropes for securing the horses when making camp. He'd grown up with horses.

Sophie and Hugo went to fetch the holdalls but as soon as they reached the bedroom, Charlotte ran in and pawed at Sophie. With her huge paws, it looked as if Sophie was being stroked by a lion.

'I'm worried too,' said Sophie, hugging Charlotte. 'Naga *really* doesn't want us to go.'

'Do you think she'll stop us?' said Hugo.

Sophie frowned. 'Before she closed her mind, I felt her frustration and dismay that we were leaving. The most powerful emotions I've felt from her.'

Right. *That* was why, after they'd rescued Freddy, Naga had only stunned them. She'd been hiring. 'She's planning something.' He checked the pistol on his belt.

'Naga wouldn't keep us here by force. She regards the use of violence as unacceptably primitive.'

'Are you sure?' said Hugo.

'Her memory of shooting us, the main emotion was … distaste.'

They put on their jackets and cloaks. Hugo fetched Freddy's jacket and cloak and folded them into a bag and added Naga's map. Sophie swung a holdall onto her shoulders, picked up Freddy's, and strode down the corridor with Charlotte.

Instead of following them, Hugo dashed into the legacy room and shut the door. Naga may have shuttered *her* mind, but might still have access to Sophie's and Charlotte's.

He lifted the time-turner pendant from its stand and stashed it deep in his bag.

Being a 'lesser being' had an upside.

Out in the passage, he lugged the holdall onto his back, but then jumped as barking and shouting erupted from the reception hall.

'Don't *shoot*,' shouted Freddy. 'For God's sake!'

'We get how important your project is,' yelled Sophie. 'They won't capture us, and I'd kill myself rather than be raped … be forced to breed an army.'

'I'm sorry,' said Naga. Her voice was flat.

Hugo's insides turned to jelly.

'We'll be careful,' said Sophie. '*Trust* me.'

A short, roaring bark slammed into Hugo's eardrums, and someone screamed. He ignored the pain in his ears, grabbed his pistol, and ran.

Sophie and Freddy were against a wall, standing close together. Naga was squirming on the floor, facing away from him, Charlotte mauling her leg.

Time slowed.

Naga pointed her buzzing device at Charlotte. No! Hugo pulled the trigger and shot Naga in the back, the bang of the bullet abrupt and brutal. Her device fell to the floor with a clatter as she slumped sideways.

Hugo gasped, his heart hammering.

'Good,' said Freddy, eying Naga with satisfaction. He picked up her device and threw it across the room. 'She meant to *murder* us. Just because of her precious work—'

The waiting staff burst in, their faces slack with shock.

'Let's go,' said Hugo.

Naga struggled into a sitting position and put up her hands, admitting defeat, her perfect mouth twisting in agony. 'Remember the timeline… and for my sake and yours, do *not* be captured alive.'

CHAPTER 33

After leaving the compound, they kept to the forest. They didn't dare light a fire or boil water, and every moment was a relentless, freezing slog.

At night, to keep warm, they huddled together, even Freddy. Charlotte unzipped her own sleeping bag with her teeth, wriggled inside it, and Sophie tugged up the zip. Given Charlotte's size, it only just closed.

They rationed the few loaves of bread Freddy had replicated before Naga had turned on them but, on the third morning, they woke up to bone-aching cold, flurries of snow — and no food.

Black Beauty nibbled at a prickly bush. 'No idea if she should eat this,' said Sophie, stamping her numb feet on smelly fallen leaves. 'On the upside, we've seen no bears.'

Freddy brushed snow from his sleeping bag. 'Even if Charlotte brought down a bear, we'd need to cook it, risk a fire.'

Gross. Sophie unzipped Charlotte's sleeping bag, and Charlotte bounded out. 'It ended badly, but I'm *so* missing the compound food.'

'Some of it was excellent,' said Hugo, 'but the coffee and the eggs … not so much.'

'How do you mean?' said Sophie.

'The coffee tasted of nothing, and the fried eggs were grainy.'

'It all tasted delightful,' said Freddy.

'Must be a gene thing.' Sophie dug about in the holdall for her notebook and pencil.

'What are you doing?' asked Freddy.

'Writing down Naga's info about Janus' walking staff. And I'll draw it too.'

Hugo nodded. 'Could be part of the lift puzzle.'

Once she was happy with the sketch, Sophie put away the notebook, and pulled Naga's map from Hugo's bag. She knelt on the snow-freckled ground and unrolled it. The hand-drawn landscape was beautiful: the Black Sea in the west, white, craggy mountains in the north, the lower land predominantly green forest. Stylised, red-roofed castles indicated major settlements. Dark dots showed smaller ones.

With a gloved finger, Freddy patted a horizontal dotted line that ran east from the coastal road, bisecting the forest. 'Are we near here?'

'I think so,' said Sophie. 'Halfway to the lift.' She'd marked the spot with her notebook pencil, a cross by the turquoise sea.

'Shame we can't access the current smoke lines on the satellite view,' said Hugo, bending to peer at the map.

Freddy touched a fortress symbol in the middle of the country and moved his finger west and down the coastal highway. 'The Mongols may have reached Kajet by now.'

Sophie got to her feet, took a kitchen knife from her holdall and, with difficulty, dug up mud in the hard ground. She smeared some on her hair.

'I'm really hungry.' Freddy pointed to a dark dot beside the sea. 'This village isn't far.'

'But it's right by the coastal road,' said Hugo. 'What about this one?' He pointed further up the map. 'I reckon we could get there tomorrow.'

'I don't know,' said Freddy.

Charlotte nudged in, and placed a heavy paw on the map, on the pencil cross beside the lift. Hugo and Freddy blinked, taken aback.

'The new Charlotte thinks we should keep going,' said Sophie.

'If we don't eat soon,' said Freddy, 'and we meet a raiding party, we'll be in no state to fight.'

An hour later, close to a settlement on a high cliff by the sea, Sophie was talking to Hugo. Charlotte's newly wired brain was still adapting to human speech, and she listened intently, catching the most important words: must be cautious, dangerous.

Charlotte rubbed her muzzle against her mistress's cloak. The wool was musty with Sophie's sweat, laced with fear, stronger than the whiff of salt floating in the sea and the scraping noise of tiny creatures burying under the earth.

The morning sun shone on the water, but bitter gusts of wind rolled off it, and the noise of the waves jarred with a clanging sound from beyond a tall wall. There were many mixed-up scents beyond the wall: poo, horses, humans, and a nasty burning smell. Charlotte pawed her mistress, meaning, 'Bad smell.'

'I'll be careful.' Sophie put her finger to her lips. 'No barking, not unless we're threatened, and stay with the boys.'

Charlotte nodded, as she'd seen humans do. Keeping

silent was a useful wolf skill. Waiting for the right moment to pounce.

Before, human speech had communicated meaning for some words, with tone and gestures, but understanding many words was better, like juicy sausages compared to grainy dogfood.

A rumbling sound signalled the approach of a laden wagon. Wine soured the heavy, horsey stench. Sophie patted Charlotte's head. 'Quiet.'

Unnecessary. Charlotte snorted.

They hid behind trees opposite the settlement, away from the cliff edge, and Freddy and Hugo tied the horses to a branch.

'I should go, determine if it's safe,' said Freddy.

Sophie's insides tightened. 'I'm not leaving Hugo just with Charlotte.'

'Oy,' said Hugo. 'More respect. If it hadn't been for me and Charlotte in the compound, you'd be dead.'

'I know.' She kissed Hugo on the cheek.

From the shelter of the copse, Sophie scanned the village. Towers with arrow-slit windows protruded out of the twenty-foot-high encircling wall, with more turrets within. The portcullis at the entrance added to the cheery architecture. She sighed. 'I miss normal villages. The sort you can just walk into.'

The portcullis creaked up and a man in a bulky coat and a bowl-shaped hat waved the cart in.

'There's my cue.' Sophie drew a steadying breath and put on the pendant. The world went silent, her companions faded, and Sophie was utterly alone.

She ran towards the village, Naga's warning ringing in

her mind. *Worn for too long, the wearer became trapped in the near past, condemned to watch forever.*

Sophie sped up and dashed under the portcullis. The sharp points at the bottom were stained, the wood darker than the rest.

The stone towers loomed over a narrow street, interspersed with ramshackle wooden buildings. A man with muscled arms, wearing only a shirt and breeches, was bashing a piece of metal with a hammer. Evidently used to the cold. Beyond him, two men heaved sacks and barrels from the wagon onto their shoulders, and more men sat at a table eating, talking in low voices. Through the prism of the pendant, they looked washed out and abstract. Dreamlike.

On the table, tankards were arranged neatly on a table mat. Quite civilised.

The emptied wagon clattered out of the village, the driver whipping the horse to speed up, and Sophie turned on her heel.

She sprinted to the boys and Charlotte and lifted off the pendant. Her friends were solid and real, and she relaxed. 'Seems normal, but if things go south, remember the plan.'

'Freddy will use the pendant to escape and take the gun,' said Hugo. Even empty, the modern weapon could be copied. 'I wish we had more bullets. Only three left…'

'If things get really dire,' Sophie said, 'I'll do my boiling.' She took the sword from Black Beauty's saddle bag and handed it to Freddy. 'If I'm carrying it, it will only draw attention.'

Hugo shot a wistful glance at the sword and Sophie kissed him lightly on the mouth. He could barely pick it up, never mind use it. 'You have other talents,' she told him.

They left the horses and their bags and walked briskly to the settlement. As they passed beneath the portcullis, Sophie whispered to Hugo, 'Stay close.' She wrinkled her nose. 'What's that smell?'

'Cooked pork but bitter,' said Freddy. 'Gone off.'

'I can't smell anything,' said Hugo.

The blacksmith stopped banging his hammer and the men at the table stood up.

Hugo called a greeting in Russian, but nobody replied. One of the men swept the tankards off the table with his arm, and the cups tumbled together, clanging and chiming. He slapped his hand on the table mat and shouted.

Fear churned in Sophie's stomach.

Hugo scanned the street. 'There should be domestic sounds from the buildings, but there's nothing.' He drew his pistol. 'No women or children. *Run.*'

They turned to flee but men in bright tunics streamed out of countless doorways, cutting off their escape. Their faces and curved swords proclaimed their Mongol heritage and they carried raised bows, ready to shoot. The fear inside Sophie exploded.

Hugo grabbed her arm. 'The Mongols must have killed all the villagers.'

'That's what I can smell,' said Freddy, unsheathing the sword. 'From when they burned the dead.'

The man who'd trashed the tankards shouted again and seized the table mat, holding it up like a poster. On it was a figure with long hair holding a sword, and a wolf.

Not a table mat. Subutai's orders—

More Mongols rushed out, a few carrying empty sacks from the wagon. Hugo's hold on Sophie's arm tightened, and she clenched her fists, trying to think straight. What were the sacks for?

Charlotte roared her terrifying bark, and the Mongols covered their ears and stopped in their tracks, but then her bark faded. Hugo fired his gun at the line of warriors. One screamed and fell.

The Mongols stared at their fallen comrade, then at Hugo.

A moment later, a gruff order sounded in their ranks, and they advanced again.

Hugo fired another bullet, and another. 'Out of bullets.'

Charlotte snarled and leaped, tearing a man's throat out. His blood spurted in shocking red, and Sophie's own throat closed in shock. Charlotte mauled another soldier, but there were too many.

Freddy waved the sword, but the Mongols just ran past him towards Sophie.

Hugo shouted, 'Stick to the plan,' stepped nearer Freddy, and thrust the pistol into his spare hand. Sophie flung the pendant over Freddy's head, and he vanished. So did the sword and the gun.

'Hugo, keep behind me,' said Sophie. 'Charlotte, escape. *Go.*'

Charlotte bolted so fast she was a blur, but the men kept coming.

Think about hot blood—

The warriors crashed into Sophie and slammed a dusty sack over her face.

Blind and winded on the ground, she could still punch and kick, but more Mongols thumped down on her, pinning her arms and legs. They pounded blows onto her face through the hood.

And then there was nothing. Only blackness.

CHAPTER 34

*H*ugo's hands were tied, linked by a coarse rope to a Mongol's horse, and his shoulders ached from the wrenching movement of the horse.

One foot in front of another. Keep. Going. Distance yourself from what was happening. There was a name for that…

Only a few hours since their capture and setting out from the village, but he was so cold and exhausted, he couldn't think straight.

Hugo stumbled to his knees and was dragged over sharp pebbles along the dirt track. He forced himself to his feet.

Sophie trudged behind a horse, a hessian sack over her head. Whether or not the Mongols believed in the red goddess, they were taking no chances. He focused on her. Try to stay strong.

His mind wandered back to the compound, to Sophie rebuffing Naga, spelling out how she felt about him.

Soulmate. They'd talked about that, and he'd *thought* about it more times than he could count: while she'd slept beside him, when she'd been adamant Freddy shouldn't cross alone. It might be irrational, but he was more certain than ever that they shared an unshakable bond. Sophie believed they did, and when she'd said *soulmate* to Naga, to a stranger, it had given him goosebumps…

The snowy path through the woods wound left and straightened. Working out where they were headed was impossible, except they were travelling inland, following a route barely wide enough for horses.

After they stopped for the night, his hands remained bound, now to a tree. Hugo managed to swallow down some hard bread and a tiny amount of sour, frothy milk. Sophie was on the far side of the campfire, the sack tied above her mouth, allowing her to eat and drink.

The horses mooched about on long tying ropes, grazing on the forest floor, and the Mongols talked and laughed, pleased with their prizes. Three men had overpowered him, though two could have done so. Did they believe he was Freddy?

A Mongol brushed past him, and Hugo shut his lips against the smell. Even in this mind-aching cold, the warrior stank of sweat and filth.

The man went over to a horse and, with a knife, sliced into its neck. The animal didn't flinch. Hugo shook his head. Were his eyes playing tricks, deceived by the spluttering light from the campfire?

The Mongol dripped horse-blood into a cup and drank. When he'd finished, he patted the injured horse before striding back. Hugo dropped his gaze. A vampire? No, a vampire would have just bitten the horse…

Rest. Sleep.

But the Mongols were noisy, drinking their sour milk.

One stood up and swaggered towards Sophie. The group's leader growled something, and the man returned to his place. Subutai had evidently issued orders that Sophie be unharmed. For now.

But their meagre possessions had been fair game. Sophie's necklace, their watches, and his coins.

Finally the Mongols slept, but took turns to stand guard.

They left the next day at dawn. The track widened, flanked by snow-covered banks. Higher up, the forest continued, the dark canopy stark against a grey sky.

The Mongol at the front of the group stopped, gesticulated, and rode up the bank. He released an arrow into the skeletal trees and cantered away.

He soon returned, his horse hauling a dead deer, and a man, his face bleeding. One of the Mongols cut loose the deer, another shot an arrow at the captive at point blank range. The force of the impact threw him against the ground.

Hugo reeled and swore under his breath.

Their party moved on down the path as if nothing had happened. Behind them, the wounded man moaned and gabbled nonsense in Russian. As he was lost to sight, he screamed.

'What's happening?' Sophie sounded terrified, disorientated.

'Nothing to us.' A blow-by-blow description wouldn't help morale.

CHAPTER 35

Freddy retrieved the horses and tied them together.

Once the Mongols left the village with Sophie and Hugo, Charlotte tracked them — from over a mile away.

At dusk, when the war party made camp, Freddy did too, keeping his distance. He couldn't see their fire smoke, so they couldn't see his.

The first three nights, he cooked small animals Charlotte caught. Unlike Charlotte, he'd eaten his share cautiously, not wanting to burn his mouth.

On the fourth day, Freddy left the horses, and risked a look at the war party. Given Charlotte understood every word he said, she'd stay quiet. They got ahead of the Mongols and lay down within the tree line to watch them pass.

Six warriors, and there were Sophie and Hugo in the centre of the group. Sophie hooded like a falcon.

Freddy's insides churned. An irrational part of him wanted to charge in and rescue them but they were too well guarded. He retreated into the woods, Charlotte leading him back to the horses.

They tracked the war party all day, and that night, after a splendid meal of almost-cooked venison, courtesy of Charlotte, Freddy spread out the map.

Charlotte placed her paw near the Atsq'uri castle symbol, the Mongol headquarters, and stared at him.

'You think we're here?'

Charlotte nodded in an unsettlingly way.

'You were remarkable *before* Naga changed you. You just couldn't show it.' Freddy zipped up Charlotte's sleeping bag and his own and sat up against a tree trunk. The forest was silent, non-nocturnal animals no doubt curled up like them.

The wind picked up, and snow dropped from a branch with a thud, but Charlotte didn't stir, managing in her sleep to distinguish between threatening and non-threatening sounds.

Freddy's mind drifted back to twenty-first century London: the gut-wrenching moment he'd knocked on Sophie's door, realised the bedroom was empty.

Hugo and Sophie had a history he didn't understand, probably never would. He was still tied to Sophie, connected by a mysterious invisible cord, but something in Freddy Lacey had changed. Adapted.

He settled in his sleeping bag and thought about Shorten. If he survived this, he'd invite suitable girls to the Manor.

The next morning, soon after dawn, concealed inside the treeline, Freddy stood beside Charlotte. The trees provided welcome shelter from the deteriorating weather. Soft snowfall had turned into a blizzard.

Hugo was staggering down the forest track, behind the

last horse in the group. Sophie was secured to the next horse along, the sack covering her head.

In the distance, on top of a sheer cliff, was a fortress from a nightmare. It looked much more formidable than on Naga's satellite image.

Atsq'uri.

Freddy addressed Charlotte. 'You haven't recovered your temple-bark yet and, yes, you might be immune from Sophie's blood-stare, but she loves you with a fierce mother's love. I can't risk you distracting her once I've taken off her hood. Even a moment could be fatal. Only leave the woods when I do this.' He gave a low whistle.

Charlotte nodded solemnly.

Freddy unsheathed the sword, put on the pendant, and skidded down a slippery bank through the fast-falling snow.

He reached Sophie, pulled off his pendant and tore the hood from her face. 'Boil them,' he said. '*Now.*'

In seconds, every man before her screamed and clutched at his head. The horses screamed too and collapsed, some on their riders.

The horse Sophie was tied to reared, threw its rider and collapsed, and Sophie was hauled violently forward. Freddy sliced through the rope with the sword, careful not to lean in front of her.

The rider from Sophie's horse lay at her feet, his body contorted and bloody. But behind Sophie, Hugo, and his captor and his horse were very much alive.

The last Mongol dismounted with a flourish, drew his curved sword, and advanced towards Hugo who was help-less, bound to the horse.

'*No.*' Freddy leapt between Hugo and the warrior.

Freddy circled the Mongol and the man's eyes glittered with menace. Yes, he had superior strength, but this was a hardened soldier. Concentrate.

Sophie faced away from them, her wrists roped together, and she moaned as if in pain. The Mongol's eyes flicked sideways, and Freddy thrust with shocking speed, his longer sword meeting cloth and flesh, and just as fast he pulled the weapon back.

The warrior slashed with his scimitar but only met air and snow, and he crumpled.

Freddy smiled in relief. Faster, as well as stronger.

Sophie dropped to her knees, consumed in a coughing fit. Finally, she muttered, 'Keep Charlotte safe.'

'She knows to stay in the forest,' said Freddy, patting the surviving horse who snorted, its breath creating hazy white plumes that faded into the white sky.

'Freddy, can you dig me out a thick patch of dirt?' asked Sophie.

Strange request. Outside her line of sight, he chopped out a hard lump with his sword, and retreated.

Sophie picked up the dirt with her tied hands, then staggered to her feet. She faced him and Hugo, her breathing quick and jerky, a thin trail of blood across her cheekbones, red-stark on her pale skin.

Freddy held his breath, but nothing happened — to him or to Hugo.

Sophie set a wiggly worm on the ground.

'What are you doing?' asked Freddy.

'I looked at the worm. It's still alive.' She put a shaky hand to her brow. 'It was the only way I could test whether the power had stopped. Before, it cut off. This time ... it didn't.'

Freddy carefully severed the rope around Sophie's wrists, then did the same for Hugo.

Hugo was rooted to the spot, stunned.

Sophie ran to him, and Hugo gathered her close. Freddy strode to the verge and cleaned the sword blade on the snowy grass. He straightened and surveyed the scene with grim approval.

'You saved me,' said Hugo. 'I thought you wanted me dead?'

Freddy's mouth twisted. 'You must think me weak.'

'You're not weak,' said Hugo.

Sophie turned to him. 'Freddy, you're incredible.'

Freddy's resentment towards her had lessened, together with his hurt pride, and he acknowledged her words with a perky grin. He scanned the treeline and whistled.

Charlotte appeared and careered over at speed, knocking Sophie over.

Sophie stood up with difficulty and hugged her.

'We should drag the bodies into the trees, so nobody finds them,' said Hugo. 'Won't be long until the snow covers the rest of the … mess.' The ground was soaked red.

'Even I can't drag the horses,' said Freddy.

Charlotte trotted up to a dead horse, took its reins in her teeth, and hauled the carcass into the woods.

'On the other hand…' Freddy threw the nearest warrior over his shoulder and strode off.

That evening, as they made camp, Freddy sorted through a Mongol saddlebag and found Sophie's necklace.

Sophie put it on. 'You did good, Freddy, retrieving the horses and our stuff.'

Modestly, Freddy nodded. 'We don't need a packhorse. We should let this one go.' He patted the Mongol's horse.

Sophie rinsed the blood from her face in the stream, gasping as the cold water met her skin. 'I'm so sorry about the village. With the time-turner on, I couldn't hear or smell, but I should have poked around more.'

'And I realised too late.' Hugo drained his travel mug of fermented milk. 'This is growing on me.'

Freddy took a swig of milk and wiped his mouth with a gloved hand while Sophie fed dried meat to Charlotte.

'You're too thin,' Hugo said to Sophie as he chewed a piece of gristle.

She filled her mug from the stream. 'Supermodel-thin?'

'*Ill*-thin,' said Hugo. 'Not a good look.'

'If something's on your mind, Hugo, just say it.' Sophie climbed into her sleeping bag.

Frowning, Hugo climbed into his. 'Killing the guards, and those Mongols…'

She drank her water.

'That must have affected you.' Hugo reached for more milk.

'Of course, it did,' said Sophie, 'but there's sod all I can do about it. It's not like I got off on it.'

Hugo put down his mug. 'Didn't you?'

She stared at him in dismay. 'I can't believe you said that.'

'Heroin addicts know their addiction might kill them,' said Hugo, 'but they don't stop.'

Sophie rolled her eyes. 'Freddy couldn't have taken them all on.'

'No, I couldn't,' said Freddy, quietly, settling himself into his sleeping bag beside his holdall.

'I get why you didn't rescue us earlier,' Hugo said to him.

'I don't,' said Sophie.

'Whenever you camped, you were surrounded,' said Freddy, glad to move on from their bickering. 'On the road, they kept you in the middle of the line. Sophie wouldn't have had a clean view. But on the track towards their castle, you were at the rear.'

'They got sloppy near their base,' said Hugo.

Freddy delved into his holdall, laid out the map, and

pointed at the Atsq'uri symbol. 'We're north of here. A few days from the lift.' He fed Charlotte a loaf of stale bread and she ate it in one gulp. 'Charlotte really is extraordinary. The first day we followed you, I said we'd have to find food, and she ran off and returned with rabbits and all sorts.'

Sophie wiggled further into her sleeping bag. 'Pre-Naga, Charlotte never killed for food.'

'The Mongols' provisions should last until the lift,' said Hugo.

Freddy gave Charlotte an appreciative glance. 'But if they don't, we ask her to hunt.'

CHAPTER 36

After two days, they turned west towards the coastal road, but Charlotte sat on the forest floor and refused to move.

'I'll go ahead on foot. Check where we are.' Sophie stashed the pendant in her trouser pocket.

Hugo opened his mouth to say something but changed his mind. He handed her his compass.

Sophie set off, following the compass, but before she reached the road, she held her scarf closer over her nose against a familiar, sickly stench. When she emerged onto the highway, it was worse.

No need for the pendant. There was no one to see her.

The queen's soldiers littered the ground, just as in the video in the compound. Birds swooped between corpses, pecking, and flapping their wings. Nausea rose in her throat, and she quickly retraced her steps into the woods.

Charlotte bounded up as she re-joined them, and Sophie described what she'd seen.

'We've come too far north,' said Hugo. 'But the lift's not far.'

The forest canopy grew lower, the light dimmer, and they dismounted. Sophie and Freddy led their horses in double file, Charlotte, Hugo and his horse behind them.

'I'll check if the highway is clear,' said Freddy, as they walked. 'The headland and the cave must be close now.'

Sophie nodded.

Frozen branches gave way with a crack under Sophie's boots, and she hurtled downwards and landed with a shattering thump. Freddy whacked down beside her and groaned.

They were in a large, deep hole with vertical sides.

Freddy scrambled to his feet, breathing hard, and Sophie gingerly stood up.

Hugo and Charlotte looked at them from the edge. 'Are you okay?'

'No bones broken,' said Sophie. The circular hole was four yards deep and the same across.

'A bear pit,' said Hugo.

'Tie the horse's lead ropes together?' said Sophie, trying to gather her wits.

Hugo disappeared and returned with them. 'Nowhere near long enough.' He frowned. 'I'll sit by the road with Charlotte. Watch for wagons and get a rope.'

'Why would wagons have a rope?' said Sophie.

'Commonplace item,' said Hugo, his eyes worried. 'I'll secure the horses again.'

A minute later, he dropped down their holdalls and the Mongol saddlebags. 'Go easy on the fermented milk, it'll dehydrate you. I'll drag the sword somewhere, hide it under fallen branches. Are you good with me taking the wind-up torch?'

'Fine.' said Sophie. 'The décor here's not going to change.'

'Be careful,' ordered Freddy.

'Charlotte, keep safe,' Sophie called. 'Hugo, I love you.'

'I love you too.'

Hugo and Charlotte disappeared from view, and Sophie bit her lip.

'Charlotte will protect him,' said Freddy. He glanced up. 'The trees should keep off most of the snow, and it's not too cold.'

'It's bloody freezing.' Sophie paced back and forth, hugging herself, then ran on the spot. 'This works better.'

But she couldn't run forever. She did five-minute spurts.

'Hugo's right, you know.' Freddy stamped his feet. 'You are too thin.'

'You're thinner too.' Rangier, his cheekbones more prominent.

He made a very-Freddy face.

The packed earth of the pit walls and floor smelled damp and heavy. Not unpleasant, protective, but the deep cold of the earth and the air was a different matter. Remorseless. Predatory.

Sophie took her notebook from her bag. 'I need a distraction.' She sat on the holdall and sketched him. Like her, Freddy's hair had grown unnaturally fast. Many months' growth, not weeks. Doing justice to his shoulder-length hair and rakish beard was a challenge.

He peered over her shoulder. 'Is that me?'

'Supposed to be.' The sketch was clumsy, made worse because she didn't remove her gloves. She stood and ran on the spot again.

Then she drew Wolf-Charlotte and Hugo.

'Hugo hasn't changed here,' said Freddy.

'Not physically.' Daylight was fading. She shut the notebook.

The forest above them was silent, except for occasional snorting from the horses, but that stopped after dusk.

Sophie gulped. 'I can't see a thing.'

'The moonlight was bright last night. Should be the same.'

Sophie squinted at him. He was a fuzzy shape.

'We could freeze to death here,' said Sophie. 'We must sleep together.'

Freddy's intake of breath was audible.

'Not *sleep together* like that. We should share one sleeping bag, inside the other.'

They sorted the sleeping bags and eventually Sophie dozed, Freddy curled around her. Something pressing into her hips woke her.

Freddy was asleep but his body wasn't. Reluctant to disturb him, she wiggled her toes and fingers and tried to sleep.

When dawn finally arrived, she struggled to stand, her legs stiff and the rest of her aching like she'd been beaten up.

Freddy groaned. 'We're still here.'

They assembled a meagre breakfast of bread, cheese, and rationed water.

Sophie carefully chewed a piece of bread. So hard, it could break a tooth.

'I didn't think I'd ever get over you and Hugo, but I have.' Freddy dug mould from a lump of cheese with a spoon. 'And even if we never get out of this…'

'Hole,' supplied Sophie.

'*I am the captain of my soul.*'

Familiar… With difficulty, she swallowed a morsel of brittle cheese. 'From the Nelson Mandela movie.'

'Nelson who?'

'Mandela,' said Sophie. 'He quoted *Invictus* to his fellow inmates in South Africa, to keep up their spirits.'

'The poem's by a British chap called William Henley. *It matters not how strait the gate, how charged with punishments the scroll, I am the master of my fate, I am the captain of my soul.*'

Sophie took a measured sip of water. Hugo believed free

will was an illusion, that no one was master of their fate, and if she had a soul, after what she'd done to protect the boys and Charlotte here… She pictured it as a tattered flag. Torn to shreds.

Night arrived, followed by another day, and yet another freezing night. Sleep was elusive, snatched in fits and starts. Dreams merged with daydreams.

Before dawn on the fourth day, they climbed out of the sleeping bags and paced the pit perimeter.

'I'm so cold,' said Sophie, her teeth chattering.

Freddy sipped from his mug and handed it to her.

No more than a dribble. She finished it.

'In the lift, Hugo said without water, we'd only survive a few days.'

'We've got the fermented milk.' She hated the stuff but needs must.

Hours later, as dusk fell, a scene from a movie Sophie had watched years ago, *The English Patient*, played inside her head. A wounded woman lying in a cave, waiting for help that never came… 'My brain's shutting down.' She removed the kitchen knife from her holdall, the serrated blade just a grey shadow in the fading light. 'We should kill ourselves.' Her fingers tightened on the handle. 'Everything hurts.'

'Stabbing would hurt more.'

'Lesser of two evils. Quicker.'

Freddy took the knife and returned it to the bag. 'We shouldn't abandon hope.'

'*Never give up. Never surrender.*' The *Galaxy Quest* joke she'd shared months ago in Shorten with Hugo. Reliving her last glimpse of him and Charlotte, she gave in to tears.

Freddy guided her into the double sleeping bag. No moonlight tonight.

She managed to zip the bags closed by touch, and he curved around her. 'When I was tracking the Mongols, being away from you helped me think. I don't know why you chose Hugo over me, perhaps I'll never know, but I understand how it happened.'

'I hope that helps.'

'It is what it is.' Freddy pulled her closer. 'Think about nice things.'

'Chocolate cake.' More tears.

'If we're going to die, can I kiss you?'

Really? Trapped in a bear pit and this was what Freddy wanted to do in their final hours?

'It might stave off the cold.'

'Good chat up line.' She turned in his arms and kissed him. A tentative kiss.

Freddy kissed her back, and his kisses had a new, ruthless edge. They progressed fast and she went with it. Superior strength and heightened senses...

A glorious last-night stand.

Three hours later, Sophie was woken by a surge of pleasure and realised her toes weren't numb.

'My darling girl.'

If they hadn't been facing painful oblivion, she'd have had a serious talk with Freddy about consent issues. Whoever he married would have been grateful in the long run. Except there wasn't a long run—

Another glorious ripple.

'I don't care if I die now,' Freddy mumbled against her mouth.

She bloody did. New tears for Hugo and Charlotte slid down her cheeks.

Sophie shifted position, and Freddy murmured something unintelligible. He moved, and she shuddered against him.

Entangled. Freddy's sleep-breathing … comforting. His hand under her clothes, cupping a breast. Possessive. Protective.

A rapid slithering sound came from above.

Sophie jerked wide awake in a panic. Too dark to see anything. '*Freddy.*'

'Whaaat is it?'

'A snake.' The noise had changed to swishing. A committed animal lover, but snakes creeped her out. She zipped open the inner sleeping bag, then the outer one and felt about for the holdall.

She found the knife.

Freddy was on his feet. 'Oh my God.' The creature was hanging down, swaying.

'Shush. Listen for it.' Sophie swiped with the knife, met only air, and a beam of dazzling light shone into her face, making her as blind in the light beam as she'd been in the dark.

She looked up, shielding her eyes. What she'd thought was a snake was a rope, swaying above her.

'Hugo, is that you?' Sophie whispered, not daring to believe it.

'Who else would it be?' Hugo peered at them.

Charlotte was beside him.

Both safe and well. Giddy with relief, Sophie returned the knife to her bag.

'I've put the rope around a tree for leverage,' said Hugo.

'You go first, Freddy,' said Sophie. 'You're taller.' The rope didn't extend far into the pit.

Freddy leapt and easily caught the rope. He hauled himself up the vertical wall, hand over hand on the rope, and scrambled over the rim, clumps of earth bouncing onto Sophie.

'I don't need the rope around the tree trunk.' Freddy rearranged the rope and threw it into the pit. It reached further.

Sophie secured the rope on the holdalls and saddlebags. Freddy lifted them out and threw the rope again.

She walked backwards, then ran forward and jumped, grabbing the rope. Freddy pulled hard. She whizzed over the edge and fell flat. The next moment, Charlotte was licking her face.

After embracing Charlotte, Sophie hugged Hugo, breathing him in.

The horses were restless, whinnying. Hugo fed them loaves from a bulging hessian sack, and they happily chomped.

'What are you giving them?' asked Freddy.

'Bread made for horses.' Hugo shone the torch at the horses' hooves. 'The sword's just there.'

Sophie retrieved the sword, they untied the horses, and mindful of bear pits, they led them cautiously, keeping near the trees.

As she walked, Sophie squirmed, reliving the last few hours with Freddy, and she adjusted her hood to hide her face. 'Rest before calling the lift?'

Freddy patted his horse. 'Agreed.'

'Can you find that forest cave?' said Hugo to Charlotte. 'The one with the water?'

She nodded her huge head.

Half an hour later, in the cave, Hugo filled travel mugs with water, and Sophie and Freddy gulped it down. He handed them bread rolls, and they ate, hardly pausing to breathe.

'The first two days, there was no traffic,' said Hugo. 'The next day, only a wagon with wine, but yesterday, we got lucky. Food and the horse bread, as well as the rope.'

Charlotte buried herself in her sleeping bag, Freddy climbed into his, but Sophie couldn't settle. She slipped off her cloak and scooped water into her mug.

Hugo stared at her chest. 'You and Freddy? *No.*'

Her ski jacket wasn't closed, and her merino top was open to the waist, revealing a gaping bodice. Sophie zipped her top shut, anguish twisting her stomach. 'Must have loosened when Freddy hauled me over the side of the pit.'

Hugo thinned his lips into a sceptical line. 'Lucky the zip didn't break.'

Sophie flushed, turned her back to scoop more water. How had she forgotten to sort her clothes—

Hugo strode over and put his fingers under her chin, forcing her head up.

She shut her eyes. She'd regret making out with Freddy for the rest of her life. Stupid, *stupid*. 'Too tired to talk. Tomorrow?'

Hugo stepped away from her, his face ashen. 'I'm done talking.'

CHAPTER 37

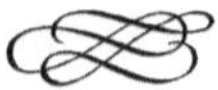

In the morning, Sophie was woken in the cave by
Charlotte snuggling closer, but she pretended to
be asleep, not ready to face Hugo. Or Freddy.

'Are you going to explain, Freddy?' Hugo's voice was
dangerously soft.

'Explain what?' whispered Freddy.

'You and Sophie.'

Silence.

'We thought you and Charlotte were dead, that we'd die. I
take full responsibility.' Freddy sounded smug, not contrite.
'She's not at fault.'

'Is your jaw broken? Have you bruises from her punches?'

'Of course not.'

'She's as strong as you. The idea that you forced yourself
on her is laughable.'

'I meant nothing of that kind,' said Freddy. 'I only mean …
I started it. We were terribly cold. We kissed and—'

'Spare me the details.'

'I'm not sorry.'

'I know.'

Sophie kept her eyes shut, reliving making out with reckless abandon… What she wouldn't give for a better time-turner, and *not* sleep with Freddy.

Someone nudged her arm, and she sat up. Freddy handed her a mug of water and a lump of mould-free cheese, and she focused on eating.

After they'd fed the horses, Sophie marshalled her courage. 'Hugo, we need to talk.'

Hugo picked up his holdall. 'I told you, I've no interest in talking or anything else.'

His indifference hit her like a punch. Freddy patted her shoulder, but she couldn't be comforted. She blinked hard.

Weeks ago, when Freddy hadn't cared if he lived or died, Sophie thought she'd understood. But now she *felt* it: hopelessness, pierced through with numb detachment.

In the woods, as Sophie led Black Beauty towards the road, Charlotte stayed close — not judging.

On the deserted highway, they rode at a steady pace under a clear sky. Up ahead, tendrils of sea mist trailed about the cliff.

Something glinted where the road curved beyond the headland.

Metal?

Freddy pulled on his reins, his horse snorting. 'Into the forest. *Move.*'

He wheeled back to the treeline, Charlotte darted after him, and Sophie and Hugo followed.

But before she and Hugo made the trees, from around the bend, riders appeared. A horn sounded, and Hugo's horse reared, spooked. Hugo fell off and lay winded.

His horse bolted, and Black Beauty tensed and snorted. Could they both ride Black Beauty? Hugo staggered to his feet.

The warriors advanced, more riders behind them. A

jarring riot of bright tunics: blue, scarlet, green. Some wore brown leather jerkins, grey armour, and fur hats. All carried weapons: scimitars, long swords, and bows. More came into view, then more.

The Mongol army.

Oh God.

If they went into the forest, these men would follow, hunt them down. 'I've got this. *Go.*'

Hugo hesitated.

Sophie drew the sword from the scabbard. '*Go.*'

Hugo dashed to the trees.

'The songs say Dali *smites invaders.*' Underneath Sophie, Black Beauty trembled. 'Let's hope it's true.'

Charlotte sprinted onto the road and stood majestically beside them.

'Your bark won't work,' hissed Sophie. 'Hide in the woods.'

Charlotte turned her head. Her large golden eyes met Sophie's, her meaning unmistakable. 'Staying.'

'I love you.' Sophie swallowed.

Sunlight glimmered on a burnished shield, a mocking reminder of 'mirroring.' What if she couldn't stop? Dread filled her, and she struggled to focus.

Just the front line. The rest will surrender.

Charlotte did a warning roar, only lasting a moment.

Sophie raised the sword high, but the soldiers set their bows. 'Stop.' Her voice rang with authority, resonating as loud as Charlotte's temple-bark. 'I am Dali.' Deep breath. 'And invading armies *piss me off.*'

The warriors put their hands over their ears, and their horses stamped and brayed.

Don't think about the horses.

She stared, pictured blood heating and boiling, thick and sweet and powerful, and screams rent the air.

Sophie was out of her body, watching from the sky. The girl on the horse with the sword was glowing. Edged in gold, like a terrifying angel. Her wolf glowed too. Men and horses before them flailed and fell. On and on, as inexorable as the waves crashing on the beach.

Stop. *Stop.*

She was back on Black Beauty, but a heat stirred in Sophie's belly, swirling and bubbling, mimicking the red whirlpool raging in her thoughts. Her senses sharpened until they sang and hurt: every shriek of agony, a taste of rust and decay, and a syrupy smell that threatened to suffocate her.

Thumping. Dead birds landed on the highway.

A pulsing energy soared through her, driving her on, and she rode through the carnage with Charlotte, seeking out survivors.

When the last man and horse dropped, Sophie looked around, surprised. She pulled up Black Beauty and Charlotte halted.

Sophie strained to empty her mind. 'No more. *End* this.'

But the image in her brain eddied and boiled and surged. She let go the sword and tumbled from the saddle, her own blood screaming for release.

CHAPTER 38

Two hours after he'd fled into the forest, Freddy cautiously emerged on foot onto the coastal highway, the pendant in his pocket. As it wouldn't work for Hugo, Freddy had ordered him to stay with the horses.

Corpses filled the road, and Freddy paused, taking it in. Only a few miles north was the remains of the queen's army. A double graveyard.

Freddy picked his way, trying not to step on men and horses and birds. Snow fell, muffling the sound of the surf on the beach.

Half an hour later, he spotted Charlotte by a horse, a live one. Charlotte was licking the face of someone on the ground.

Please God. No.

Sophie was on her back, the hood of her cloak pinned under her.

Her face was screwed up, whether in pain or concentration, Freddy couldn't tell. A wide scarlet strip ran across her cheekbones.

The sword lay beside her, the blade filthy with dirt from the road.

'My darling girl. Wake up. Please wake up.' He knelt and touched her face. The red mark was part of her skin. A tattoo.

She was cold as marble. But for that, she could have been sleeping. Grief blotted out the scene surrounding him, and he lowered his head towards his knees.

Charlotte nuzzled into him, and he forced himself to stand. He draped Sophie's body over her horse, returned the sword to its scabbard on the saddlebag, and retraced his steps, Charlotte leading the way. Snow blew in gusts around them, but Freddy didn't notice, walking in a daze.

Just before they left the road, Sophie moaned. *Not* dead. Freddy leaned against the horse and cried.

In the forest, Hugo jumped up from a fallen tree he'd been sitting on. 'She's—'

'Alive, but that's all.' Freddy laid Sophie down, eliciting another moan.

Hugo trickled water from his travel mug into her mouth. She spluttered and opened her eyes, staring but unseeing. He tipped in more and she swallowed it.

'Not real. Gone. Gone.' Her eyes rolled.

'What's gone?' said Hugo.

'Even the birds.' She held her head in her hands.

'She wiped out the whole army,' said Freddy. The memory would haunt his dreams.

Sophie rocked like a lunatic in Bedlam. 'My voice was as deep as Charlotte's temple bark. So loud…'

Hugo set out a sleeping bag, and Freddy carried her over to it and zipped her inside. Eventually, she fell asleep.

'You found your horse.' Freddy tied up Sophie's horse by the others.

'Yes.' Hugo sat on the fallen tree. 'Hadn't gone far.'

'We can put this behind us.' Freddy wanted with all his heart to believe that. He sat on the tree too.

'I don't know her.' Hugo stared at Sophie, asleep in the sleeping bag. 'Perhaps I never did?'

'She's still Sophie. It's this place. It's done something to her.'

'This world only gave her the ability,' said Hugo, his expression grim. 'She *chose* to use it.'

CHAPTER 39

Sophie slept through the night.

But she woke up struggling to think straight. Dawning consciousness from an unnaturally deep sleep brought disbelief — and mounting horror. All those men and horses dying... No, not real.

She could hear soft breathing. Charlotte was asleep, lying next to her, and so were Freddy and Hugo.

The pure scent of water and the rich sound of it running over stone were familiar. She was in the hidden cave in the woods — not far from the lift.

Her mouth tasted strange, and something was caked on her lips. She rubbed it off with the back of her hand. Dried blood. She touched her tongue. The tips of her fingers came away sticky and red. She sat up with a jolt. The last man falling, his eyes bulging, bleeding, then *nothing*.

She unzipped her sleeping bag, ran to the rear of the cave, and frantically scooped water into her mouth.

'Sophie.' Freddy jumped out of his sleeping bag and strode over to her. She straightened, and he gathered her into his arms. She tried to relax against him, but the cries of the dying filled her mind — on and on. Would they ever stop?

He stroked her hair. 'Let's go home.'

Hugo discarded his sleeping bag and walked out of the cave without speaking or looking at her, and she sobbed into Freddy's chest.

By the time Hugo returned, she'd pulled herself together. Crying had been cathartic, and the screams in her head had stopped.

She patted Charlotte and squared her shoulders. Nearly at the lift. Focus on home.

They saddled up and left the forest.

The sky was clear, the morning tide was out, and there was beach all the way to the lift cave.

'The road's too difficult for the horses,' said Sophie. Not about to go there. The corpses were too close together.

Charlotte rushed ahead, joyfully racing in front of the waves, and Sophie guided Black Beauty down a grassy bank onto the sand.

Hugo was ignoring her, and despite Freddy's comforting embrace, he seemed distant too. Why was that a surprise? What she'd done was horrible. Beyond horrible. But she'd saved them and Charlotte, all the while being certain she would die. Surely, that should count for something. Yes, yes it did. Yet the fact remained: she *deserved* to die for what she had done.

The taste of blood lingered in her mouth, cakey and steel-sweet. She leaned to the right and spat on the sand. Naga's 'mirroring' tale was a centuries-old lie, invented to deter women from using this power — or curse. She closed her palm over the pendant stone in her pocket. Likely, the 'getting trapped in the near past' warning was also fiction.

The sea sparkled in the winter sun, and she breathed in the clean, icy air, invigorated. Invincible.

She tugged on the reins, Black Beauty stopped, and Sophie's thoughts returned to Naga. Wiping out the Mongol army had well and truly trashed the timeline, so why not trash it more? If she chose to, she could overthrow the queen… End executions and torture, protect the innocent. Bring in a golden age of science and reason—

'Sophie?' Hugo had turned around, pausing his horse.

'I thought you weren't interested in talking.'

'Don't become the red goddess.' Hugo met her eyes. 'Just because you can.'

Sophie broke eye contact. It sucked that he'd guessed her thoughts.

Hugo charged towards the cave, his cloak flying up behind him. Freddy was almost at the entrance, Charlotte beside him.

Outside the cave, released by Hugo and Freddy, the horses galloped riderless along the beach. Black Beauty snorted, wanting to join them.

Moments later, the cave interior lit up. Freddy must have said 'Janus' out loud. Evidently, that worked fine, regardless of what choices she and Freddy had made.

But Sophie didn't move Black Beauty on, needed to think.

The memory of yesterday turned her stomach — that part of the ability was *not* addictive — but now, her reputation alone could help people. She relished the sea air in her lungs and stretched her arms up to the sky. Obviously, she'd need to kill the queen…

Don't become the red goddess, just because you can.

Her dead parents' faces appeared in her mind. How proud they'd been of her… She bowed her head.

How she'd physically changed here was messing with her brain. She wasn't divine. Only a flawed human with a saviour complex.

Reach the lift. Get home.

But where was home? Not Hugo's house. The Manor in Shorten? Her aunt's house in Buckinghamshire?

Sophie urged Black Beauty into a gallop by the breaking waves. Her hood fell back, her hair loose, and she enjoyed the moment.

Until she spotted movement on the road.

She slowed Black Beauty to a walk. Mongol reinforcements swarmed like flies over their fallen comrades. And they'd spotted her, several riding over the dunes.

Sophie drew her sword and held it aloft. 'Stop.' Her command boomed over the shore.

The warriors covered their ears, their horses bumping into each other.

She coaxed Black Beauty into the sea. The horse whinnied in protest. Still holding the sword, Sophie dismounted and gasped as the icy water hit her thighs. She grabbed her holdall. 'Run free.' She patted her gratefully and Black Beauty shot off down the beach.

The soldiers muttered to each other and pointed at her. She secured the rucksack on her shoulders and waded out of the surf, holding up the sword. Before she reached the shoreline, she slipped on the pendant. Hopefully, the disappearing act would divert the Mongols from the lit-up cave.

The faded soldiers advanced cautiously, and Sophie ran past them. Her sodden boots pushed against the sand, her wet skin burned with the cold, but not far to the lift—

A blonde girl and a wolf materialised in front of her, and Sophie careered to a halt in shock.

The wolf was bigger than Charlotte, sleek and black, with a bejewelled collar and a gold chain about its neck. The girl was tall, her long hair thick and wavy. On her wrist was a bracelet of the same design as the wolf's collar and, seemingly impervious to the temperature, she wore strappy sandals and a silk red dress that undulated in the wind. She carried a curved bow of burnished wood and a sheaf of arrows.

Sophie tried to gather her wits. 'Where have you come from? How can you see me?'

The girl touched a pendant around her neck. The ruby tourmaline gem glittered.

Another time-turner. And the chain on the wolf must be another. This wasn't an apparition, but a flesh and blood person, a nano-second in the past like her.

'We are sisters, you and I.' The girl's words had the same mechanical clipped cadence as Naga's, and she had a similar feline grace, except her pale skin had a youthful glow.

What had Naga said? '*When I first arrived, there were faulty 'priority interest' alerts, but they quickly recalibrated.*' This girl and the wolf had been living here for centuries, right under Naga's nose.

'There can only be one Dali.' The girl set her bow and shot Sophie.

The arrow tore through Sophie's clothes and pierced her thigh with a thwack. In a trice, the girl darted forward, wrenched off Sophie's pendant, and vanished.

The feather fletching and shaft sticking out of Sophie's cloak quivered. Disbelief gave way to panic.

No, she'd be okay. The lift would sort this. *Move.*

Inside the cave, Hugo and Freddy were standing on the lift threshold with Charlotte.

'*Sophie.*' Freddy's smile died when he saw the arrow.

A pins and needles sensation pooled in her leg and she toppled sideways. The sword landed on the cave floor with a clang.

Freddy cradled her in his arms, and carried her in, Charlotte at his heels. Hugo dragged the sword inside.

As Freddy laid her down, agonising pain ripped through her guts, and she doubled over.

'Hell…o,' said a melodious baritone voice. 'Always such a pretty one.'

Dizzy and nauseous, Sophie managed to say, 'Wolfsbane.'

'Cure her,' said Freddy.

'Janus cannot.' The deep voice held no regret.

CHAPTER 40

$\mathcal{A}$s the lift doors rattled shut, Sophie writhed in agony, her screams echoing in the enclosed space.

Hugo fought to think straight as her cries pierced and splintered inside his head. The memory of the Mongols' prisoner, shot with an arrow and left to die in the woods, played in his mind, the sound of the man's screams mixing in with Sophie's.

Hugo sobbed. Helplessness, anguish...

He would *not* let Sophie die in such pain. The dagger in his holdall... A terrible choice. But killing her quickly would stop her agony—

'*Why* can't you save her?' shouted Freddy over Sophie's screaming.

'You cured me and Charlotte before,' yelled Hugo. '*Please cure her.*'

Janus didn't answer.

'Answer Hugo as you would me,' ordered Freddy.

'A simple task to suture Charlotte's wound,' said Janus, 'or straighten your broken nose.' A mechanical arm shot out of a wall, its metal hand fitted with alarming sharp tools. Charlotte leapt out of the way, barging into Freddy.

'Time healed you before,' said Janus. 'A friend. Wolfsbane spreads in but a few breaths. Time is Sophie Arundel's enemy.' The metal arm folded back.

Hugo steeled himself and took the dagger from his bag.

'Surely you can stop time or pause it?' Freddy noticed the dagger and froze.

'Deep stasis would slow change,' said Janus. 'Pause the poison.'

'Do that,' said Freddy, his voice cracking. '*Now.*'

A faint azure barrier appeared around Sophie, outlining the shape of her, including the arrow. Her screaming stopped abruptly.

Hugo was still gripping the dagger. 'Is she asleep? Has the pain gone?'

'She feels nothing,' said Janus. 'Suspended between breaths.'

Trembling, Hugo returned the dagger to the holdall and gave in to more tears — of relief. Freddy watched him, blinking hard.

In stasis, Sophie was curled up, her skin grey, the red line across her face gone.

The arrow jutted out of her cloak like a snapped bone. Hugo closed his eyes against the image. Should *never* have left her alone on the beach—

'Can we take the arrow out?' Freddy shrugged off his cloak and jacket and sat near Sophie.

'To remove the arrow, time for Sophie Arundel must restart.' Janus' voice was gravel-deep enough for a Hollywood movie trailer, except his accent was clipped and British, presumably based on Freddy's accent.

'Don't touch the arrow,' said Freddy. Charlotte sat beside him and placed a large paw over his hand.

'She lives, Freddy Lacey,' said Janus. 'Do not grieve yet.'

Hugo removed his cloak, jacket and merino top, and rolled up his shirt sleeves. He sat down on the floor, resting his head against the wall, fear and stress draining him of energy. 'How long can you keep her in stasis?'

'Until the last universe ends.' Janus' attitude was smug. 'In a quantum state, time has no meaning.'

Hugo thought about Janus' bizarre greeting to Sophie. *Always such a pretty one.* 'You see beyond linear time in multiple universes?'

'I do.'

'Has this happened to Sophie before?' asked Hugo. 'Other versions of her?'

'It has.'

'So, you know,' said Hugo, 'whether she survives?'

'Sophie Arundel lives, or dies, longs for death, or chooses to die. All has happened, is happening, and will happen. Probability is in flux. Janus cannot alter what is.'

Unhelpful, and referring to yourself in the third person, even allowing for software translation, wasn't a good sign.

'We must work to affect the probability,' said Freddy. 'Janus, what do you know about wolfsbane?'

'*Aconitum napellus.* Also named monkshood. Efficient poison, widely used.' Janus' eager tone suggested delight in showing off his knowledge and — eerily like Naga — zero empathy.

'Why is it called Monkshood and Wolfsbane?' Freddy's eyes were fixed on Sophie.

'The flowers resemble a monk's hood,' said Janus. 'The Latin word, Aconite, comes from the Greek ἀκόνιτον. "Without dust, without struggle." Even werewolves succumb.'

'Werewolves are real?' blurted Hugo.

'In some universes. In others, your brethren use wolfsbane for executions.'

Freddy shook his head. 'We don't—'

'Do not question.' Janus' booming voice hardened, making the hairs on Hugo's neck stand up.

'When I walked among you, Janus saw all. Remembers all.'

'Is there an antidote?' said Freddy.

'In some worlds,' said Janus.

'So, if we went to one of those,' said Hugo, 'she'd survive?'

'Creatures do not help those who appear different, who cannot communicate intentions or need.'

'Would a hospital in my universe save her?' said Hugo.

'Possibly.'

'Take us to the twenty-first century,' said Freddy, as if instructing his chauffeur.

'To be specific,' added Hugo, 'universe 666.'

'Yes,' said Freddy. The lift tilted. 'Should we tie Sophie to the rail?'

'Sophie Arundel is tethered,' said Janus, 'and Charlotte needs no assistance.'

Charlotte was holding onto a rail with her front paws. In the midst of astounding things, not so astounding. 'When we land,' said Hugo, 'can you keep Sophie in stasis after you open the doors, right until the moment I fetch medics?'

Freddy nodded.

'Of course.' Janus sounded bored.

'You've seen so much, know so much,' said Hugo, hoping flattery would glean more information. 'Is there anything else that could save her life?'

'Her fate lies in your hands.'

Annoyingly cryptic.

'How long before we get there?' asked Freddy.

'That depends.' Janus' words were ponderous, theatrical. 'Rotating black holes allow matter to slip from one universe to another, but they're unstable.'

'We're in a black hole?' Hugo gulped.

'We are,' said Janus. 'At the centre, there is an opening, but the exit is tricky to navigate. The end of the passage thrashes like a snake's tail.'

Hugo hugged himself. 'Why does the length of crossings vary?'

'Janus cannot control time outside. Only within. If travellers are hurt, time accelerates to heal an injury, while separately slowing for the rest of their body.'

'That's remarkable,' said Freddy.

Stay with the flattery. 'You're the Master of Time.'

'Janus is the first and the last. My builders dictated my choices, always to benefit *them*, but they feared sentience. After Janus, ships were hamstrung, mere rowing boats.'

Not quite what Naga had told them.

'Since you've been sentient,' said Freddy, 'you've still chosen to help travellers, to protect them?'

'As biological creatures have primary elements, so has Janus.'

'Why didn't you wait to release the doors,' said Hugo, 'until the tide was out?'

'You were not harmed.'

So, Janus couldn't act — or fail to act — to cause actual physical harm, but Naga's take on him had been spot on. *He seeks entertainment. Travellers and their struggles provide that.*

'You access the thoughts of individuals with the gene,' said Hugo, 'but not those without it?'

'There is no need with lesser beings.'

Yet again, pet status had advantages.

Freddy sighed. 'Can you make it a little less hot?'

'You only have to ask,' said Janus.

'Twenty-two centigrade,' clarified Hugo. 'Seventy Fahrenheit.'

'A nice temperature,' said Freddy. 'Why did you send us to Georgia?'

'*Do your worst* is not a destination. You gave Janus discretion. A rare pleasure. Janus was … benevolent.'

Hugo shuddered. Freddy had given Janus an a la carte menu of the worst periods of history.

'Why didn't you appear when I called you in my head?' said Freddy.

'Your longing for death was stronger than your companions' wish to travel.'

Freddy flinched.

'Sleep now.'

Hugo sprinted out of the lift into a crowded students' union and collided with a dark-haired girl in torn jeans and a black T-shirt.

She glanced up from her phone, surprised.

'Sorry, I need to call 999.' A whiff of her flowery perfume made him sneeze. 'Can I use your phone?'

'Okay…' She reluctantly handed it over. 'How's the games convention?'

'What?'

'I'm guessing you're into Lord of the Rings. Cool Gandalf cloak.'

'Thanks.' Hugo hit the numbers. He must have put on his ski clothes and cloak when he'd woken in the lift, though he had no memory of doing so.

'What service do you require?' A woman's voice. Calm, practised.

'Ambulance. No, air ambulance.' He stumbled over the words.

A click and a different voice. 'Where are you?'

'The students' union in Little Shorten, Derbyshire. My

friend has been poisoned with wolfsbane. It's quick acting. Fatal.'

'What's your name?'

'Hugo Harrington. I'm using a stranger's phone.'

'Thank you. We're experiencing delays—'

'She's *dying*.' Dealing with someone who couldn't deviate from a script, Hugo's resolute calm shattered.

A click, then a new call handler. 'Did she ingest the poison?'

'No. Poisoned arrow.'

An intake of breath down the line. 'Has the arrow pierced the flesh?'

'Yes.'

'What is the patient's age, gender, and medical history?'

'Twenty, female, no medical problems.'

'Is she unconscious, breathing or not breathing?'

'Unconscious.' He had no idea whether Sophie was breathing, but hopefully once she came out of stasis, she would be. 'Breathing.'

'Where is the injury?'

'Thigh.'

'Any serious bleeding?'

'I don't know.'

'Is the area safe?'

'Yes.'

'Can you stay on the line?'

Hugo looked at the girl for confirmation and she nodded. 'Yes,' he blurted into the phone, beyond glad Sophie was in stasis.

Inside the open lift, the barrier surrounding Sophie shimmered, azure but faint under the bright chandelier. Freddy was pacing in his cloak while Charlotte sat in guard-mode, still and alert next to Sophie.

'Where's your injured friend?' The girl looked around, her eyes sliding past the lift, oblivious.

'I don't want to move her,' said Hugo, 'not till the ambulance arrives.'

'Messing with a poisoned arrow is dumb.' The girl frowned.

Hugo struggled to think, stress dulling his brain. *Shot in a parallel universe* would get him sectioned. 'We're studying the use of plants in warfare. She was analysing the arrow in the lab and slipped.'

He spent the next thirty minutes listening to the call-handler's updates on the ambulance, confirming his location by the lifts, and fobbing off the girl's questions about plant-based poisons.

The noise of a helicopter sounded outside the hall. Hugo handed back the phone.

Medics in fluorescent jackets ran towards them and Hugo called to Freddy. 'It's time.'

Janus dropped the stasis field and Freddy picked up Sophie. He staggered out, Sophie thrashing in his arms, her screams rending the air.

Freddy set her down on the students' union floor, careful not to knock the arrow protruding through her cloak. The medics ran forward, and students scurried to let them through. Sophie's screams had silenced the hall.

Hugo fought an irrational urge to push the ambulance crew aside to comfort her. He bunched his fists. *Please, please stop the pain.*

The medics transferred Sophie to a stretcher and jogged with her to the helicopter, and Hugo slumped onto a plastic chair.

Charlotte pawed at him in distress, and he stroked her. She'd shrunk to her normal size and the silver streaks in her brown fur had gone.

Freddy was back inside the lift. Going to Shorten? *No. Too upset—*

But Freddy came out, pulling the holdalls along the floor. He left them, wiped his eyes, returned to the lift, and re-emerged, dragging the sword behind him.

The hall was noisy again. Students were talking and pointing at Freddy, filming him.

'Come on,' said Freddy.

Hugo forced himself to his feet. 'Come on … where?'

'Elliot and Lorna's flat.'

Hugo hoisted a holdall on to his shoulders and held another. Freddy grabbed the last bag with his free hand and Hugo followed him and Charlotte across the hall, keeping his distance to avoid the dragged sword.

In a dingy corridor, Freddy knocked on a plywood door numbered 0001. The first 0 was loose and swung slightly.

Elliot opened the door and gaped.

'Apologies for calling unannounced,' said Freddy. 'May we come in?'

Inside, Freddy laid down the sword. 'It's rather heavy.' He shrugged off his cloak.

Charlotte bounded in and Hugo shut the door, taking in a neat flat. He removed his cloak and jacket. 'Sophie's been poisoned.'

'Oh, God,' said Elliot, 'Novichok.'

After weeks of interpreting Russian, Hugo automatically translated, though it made no sense. 'New boy.'

Elliot frowned. 'No, the Salisbury poisonings.'

'Sorry?' said Hugo.

Elliot tapped his phone and showed it to Hugo. *It is now clear that the Russian defector Sergei Skripal and his daughter were poisoned with Novichok. The nerve agent can be inhaled, could have killed thousands...*

'What's the date today?' asked Hugo.

'23rd March,' said Elliot. 'Friday.'

The door swung open, and Lorna walked in with Fudge. Charlotte rushed to greet them, almost knocking Lorna over. Lorna regained her balance and patted her. 'There's been another poisoning, right here, in the students' union.'

'Nothing to do with Salisbury,' said Hugo. 'Sophie's been poisoned with wolfsbane.'

Lorna shook her head. 'Is that better or worse than Novichok?'

'I guess … better,' said Hugo. 'It won't poison anyone else.'

'Here's the stuff Sophie gave me for safekeeping.' Elliot rummaged in a kitchen cupboard. As he handed the plastic bag to Hugo, Elliot's phone bleeped. 'Message from the dean. Suspected Novichok attack.'

Elliot gulped. 'We're in lockdown.'

CHAPTER 42

For four days, Freddy and Hugo were obliged to stay with Lorna and Elliot, sleeping on their living room floor. Along with the other students living in the tower block, they subsisted on sandwiches delivered by people in grey chemical suits. On the fifth morning, the government's facility at Porton Down finally ruled out Novichok, and they were free to leave.

Straight away, they called a taxi to the hospital, leaving Lorna to watch Charlotte.

Twenty minutes later, before they reached the reception desk, Hugo grabbed Freddy's arm. 'Remember, as far as the hospital's concerned, you're Sophie's husband and I'm her brother.'

Directed upstairs, they eventually found the intensive care ward. A slight girl was connected to machines, a shiny mask over her face.

'Is that her?' said Freddy, his heart sinking.

Hugo pointed to a card on the wall above the bed. *Sophie Arundel.*

'Her hair's thinner and straighter,' said Freddy, fighting

tears. Sophie's blonde tresses lay loose over the pillow. 'Not like a goddess.'

Hugo blinked. 'No. Just a girl.'

~

Later that morning, Freddy stood up from the hard chair beside Sophie's hospital bed, stretched, and sat down again. His anguish ebbed and flowed, his emotions swinging between boredom and despair. The air smelled of disinfectant, and bleeps and blinking lights came from the machines, but Sophie's eyelids didn't flicker, and her mouth was slack. He held her limp hand. Warm. Try to take comfort from that—

'We've been here for two hours,' said Hugo.

'Seems *much* longer.'

'I think hospitals have time-turners. One for medics where time races, one for relatives where it crawls.'

A tall man in green trousers and a matching tunic came in. 'Consultant for critical care. Which of you is Ms Arundel's partner?'

Partner?

'Husband,' said Hugo.

Freddy jumped to his feet.

'Sophie's very poorly, I'm afraid. She's not able to breathe independently, but the main problem is her heart. Her blood pressure's low and her heart rate is highly elevated. If that doesn't change, you need to prepare yourself for the worst.'

Freddy's brain went blank, and he couldn't take in the man's words.

'... rhythm abnormalities,' said the consultant. 'We're treating her with Amiodarone and electric therapy and she's on extracorporeal life support.'

'What sort of support?' asked Hugo.

'Cardiopulmonary bypass, sustaining her lungs and heart.'

After the consultant left, Freddy took Sophie's hand. The machine keeping her alive bleeped, detached and constant, but Freddy found no consolation in its efficiency. 'This helpless limbo is unbearable.'

Hugo didn't reply. Sitting on the other side of the bed, his tall frame was hunched and his face gaunt.

When a nurse cajoled them into visiting the hospital café, Freddy nibbled at a sandwich, and Hugo gave up on his. Eating, doing *anything* normal, seemed … wrong.

'What I prayed for has happened,' said Freddy, dropping his half-eaten meal in a bin.

They walked towards the stairs that led to intensive care.

'*Do your worst.*' Freddy frowned in despair.

'Janus took us to medieval Georgia, but he has no agency outside the lift,' said Hugo. 'Whoever shot Sophie on that beach bears responsibility, *not* you.'

'After you came to Shorten, everything that's ensued since then…' Freddy wiped his eyes, anger joining despair. 'Was this always where it was going to end?'

Hugo hesitated. 'When I was at school with Sophie, I knew we were somehow connected. But I didn't believe in fate. I didn't want to.' They climbed the stairs side by side. 'I only crossed universes because my life is so entangled with hers, in the past, in the present and in the future.' At the top of the stairs, Hugo paused, his expression grim. 'You're connected too.'

'There's a tugging feeling, drawing me to her. Will that go, if—'

'I don't know.' Hugo's voice faltered. He turned and hurried to the ward and Freddy followed.

A thin woman with grey bobbed hair and a pointed chin was standing by Sophie's bed, writing on a chart. 'I'm Miss Weir. The toxicologist.' She gestured for them to leave the ward and they stepped into the corridor. 'Wolfsbane poisoning is very rare. Not ingested is even rarer, and the wolfsbane is an unknown variety.' She sighed. 'This is a wait and see.'

Hugo nodded, as if what the woman had said was helpful.

Back in the ward, Freddy sat in the bedside chair. *Wait and see.* For days? Weeks? He rocked on the chair, only stopping when Hugo's hand rested on his shoulder. Before he registered what he was doing, Freddy patted Hugo's hand.

Hugo sat on another chair, and Freddy made himself take slow breaths. After a while, though Naga's revelations had undermined his faith, he prayed.

Hours later, the nurse told them to go home.

'Home is far away,' said Freddy.

The nurse gave him a leaflet with a list of local hotels.

Freddy drew up his knees on the hotel bed. The inane chatter on the television in the evenings distracted him from thinking about Sophie.

They'd been staying in the 'chain hotel' as Hugo called it for a week. During the day, they sat with Sophie in the hospital, read to her, or played music. A horrible re-run of his own near-death experience. During the evening, time dragged even more. He hated the hospital, but he hated *not* being there. What if she woke up when they weren't there? What if the machine preventing her dying went wrong?

'In this universe, medieval Georgians didn't speak Russian, and at lot of Georgian cuisine is vegetables.' Hugo scrolled on his phone. 'And their wine is world famous. Interesting.'

In other circumstances, it would have been. Reciting new facts at least passed the time. Freddy tapped on his phone.

'The Mongol hordes drank horse-blood here. They'd slit a minor vein, drink it neat or mix it with milk or water.'

'In the end, Sophie made the right choice.'

'Choosing to be with me, you mean?' said Freddy. 'So much has happened…'

'No, choosing to come back.'

'What will you do, if…' Freddy looked down at his knees.

'I guess I'll go home. I can't think beyond that.' Hugo pushed his fringe away from his eyes. 'You should wait a few months before trying to cross.'

Freddy raised his head. 'You'd let me stay with you?'

'Of course, Freddy. Of course.'

Two days later, at ten in the morning, they approached Sophie's ward. Miss Weir was there and asked them to accompany her into a small, empty room.

Hugo's face fell. 'Side rooms are used to tell people bad news.'

Freddy steeled himself and sat beside Hugo at a desk across from Miss Weir.

But Miss Weir gave them an encouraging smile. 'Sophie's breathing on her own and she's awake.'

'What about her heart?' said Freddy.

'Almost normal, and the final test results included a surprise. She's pregnant.' Miss Weir smiled again. 'I hope that's welcome news. Around five weeks.'

'Pregnant,' said Hugo.

Freddy opened his mouth, but no words came out.

Miss Weir left the room, and Freddy said half to himself, 'How on earth can Sophie be *pregnant*?'

Hugo stood up abruptly, the metal chair legs scraping on

the hard floor. 'I imagine in the usual way.' He chewed his lip. 'Apart from conceiving in a bear pit.'

Freddy shook his head. 'But if she's *five* weeks pregnant—'

'You're the maths genius. We've been back two weeks, so we must have been in the lift for three weeks.'

A surge of joy flooded through Freddy, and he leapt to his feet. 'That means … she's carrying my baby!'

Hugo compressed his lips. 'Yes, that *is* what it means.'

'She'll be pleased,' said Freddy. 'Ladies like babies.'

Hugo briefly closed his eyes, seemed pained. 'I have no idea how she'll react, but for now, unless Sophie brings it up, don't mention it. She'll be in no state to cope with this.'

CHAPTER 43

That afternoon, Sophie was wheeled out of intensive care on a trolley. The pain in her stomach and chest, the pins and needles, the blurred vision overlaid with a purple haze … all gone. Her consultant had said she'd stopped breathing, and other stuff she couldn't remember, but she'd been given the all clear.

The last thing she remembered from before the hospital was Freddy carrying her out of the lift. She wiggled her toes under a white cellular blanket, relieved to be alive, but more relieved to be free from pain. And thanks to the morphine patch on her back, she was happy, floaty.

The new ward had three other patients. A nurse helped her onto the unoccupied bed and tugged a curtain around it. 'Time to remove the patch, dear.'

Sophie didn't want it removed, but she pulled up the flimsy gown, and the nurse peeled it off. Once Sophie was settled in the bed, the nurse swished aside the curtain and set a plastic cup of water on a side table.

The water was welcome, and Sophie drank it all, but her

hand tightened on the cup. There was something wrong, just out of reach…

'Your husband and your brother will be here soon.'

Sophie narrowed her eyes. 'I'm single and an only child.'

'Confusion's normal. You've had enough Fentanyl to knock out a bear.'

A bear … *the bear pit*. Making out with Freddy, the soldiers, the girl on the beach. But not a husband and brother—

'Hey.' Hugo stood in the ward doorway. Clean-shaven, like her old Hugo. No, not *her* Hugo.

Freddy came in, sporting a neatly trimmed beard. He rushed forward but paused, as if afraid to touch her.

Sophie put the plastic cup aside. 'You're my husband and brother?'

'That's us,' said Hugo. '*Next of kin.*'

'Does my aunt know I'm here?'

'Everybody knows,' said Freddy.

Conscious of the thin hospital shift over her bare body, Sophie adjusted the white blanket over her chest. 'Where's Charlotte?'

'Safe,' said Hugo, 'with Lorna.'

'The red goddess *shot* me.'

Freddy made a disbelieving face and Hugo frowned.

'One of Naga's people, living under the radar the whole time.' Everything about Georgia seemed so distant, like it had never happened.

'Your phone.' Freddy placed it by the bed with a charger. 'And your money card.'

Sophie took the phone, welcoming the familiar feel of it. 'How long is it since we left the lift?'

'Seven days,' said Hugo.

'We know the crossing lasted three weeks,' said Freddy, 'because—'

Hugo silenced him with a look.

She knew that look. They were hiding something. But it couldn't be anything important. What was more important than not dying?

'It's been difficult,' said Hugo, 'when we thought…'

'But the hotel beds are wonderfully comfortable,' said Freddy.

'What hotel?' Sophie laid her head on the pillow.

'Rest,' said Freddy, and he strode off with Hugo.

After lunch, Miss Weir called by. 'You were confused,' she said, reading the nurse's notes, 'but you're fine now.'

Sophie's sense of smell and her hearing were dull, muffled, and she wasn't super-strong. She'd miss that. She poured herself more water and, ensuring no one was in her line of sight, gave the liquid a hot-tea stare.

Not a ripple.

She sat against the pillows, buoyed with relief, but then her mind wandered. *Hugo.* She rubbed her temples, tormented by 'if only.'

Miss Weir was still talking. '… blood tests … scan … pregnancy.'

'Sorry,' said Sophie. 'Could you repeat that?'

'The embryo is developing as it should at five weeks.'

The noise of the ward — the clink of hospital equipment, the chatter of visiting family members — faded. Sophie gripped the bed rail. 'I'm *pregnant*? Are you sure?'

'Quite sure.' Miss Weir gave her a sympathetic smile and ticked something on her clipboard. 'The critical care consultant will sign your release form on Monday.'

'What day is it today?'

'Friday. Not long before you can go home.'

Sophie's thoughts scattered. *Home.*

Aunty Wendy would have her back.

For more than an hour, Sophie lay in bed, staring at the

ceiling. Her stomach was flat, and her insides felt no different ... but Miss Weir had been breezily certain.

Face this. Be brave. But how could she possibly support a baby?

Only five weeks pregnant. No, she batted that option away. This baby was *Freddy*'s, conceived in a desperate time and place. With love.

She tried in vain to picture Freddy's reaction. Would he feel obliged to marry her, or bolt? Tears welled up. She'd have to get a job, any job. Save for when the baby's born...

Fatigue overwhelmed her, shutting down her brain, and she closed her eyes.

Over the weekend, Sophie slept through the boys' visits, and on Monday afternoon, she wasn't so exhausted, and should have got out of bed. Instead, she stayed put, teary and unsettled. Should she call an Uber, collect Charlotte and go to the station? No, say goodbye to Freddy and Hugo first.

As if she'd summoned them, they trooped in. Freddy shot her a wide, glad smile. He had a bounce in his step and despite his edgy beard, he looked boyish and upbeat. Hugo was as distant as ever, his expression impossible to read. Did they know? She fought a childish urge to hide under the bedding.

Freddy handed her a parcel and Sophie opened it. The clothes she'd ordered online before Georgia, with her faithful cardigan and new walking boots.

'Thank you,' said Sophie. 'I guess the outfit I wore in Medieval World could do with a wash.'

'All gone,' said Freddy. 'Incinerated.'

'*What*? Why?'

'They were a contamination risk,' said Freddy.

Sophie gulped.

They left the ward so she could change, and she selected jeans and a top. Her legs were shaky, and she sat down to pull on the boots.

When she was done, the boys returned, and Freddy helped her up, his arm gentle around her shoulders. 'We've hired a car.'

Hugo carried the clothes parcel, his face unreadable, while Freddy guided her towards the ward door.

'Where are we going?'

Freddy's arm was firmer about her shoulders. 'London.'

London? Hugo's house? As Freddy steered her out of the hospital, her thoughts flew off in a panic. If they knew about the baby, they'd have said. She stumbled and swore under her breath. For Hugo, this would only cement her betrayal, deepen his contempt. And Freddy would be horrified or glad or conflicted…

She'd tell them tomorrow. Pick her moment.

Two hours later, Hugo glanced in the rear-view mirror. Shortly after driving off from Lorna and Elliot's flat, Sophie had fallen asleep on the back seat and hadn't stirred.

The sword was stashed in the seat well, and Charlotte was dozing beside Sophie.

They'd agreed that Charlotte's new talents should never be shared, or she'd be prodded and analysed in a lab. When Elliot had remarked that Charlotte seemed to understand English, they'd brushed it off.

Freddy glanced over at Sophie. 'We should return to Shorten. Marry as soon as possible.'

'Don't get ahead of yourself.' Sophie was barely out of her teens, and she'd not spoken a word since the hospital. He turned off the motorway into a fast-food drive-through and ordered two burger meals and a veggie one.

Freddy tore into his burger and Charlotte shuffled forward and sniffed. 'The baby changes things. I'm clear what to do.'

'Going to the 1920s to give birth would be dangerous and stupid,' said Hugo.

'She'd be more comfortable at the Manor than in a hospital.'

'I have no idea what Sophie will do about this pregnancy, or you,' said Hugo. 'Wait, and let her have some space.'

Sophie sat up.

Freddy snorted. 'It's none of your business—'

'Bin the testosterone fest,' said Sophie. '*Please.*'

'How are you?' asked Freddy, half turning towards her.

'Shocked, knackered.' She met Hugo's eyes in the mirror. 'A ton of regret.'

Hugo held her gaze for a moment before focusing on the road. The hours and days when she'd almost died had entirely dissolved his fury. And even after wiping out an army, even after the bear pit, he wanted her. Acting on that realisation though, was too complicated.

Freddy reached for the paper bag by his feet and handed it to Sophie. The packaging rustled as she tore it open.

Charlotte's nose twitched and Hugo smiled at her in the mirror. He recognised that dog-expression. *Give Me Your Food*. The old Charlotte was still in there.

CHAPTER 44

The following morning, just after six, Sophie woke in Hugo's guest bedroom, her mind full of the pictures on the lift doors. She'd been dreaming about them.

She jumped out of bed, found her notebook in her holdall, pulled on Isobel's pink dressing gown, and relaxed against the pillows. Beside her, Charlotte stretched.

Sophie found the picture of the galloping horses on the beach. 'These riders are the boys and me.' She pointed to the wolf. 'And that's you.' Charlotte sat up straighter. 'Did you see that on the lift?'

The Charlotte nod.

Unnerving. Sophie had adapted surprisingly fast to Wolf-Charlotte pulverising city walls and battling Mongols. Now, back in the regular world, she was still getting used to the new Charlotte.

On the next page was the girl with the sword. 'Crazy.' Sophie turned the page. 'The forked road symbolises me choosing to come home, and Freddy killing the Mongolian soldier, saving Hugo.' Charlotte put on her serious face. 'The man by the cot is Freddy, and the baby is mine and his.'

The last page had the sketches she'd scribbled down in the students' union before they'd left: the two unknown signs. Sophie grabbed her phone. 'Hugo thinks the lift works on sub-atomic software.' She searched for 'quantum mechanics symbols,' and there they were: the five-sided shape and criss-crossing lines inside a rectangle.

Charlotte nuzzled into her. Sophie set the phone and notebook aside, and thought about Jack the retriever. 'We'll travel to Shorten after the baby's born, and you'll be with Jack.' Charlotte leaped off the bed and whirled around in a circle, chasing her tail, and Sophie laughed.

A knock on the door. Someone was up early.

It was Hugo, in his towelling dressing gown. Charlotte bounced up in the doorway. He ruffled her head, then locked the door.

'What are you doing?'

'We need to clear the air, *without* Freddy taking notes.' Charlotte settled on the floor.

'This horrible politeness is the pits.'

He raised his eyebrows.

'I half-wish you'd got drunk and thrown things.' She plumped a pillow.

'Not an option in that cave in Georgia,' said Hugo, 'or in the hospital.' He sat on the edge of the double bed. 'You don't need to decide about the pregnancy. You have time.'

'I don't need time. I couldn't do that to Freddy. He's obsessed with the baby, like he was with me.'

'*I* needed time, Sophie, after the bear pit. It tore my insides out.'

She winced. 'I'll go with Freddy to my aunt's house, then cross with him to Shorten when the baby's old enough.'

'You should think about this. Not make any hasty decisions.'

'It's not really a decision. It's what's best for the baby.'

'You should choose what's best for *you.*' He exhaled. 'I can put this behind us, *if* you want to.'

She gaped. He was serious. 'How can that work, with Freddy's child?'

Hugo stood up, then sat beside her on the bed. 'Freddy's asleep, probably dreaming about the baby, teaching it maths.' He fidgeted, adjusting a pillow. 'Your baby will be loved, whatever you decide. Whether you stay with Freddy — or me.'

Sophie avoided his gaze, humbled. 'I'm sorry, I don't know what to say.'

'When you say you're sorry—'

'I can't wish away Freddy's baby. He's so happy.' She looked directly at him. 'I want to be with you.'

Relief showed in his face.

'But you'll never trust me.'

He met her eyes. 'You shouldn't take up law, train for the bar.'

'What?'

'You've missed the strongest point in your defence. Extreme circumstances.'

Sophie swallowed.

'There aren't any bear pits in London,' said Hugo, 'so we have a good chance, second time around.'

She blinked, welling up.

'And there is an upside to you being pregnant.' He kissed her lightly on the forehead. 'We don't have to be careful. You can't fall pregnant again.'

She managed a nervy giggle. 'I could have twins, one baby for you and one for Freddy.'

'It doesn't work like that.'

'I know.' Trying to keep it together, she flicked through the sketchbook to the symbols she'd googled. 'Corroborates your idea that the lift uses quantum mechanics.' She glanced over at Charlotte, who was yawning, half-asleep. 'I'll still go and collect Jack.'

Hugo nodded, his expression sombre. 'Without Charlotte, we'd never have made it out.'

'And that boiling-blood power did mess me up. If I had a saviour complex before, it grew … out of control.'

He smiled. 'So, you admit I was correct—'

Sophie kissed him, and when he kissed her back, she lost herself in the moment.

Decisions about the future would have to wait.

This moment, right here, right now, was mighty fine.

IF YOU ENJOYED EXILE
LET PEOPLE KNOW

Reviews are the most effective way of building awareness of a book you've enjoyed.

While I love telling people about the *Shorten Chronicles,* honest reviews bring books to the attention of other readers.

If you didn't find *Exile* on my Bookshop, I'd really appreciate it if you'd leave a review (short as you like) where you bought it.

Thank you!

The next book in the *Shorten Chronicles, Intermezzo, Book 3. 5* is waiting...

Okay, you might be thinking, 'That looks like a rom-com novel, not the next book in this fantasy series.'

It *is* the next book in the *Shorten Chronicles*, though it's a little different from the main books. This lighter, fun novella is set in modern London before the gang cross universes again in *Defiance* (Book 4).

You see, the baby might not be Freddy's...

Pregnant. Paternity Unclear. Trouble.

Sophie's condition isn't compatible with crazy adventures, so she's taking a break from crossing between universes. Obviously.

After her baby's born, a simple paternity test will ID the father, but in the meantime, life's … complicated.

Join Sophie as she navigates motherhood, conceals her dog's unusual talents, and copes with two seriously fit soulmates!

Intermezzo is only available from my Bookshop: *https://bookshop.rosalindtate.com.* Click on 'Exclusive To this Book-shop' to choose your preferred format.

ABOUT THE AUTHOR

Rosalind Tate lives in Gloucestershire, England, and holidays on the Cornish coast. She served in the British military, then worked as a journalist and a lawyer.

Rosalind's enjoys speaking at authors' and readers' conferences, talking about publishing and encouraging new authors. When she's not behind her computer, you can find Rosalind reading her favourite books, walking her dogs, swimming, or watching sci-fi and fantasy shows.

Rosalind has three grown up children, a tolerant husband, and two utterly gorgeous dogs.

ACKNOWLEDGMENTS

To my husband, Ian. Thank you for your patience, support, and sharp, proofreading eyes.

To my mother, who showed me how to be a writer.

To my editor, Debi Alper, and my fabulous readers in *Team Charlotte*.

Thank you to our labradoodle, the wonderful Bella. You inspired the *Shorten Chronicles* after all.

And thanks also to Bella's goldendoodle kid sister, for her author guarding skills. She's called … Sophie. *What?* Okay, when we adopted her, I was obsessed with Sophie Arundel, and our energetic puppy has some things in common with her literary human counterpart. She's sassy, runs fast and is far too impulsive.

Finally, Toby deserves a mention. He was our first labradoodle and is no longer with us.

Well, in this world.

Rosalind Tate
Gloucestershire 2022

EXILE

BOOK THREE OF THE SHORTEN CHRONICLES

www.rosalindtate.com
TOB Publishing

www.ingramcontent.com/pod-product-compliance
Lightning Source LLC
Chambersburg PA
CBHW060656190726
48289CB00002B/437